THE TWIST OF A KNIFE

Also by Anthony Horowitz

The House of Silk
Moriarty
Trigger Mortis
Magpie Murders
The Word Is Murder
Forever and a Day
The Sentence Is Death
Moonflower Murders
A Line to Kill
With a Mind to Kill

THE TWIST OF A KNIFE

a novel

anthony
horowitz

NEW YORK • LONDON • TORONTO • SYDNEY • NEW DELHI • AUCKLAND

HARPER PERENNIAL

This book is a work of fiction. References to real people, events, establishments, organizations, or locales are intended only to provide a sense of authenticity, and are used fictitiously. All other characters, and all incidents and dialogue, are drawn from the author's imagination and are not to be construed as real.

Originally published in the United Kingdom in 2022 by Century Penguin Random House UK.

A hardcover edition of this book was published in 2022 by HarperCollins Publishers.

HarperCollins books may be purchased for educational, business, or sales promotional use. For information, please email the Special Markets Department in the U.S. at SPsales@harpercollins.com or in Canada at HCOrder@harpercollins.com.

FIRST HARPER PERENNIAL EDITION PUBLISHED 2023.

Library of Congress Cataloging-in-Publication Data has been applied for.

Library and Archives Canada Cataloguing in Publication information is available upon request.

ISBN 978-0-06-293819-0 (U.S. pbk.)
ISBN 978-1-4434-5914-3 (Canada pbk.)

23 24 25 26 27 LBC 5 4 3 2 1

For Sophia and Iona, joining the family

Contents

1

Separate Ways

'I'm sorry, Hawthorne. But the answer's no. Our deal is over.'

I hated arguing with Hawthorne. It wasn't just that I invariably lost. He managed to make me feel bad about even trying to win. Those murky brown eyes of his could be quite ferocious when he was on the attack, but the moment I challenged him they would suddenly become hurt and defensive and I would find myself backtracking and apologising even though I was quite sure I was right. I've said this before, but there was something childlike about his moods. I never really knew where I was with him, which made it almost impossible to write about him and that, as it happened, was exactly what we were discussing now.

I had followed Hawthorne on three investigations and these had led to three books. The first had been published. The second was being read by my agent (although she'd had it for two and a half weeks and I hadn't heard a word). I would start writing the third at the end of the year and I was confident it wasn't going to be difficult because of course I'd already lived through it and knew what happened in the end. I had agreed to a three-book contract and as far as I was concerned, three was enough.

I hadn't seen Hawthorne for a while. From the amount of crime fiction you'll find in bookshops and on TV, you'd think someone is being murdered every hour of the day, but fortunately real life isn't like that and several months had passed since we had got back from the island of Alderney, leaving just three bodies behind. I had no idea what he'd been up to in that time and, to be honest, he hadn't been very much in my thoughts.

And then, quite suddenly, there he was, on the telephone, inviting me round to his London flat – and that in itself was remarkable because usually if I wanted to get in, I had to ring someone else's doorbell and pretend to be from Ocado. River Court was a low-rise block of flats built in the seventies close to Blackfriars Bridge, and Hawthorne had a space on the top floor. *Space* was the operative word. There was almost no furniture, no pictures on the walls, no possessions of any sort apart from the Airfix models he liked to assemble and the computer equipment he used to hack into the police database, helped by the teenager who lived one floor below.

This was something that had shocked me when I had first stumbled into Kevin Chakraborty's bedroom and discovered him cheerfully displaying a private photograph of me and my son as his screensaver. Kevin admitted he had stolen it from my phone and then went on to explain that he had also helped Hawthorne break into the automatic number-plate recognition system used by the police in Hampshire. I hadn't remonstrated with him, partly because he had provided us with useful information, but also because, at the end of the day, how do you pick a fight with a teenager who's in a wheelchair? Nor had I ever mentioned it to Hawthorne. After all, this was a man who had been thrown out of the police force for pushing a known paedophile down a flight of stairs. He might have a moral compass, but he was the one who would decide which way it pointed.

He didn't own the flat, by the way. He didn't even rent it. He had told me that he was a caretaker, employed by a London estate agent who was 'a sort of half-brother'. That was the thing about Hawthorne. He couldn't have a relative who was something simple like a sister-in-law or a first cousin or whatever. He was separated from his wife, but he was still close to her. Everything about him was complicated and it didn't matter what questions I asked because the answers led me exactly nowhere. It was all very frustrating.

The two of us were sitting in his kitchen, surrounded by gleaming chrome and pristine work surfaces. I had walked down from my own flat in Clerkenwell: we only lived about fifteen minutes apart, which made the emotional distance between us all the more striking. Hawthorne was wearing his usual combination of a suit with a white shirt, although, just for once, he had put on a grey round-neck jersey instead of a jacket. The casual look. He had offered me a cup of tea and he had been thoughtful enough to provide biscuits: four of them, to be precise; two-finger KitKats criss-crossing each other on a plate as if set up for a game of noughts and crosses. He was drinking black coffee with his ever-present packet of cigarettes close by.

He wanted me to write a fourth book. That was what the meeting was about, but I had already decided against it. Why? Well, first of all – and ignoring the visits I had made to the casualty wards of two London hospitals – Hawthorne had never been very kind to me. He had made it clear from the start that this was going to be a business relationship. He wanted someone to write about him because he needed the money and, to make matters worse, he had let me know that I wasn't even his first choice. For my part, I'd made my decision before I'd come here. Enough was enough. I was fed up of being treated like an appendage. There were lots of stories I wanted to write where I would be in charge and this was something he would never understand. Authors don't write their books for other people. We write for ourselves.

'You can't stop now,' Hawthorne said. He thought for a moment. '*The Word Is Murder* was really good.'

'You read it?' I asked.

'Some of it. But the reviews were great! You should be pleased with yourself. The *Daily Mail* said it was splendidly entertaining.'

'I don't read reviews – and that was the *Express*.'

'Your publishers want you to do more.'

'How do you know that?'

'Hilda told me.'

'Hilda?' I couldn't believe what he'd just said. Hilda Starke was my literary agent – the same agent who had advised me against getting into all this in the first place. I could still remember her face when I'd told her I would be sharing the profits fifty-fifty with Hawthorne. She'd met him recently at Penguin Random House and I'd seen him charm her, but it was still a surprise that the two of them had been having conversations without me. 'When did you talk to her?' I asked.

'Last week.'

'What? You rang her?'

'No. We had lunch.'

My head swam as I took this in. 'You don't even eat lunch!' I exclaimed. 'And anyway, what are you doing meeting Hilda? She's *my* agent.'

'She's mine now too.'

'You're serious? You're paying her fifteen per cent?'

'Actually, I managed to knock her down a bit.' He moved on hastily. 'She reckons we could get another three-book deal. And a bigger advance!'

'I don't write for the money.' I didn't mean to sound so prim but it was true. Writing for me has always been a very personal process. It's my life. It's what makes me happy.

'Anyway, it doesn't make any difference,' I went on. 'I can't write another book about you. You're not working on any new cases.'

'Not at the moment,' he admitted. 'But I could tell you about some of my past ones.'

'When you were with the police?'

'After I left. There was that business in Riverside Close in Richmond. A man hammered to death in a posh cul-de-sac. You'd like that, Tony! It was my first private investigation.'

I remembered him talking about it when we were both in Alderney. 'It may be a great story,' I said. 'But I can't write about it. I wasn't there.'

'I could tell you what happened.'

'I'm sorry. I'm not interested.' I reached out for one of the biscuits, then changed my mind. They were somehow unappetising. A chocolate hashtag. 'Anyway, it's not just about the crimes, Hawthorne. How can I write about you when I know almost nothing about you?'

'I'm a detective. What else do you need to know?'

'We've already been into this. I know you're a very private person. But you've got to see things from my point of view. You can't have a main character who doesn't give anything away, and frankly, being with you, I feel I'm up against a brick wall.'

'What do you want to know?'

'Are you being serious?'

'Ask me!'

'All right.' About twenty questions arrived at the same moment, but I asked the first one that came into my head. 'What happened at Reeth?'

'I don't even know where that is.'

'When we were in that pub in Yorkshire, a man called Mike Carlyle said that he knew you from Reeth, although he called you Billy.'

'He'd got the wrong person. That wasn't me.'

'And there's something I didn't tell you.' I paused. 'When I got back from Alderney, a postcard came. It was from Derek Abbott.'

Abbott was the convicted child pornographer we'd met in Alderney. He was the man who'd supposedly fallen down the stairs while he was in police custody.

'He wrote to you from hell?' Hawthorne asked.

'He wrote to me before he died. He told me to ask you about Reeth.'

'I don't know anything about Reeth. It's a place. I haven't been there.'

I knew he was lying, but there was no point in challenging him. 'All right, then,' I said. 'Tell me about your wife. Your son. What about your brother, the estate agent? How old are you really? You said you were thirty-nine in Alderney, but I think you're older.'

'That's not very nice.'

I ignored him. 'Why do you make all these models? What's that all about? Why don't you ever eat?'

Hawthorne looked uncomfortable. His hand edged towards the cigarette packet and I knew that he wanted to light up. 'You don't need any of this,' he complained. 'That's not what the books are about. They're about murder!' He made it sound attractive, as if violent death was something to be desired. 'If you really want to put in stuff about me, why don't you just make it up?'

'That's exactly my point!' I exclaimed. 'I prefer making things up. I don't find it easy writing books when I don't know the ending. I don't like walking three steps behind you like the murder-mystery equivalent of the Duke of Edinburgh. I'm sorry, Hawthorne. But this hasn't been much fun for me. I've been stabbed twice! I've never come anywhere close to getting anything right. And even if I did want to continue, you haven't got any more cases for us to investigate together – besides which, I made a mistake with the titles.'

'You should have called the first one *Hawthorne Investigates*.'

'That's not what I mean.' I snatched one of the KitKats after all. I didn't want to eat it. I just wanted to spoil the pattern. 'It's the concept. It doesn't work.'

I'd decided that all the titles would have some sort of literary reference. After all, I was a writer; he was a detective. *The Word is Murder*, *The Sentence Is Death*, *A Line to Kill*. It had seemed like a good idea at the time, but I'd already run out of grammatical allusions. *Life Comes to a Full Stop*? It wouldn't make sense in America, where they have periods.

The Case of the Missing Colon? It would only work if a body part went missing from a morgue. No. Even the titles were telling me that I had agreed to a trilogy and that was as far as it would go.

'You can find someone else,' I suggested, weakly.

He shrugged. 'I like working with you, mate. You and I get along . . . somehow. We've got an understanding.'

'I'm not sure I understand anything,' I said. It was strange. I hadn't expected this meeting to become so gloomy. I'd thought it was just going to be a simple parting of the ways. 'It's not the end of our relationship,' I continued. 'There are two more books still to come out. We'll meet at the publishers. And maybe there'll be more literary festivals – although after the last one, people may be nervous about inviting us.'

'I thought we did all right.'

'Three people got killed!'

I had never seen Hawthorne so defeated. At that moment, I realised that whatever I might have said, some sort of bond had grown between us. At the end of the day, it's not possible to investigate the deaths of seven human beings without becoming close. I admired Hawthorne. I liked him and I'd always tried to make him likeable when I was writing about him. Suddenly I wanted to leave.

I didn't eat the KitKat. I finished my tea and stood up. 'Look,' I said. 'If something comes up, another investigation, let me know and maybe I'll think again.' Even as I spoke the words, I knew I wouldn't. At the same time, I was quite sure he wouldn't get in touch with me either.

'I'll do that,' he said.

I walked towards the door but before I reached it, I turned back. I wanted to end on a more cheerful note. 'My play opens next week,' I said. 'Why don't you come to the first night?'

'What play is that?'

I was sure I'd mentioned it to him. '*Mindgame*. It's a sort of thriller. It's got Jordan Williams and Tirian Kirke in it.' They were both well-known actors but Hawthorne didn't appear to have heard of either of them. 'You'll enjoy it. It's on at the Vaudeville Theatre.'

'Where's that?'

'It's in the Strand . . . opposite the Savoy. There'll be a party afterwards and Hilda will be there.'

'So what night is it on?'

'Tuesday.'

'Sorry, mate.' The answer came straight back without a moment's pause. 'I'm busy that night.'

Well, if he was going to be like that, I wasn't going to persuade him otherwise. 'That's too bad,' I said, and I left.

I was feeling a little dejected as I walked along the River Thames towards the bridge, heading back to my flat in Clerkenwell. I knew I'd made the right decision about the books, but still I had a sense of a task that I hadn't completed, of an opportunity I'd allowed to slip away. I really had wanted to know more about Hawthorne. I'd even been thinking of making the journey to Reeth. Now it was almost certain that I'd never see him again.

Here's the annoying thing . . .

Despite everything I've just written, it's obvious that there's going to be another murder because if there hadn't been, why would I have written anything at all? The very fact that you're holding this book, complete with compulsory bloodstain on the cover, rather spoils the surprise. It proves how handicapped writers are when they're dealing with the truth, with what actually happened.

There was one thing that I didn't know, however. Although the first three books had caused me enough upsets, this one was going to be much, much worse.

2
Mindgame

I love theatre. When I look back at my life, I can remember – vividly – evenings when I have felt myself to be in a state of complete happiness; when performance, music, costume, direction and, of course, writing have combined to make an experience that I know will stay with me for ever. The National Theatre's 1982 production of *Guys and Dolls*. *Nicholas Nickleby* at the RSC. Michael Frayn's brilliantly constructed comedy *Noises Off*. Ian Richardson and Richard Pasco swapping parts every night in John Barton's *Richard II*. I went to that when I was eighteen years old and I can still see them holding the 'hollow crown' between them, gazing into the mirror that it has become. Theatre, at its best, is a candle that never goes out and all of these productions, along with many more, still burn in my memory.

In my early twenties I worked as an usher at the National and saw Harold Pinter's *Betrayal*, Peter Shaffer's *Amadeus*,

Arthur Miller's *Death of a Salesman* and Alan Ayckbourn's *Bedroom Farce* perhaps a dozen times each and I was never bored. Earlier in the evening, I would sit down in the backstage canteen wearing my grey nylon shirt and slightly camp mauve cravat and I might find myself a few places away from the likes of John Gielgud or Ralph Richardson, both of them imperious even in their tracksuits and trainers. Of course, I never spoke to them. They were gods to me. Donald Sutherland once tipped me twenty pence when I was working in the NT cloakroom. I still have it somewhere.

Before I started writing novels, I wanted to work in the theatre. I acted in plays at school. I directed them at university. I went to shows three or four nights a week, often standing at the back of the stalls, which would cost as little as two pounds. I tried to get into drama school and I applied for jobs as an assistant stage manager, which in those days was a recognised way into the profession. It never worked. I began to see there was something about me that not only didn't fit in with the world I so wanted to enter, it somehow barred me from it. '*Ambition, madam, is a great man's madness*,' says Antonio in Webster's *The Duchess of Malfi*, a play I first saw at the RSC in 1971 with Judi Dench in the title role. But it's accepting that you will never achieve your ambition that can really drive you mad.

Perhaps that was part of the reason why I wrote *Mindgame*. I was keeping the flame alive.

Mindgame was actually inspired by another play I'd seen in my teens and which had obsessed me ever since. *Sleuth* by Anthony Shaffer (brother of Peter) was both a parody of Agatha Christie and a completely original murder mystery, as inventive as anything she had ever created. There were only three characters – a wealthy writer, his wife's lover and a lugubrious detective called Inspector Doppler – but in the space of two acts the play managed to pull off a series of extraordinary surprises, doing things on the stage that had never been done before and leaving the audience gasping. It was a huge hit. It ran for over two thousand performances. It won major awards. It was filmed . . . twice. To this day, it remains a theatrical landmark.

It goes without saying that there have been attempts to replicate the success of *Sleuth*, but apart from Ira Levin (*Deathtrap*), nobody has come close. When you think about it, there's not a great deal you can do on the stage. Magic and illusion may have a part to play, but so much of theatre is words: people moving about a space, talking to each other. Shaffer broke the physical rules – just as he did with *Black Comedy*, a farce that takes place during a power cut, the stage lights coming on only when the blackout supposedly begins. The trouble is, once the rules have been broken, nobody will be excited when someone else does it a second time. If something is unique, it can't be done twice.

Even so, it had become an obsession of mine to do exactly that: to write a play with a small cast and a series of twists and turns in the manner of a traditional murder mystery, but using the stage in an entirely new and surprising way. Whenever I found myself between books or TV scripts, I would scribble down ideas and over the years I had completed three plays before I came up with the idea for *Mindgame*. I had, incidentally, had limited success. One of my works, a one-act play called *A Handbag*, was performed as part of a local festival. The other two were never produced.

Mindgame itself would never have reached the stage but for my sister, Caroline, who at the time was running a small but successful theatrical agency, representing actors and actresses. She read it and liked it and, without telling me, showed it to a producer she knew called Ahmet Yurdakul. A few days later, he phoned me and asked me to come round for a chat.

I will never forget that meeting. Ahmet worked out of an office near Euston Station, so close to the railway lines that it vibrated every time a train went past, like something out of one of those old black-and-white comedies starring Sid James or Norman Wisdom. He offered me a cup of tea that tasted of engine oil and biscuits that danced on the plate. Ahmet was a small, neat man with jet-black hair. He spoke very quickly and bit his nails. There was a button missing on his suit jacket and throughout our discussion I couldn't keep my eyes off the patch where it should have been, the three threads hanging down. He had an assistant, Maureen Bates, dressed in a cable-knit cardigan with silver hair and glasses on a chain around her neck. From the way she bustled around him, she could have been his aunt or perhaps an elderly bodyguard. She seemed to be endlessly doubtful and suspicious, taking notes in tiny handwriting, but she barely said a word to me. They were about the same age – in their fifties.

The office did not inspire confidence. Situated in the basement of a three-storey house, it had a window too dusty to see through and furniture that was ugly and mismatched. I remember casting my eye over the posters on the walls and wondering if I had found the right home for my masterpiece. *Run for Your Wife*, a farce by Ray Cooney that had opened in Norwich. *It Ain't Half Hot Mum*, adapted from the long-running BBC sitcom, at the Gaiety Theatre on the Isle of Man. Rolf Harris in *Robin Hood* at the Epsom Playhouse. *Macbeth (Abridged)* performed in the open air at Middleham Castle with a cast of six.

To be fair to him, Ahmet loved my play. When I came into the room, he rose up to embrace me, overwhelming me with the smell of aftershave and tobacco. As we sat down, I noticed the packet of American cigarettes and heavy onyx lighter on his desk.

'This is a great play. A very great play!' They were almost his first words to me. The typescript was in front of him and he emphasised his words by striking it with the back of his hand. He was wearing a heavy signet ring that left dints on the first page. 'Do you not think so, Maureen?'

Maureen said nothing.

'Ignore her! She doesn't read. She doesn't know. Anthony, let me tell you. We will take this play out on tour. Then we will come into town. I love your sister who brought this to me. I cry with happiness to meet you.'

Ahmet was Turkish. I think he quite revelled in the part, using deliberately ornate phrases as if to illustrate his 'otherness'. Once I got to know him a bit better, I realised that he actually spoke English perfectly well. His parents were Turkish Cypriots who had emigrated to the UK in the seventies, fleeing ethnic fighting and terrorism. Ahmet was ten years old when they arrived, moving into a small flat in Enfield, north London, from where he took the bus each day to the local comprehensive while they set up a clothing business. He mentioned that he'd studied computer science at Roehampton University and that he'd lived with his parents for ten years, working as a software developer for Enfield social services. Every time we met, he told me a little more about himself and I got the feeling that he was hoping I'd write a book about him . . . just like Hawthorne. I listened politely, but, to be honest, I was more interested in his plans for the play and his ability to achieve them.

Maureen had already typed up an outline of the tour that they were planning and slid it in front of me. Bath, Southampton, Colchester, York – they were all good-sized cities with excellent theatres, and I should say at once that Ahmet was as good as his word. He managed to entice a well-known director, Ewan Lloyd, to come on board and over the next few weeks I received regular updates. The money had been raised. Jordan Williams was interested in the part of Dr Farquhar. The theatres had been signed up. They were starting work on the designs. Jordan Williams had accepted the part of Dr Farquhar. A rehearsal space had been booked. I'm condensing the events of several months into just a few lines because I want to get on to what happened in London, but I can't overstate how exciting this all was for me. It was my earliest dream, my first ambition, still somehow alive.

This is the plot of *Mindgame*:

Mark Styler, a journalist and 'true crime' writer, is visiting a lunatic asylum called Fairfields where he hopes to interview a notorious serial killer, Easterman, for a book he is writing. First, he has to persuade the unwilling and unhelpful director of the institute, Dr Farquhar, to allow him access to his patient. Quite quickly, Styler comes to realise that not all is as it should be at Fairfields. For no good reason, there's a full-length human skeleton hanging in Dr Farquhar's office, and his assistant, Nurse Plimpton, is clearly frightened of something and tries to warn Styler to leave while he still can. As the action continues, the sense of uneasiness erupts into violence until it is revealed that the lunatics have taken over the asylum. The real Dr Farquhar is dead. Styler is trapped.

My big idea – and my nod to Shaffer – was that since nothing was as it seemed, this should be literally true for the audience.

So, as the play continues, the set plays a series of tricks. A door that had opened into a cupboard suddenly leads into a corridor and later into a bathroom. The view out of the window is gradually blocked as a wall rises up, brick by brick. The pictures on the walls change subject. The curtains change colour and the furniture is secretly replaced. Originally, the play was called *Metanoia*, a word used in psychology to describe the abandonment of the false self . . . but this was quickly jettisoned by Maureen. 'Why should I pay to see it when I don't even know what it means?'

Mindgame opened in Colchester and did surprisingly well. It got some good reviews in the local press and the audiences loved it. I can say this with confidence because I watched several performances in the first week and got into the habit of slipping into the bar in the interval to hear what people were saying. The first act ends on a knife-edge. Easterman has escaped and assumed the identity of Dr Farquhar. He has murdered Nurse Plimpton. Holding a scalpel, he advances on Mark Styler, who is helpless, strapped into a straitjacket. There seems to be no possible escape. Curtain. And it worked. I listened to people chatting and they really were engaged, wondering what was going to happen next. There were no walkouts.

For the next five months, from November through to March, the play faded into the background as it continued its tour and I got on with my other work. It was easy to forget that it was happening at all unless Ahmet happened to ring me – which he did occasionally when there were good reviews or when things went wrong. The big news, though, came at the end of February. After going through the box-office receipts with his accountant, he had decided to open in the West End and somehow he had managed to raise the money for an initial twelve-week run at the Vaudeville, a handsome nineteenth-century theatre in the Strand, not far from Trafalgar Square. There would only be three weeks' rehearsal. One of the actors had decided to drop out. But Ewan Lloyd was still on board as director. We would open in the second week of April.

Before I knew it, we were rehearsing in a converted warehouse in Dalston and this time I was allowed to join in. The rehearsal room was exactly what I would have imagined: a large, empty space with a triple-height ceiling and flaking walls, a kitchen area with an assortment of mugs, a kettle, tea and biscuits. Four plastic chairs were arranged in a circle for the director and cast and made me think of an AA meeting. The shape of the set had been chalked out on the bare floorboards, with traffic cones used for the doors and windows. The various props had been arranged on trestle tables. Styler's straitjacket hung on a rail. There were more chairs at the edge of the room for the assistant director, the lighting designer, the costume assistant and various other backstage staff. The atmosphere was always highly charged . . . intense.

It was during this time that I got to know Ewan Lloyd and the cast a little better. I won't say I was part of the team.

I was sitting in the outer circle. But we did occasionally have a drink together once we'd finished for the day and something vaguely resembling a friendship sprang up between us.

When I'd first met Ewan, I'd assumed he was gay. He was quite effete, dressing like Oscar Wilde with a wide-brimmed hat and a scarf. If he'd smoked, I could imagine him using an ebony cigarette holder. I was quite surprised when Ahmet told me that although Ewan was now divorced, he had been married to an actress and they'd had four children.

Ewan was in his late forties and completely bald, although it looked as if he had shaved off his hair rather than lose it strand by strand. He was quite fastidious, almost prissy, when he was talking about his work and it didn't help that he spoke with a slight stutter. He wore glasses with very thin frames and he would use them like a conductor's baton, tapping the script or jabbing them at me when he was making a point. Maureen had shown me his CV and I had seen that he had worked in a number of well-respected theatres, although I couldn't help noticing that his CV had become a lot thinner in recent years. He had mounted several productions with a fringe theatre company in Antwerp, but had returned to England to direct *Macbeth* for Ahmet.

We went out for a Chinese meal one evening, just the two of us, and after telling me about some of the plays he'd directed and the awards he'd won, he suddenly launched into an extraordinary tirade. Maybe it was the wine that did it. He'd worked all over the world, he said. He was huge in

Belgium. But he had never been fully accepted in his own country. He had never been given the credit he deserved. He would have liked a spell as the artistic director of one of the good provincial theatres, but he knew that was never going to happen. Everyone was against him.

We were on our second bottle by now and I sat silently, feeling uncomfortable as the anguish poured out.

'It was all because of Chichester. Bloody Chichester! Theatre people are the worst in the world. There's so much malice. Everyone's at each other's throats. They're always waiting to get you and the moment they get the chance, they pounce!'

According to Ewan, his problems had begun eight years ago at the Chichester Festival Theatre. He had been directing George Bernard Shaw's *Saint Joan*, starring Sonja Childs in the title role. We don't usually see the burning at the stake. This happens offstage. But Ewan had decided to open with a striking tableau of the flames, the smoke, the great pile of firewood, the bare-chested executioner, the crowd. He wanted it to prefigure what was going to happen, to illustrate the fate of the main character.

On the opening night, it had all gone terribly wrong.

'It wasn't my fault,' he told me. 'It was all so bloody unfair! I did everything by the book . . . producer's notes, control and management procedures, emergency plan. We'd spoken to the police, the local authority, the local fire authority . . . I couldn't have done any more. There was a full investigation afterwards. I spent hours being questioned and, in the end, everyone agreed that I was in no way to blame. Of course, the play closed immediately . . . not that it mattered. I will never forgive myself for what happened to Sonja. It was horrible.'

'Was she killed?' I asked.

'No.' He looked at me sadly over his glass. 'But she was very badly injured: it was the end of her career. And mine! Nobody wanted to know me after that. I had two productions cancelled even though I'd already signed the contracts. It was as if I'd lit the bloody match! And look at me now. I mean . . . Ahmet's decent enough, but he's not exactly Cameron Mackintosh, is he!'

And what of the cast?

I have already mentioned Jordan Williams, who had agreed to play Dr Farquhar and was undoubtedly the star of our show. He was a Native American, the first I had ever met; a Lakota to be exact. I'd looked him up on Wikipedia and discovered that he had been born on the Rosebud Reservation in South Dakota in the USA. He had spent ten years working in Los Angeles and had received an Emmy nomination for his role as a psychopathic killer in *American Horror Story*. He had married his make-up artist, who happened to be English, and that was what had brought him to the UK. When he had first arrived, many of the newspapers had suggested that he might take over from Peter Capaldi as the first ethnically diverse Dr Who, but this hadn't happened. Instead, he had taken on multiple roles in theatre, film and TV and if he wasn't quite a household name, he was certainly respected.

I never feel at ease with actors and this was particularly true of him. He was a thickset, broad-shouldered man with extraordinarily intense eyes; I could feel them boring right into me every time we spoke. His face was defined by features that had a sort of mathematical precision, with a very straight nose and a square chin. He had greying hair that wasn't quite long enough to be called a ponytail, but which he still tied back with a coloured band when he wasn't onstage. He was by far the oldest member of the cast, but he wore his age well, sloping into rehearsals in tracksuits or jeans, his hands deep in his pockets, his thoughts far away. When he spoke, he chose his words carefully, with no trace of an American accent. It was as if he was performing . . . and this was in fact his defining characteristic. It was very hard to tell when he was acting and when he wasn't – sometimes with unfortunate consequences.

We had quite a nasty incident at the end of the first week in Dalston. We were rehearsing the scene when Dr Farquhar attacks Nurse Plimpton and Jordan had grabbed hold of Sky Palmer, the actress playing her. I watched the two of them in the middle of the chalk outline, surrounded by the entire team. He was holding her, his hands clamped on her arms, his face very close to hers. He was shouting at her, in a rage. They must have done the scene a hundred times by now, but suddenly Sky began to scream. At first, I thought she was ad-libbing, trying something new. Then I saw the alarm on Ewan's face and realised that this was serious, she really was in pain. At that moment, Jordan had *become* Dr Farquhar and he only released her when Ewan shouted at him to stop and everyone rushed forward to bring the action to a halt. Sky fell to the floor and I saw the bruising on her arms. She had been hurt and she had been frightened. That was the end of rehearsals for the day.

As we left, Ewan told me that this wasn't the first time Jordan had behaved in this way. Apparently, he had quite a reputation. He was a method actor who took his roles very seriously. When he had been cast as the highwayman Dick Turpin in a BBC drama, he had not only learned to ride a horse, he had insisted on re-creating the famous two-hundred-mile ride from London to Yorkshire and had almost been killed crossing the M1. On another occasion, playing King Lear at the Hampstead Theatre, he had often spent the night sleeping rough on the Heath.

To be fair to him, he could be generous too. He was mortified by what had happened and when we came back the following Monday, he presented Sky with a bunch of flowers so huge that it filled two vases.

Sky Palmer herself was something of an enigma.

I'd seen her perform many times, but I can't say I knew her particularly well, which was hardly surprising as she was in her mid-twenties – three decades younger than me. Outside the play, we had nothing in common. When I first met her I had been struck by her intense, dark eyes, her self-assurance and, most of all, by her luminous pink hair – which she'd had to wash out once she'd started playing the part. She'd also lost her nose stud and multicoloured fingernails. She didn't smoke but during rehearsals she vaped, blowing out little clouds of steam that evaporated immediately, leaving a faint smell of menthol in the air. I'd been worried that the part of Nurse Plimpton might be difficult to cast. The way I'd written the character had been undeniably sexist . . . but then I'd deliberately based her on the sort of character who might have appeared in an old Hammer film. Sky didn't seem to care. She never asked me questions. She did everything Ewan told her. It was hard to tell if she was enjoying herself or not.

This was mainly because, whenever she wasn't working, she was plugged into her iPhone. It was the very latest model, the iPhone 8, in rose gold with a protective cover that sparkled with crystal glitter. She played games – Minecraft and Monument Valley – and she was forever checking her Twitter account. I never actually heard her speak to anybody, but she was endlessly texting, obviously in a relationship with someone. Her phone would ping in the middle of a scene and drive Ewan Lloyd to distraction. She would apologise sweetly even as she was firing off a reply. I had never seen anyone's thumbs move so quickly.

Nothing about her quite connected. For example, the sweatshirts and leggings she liked to wear had come straight out of Sports Locker, but she also had a Cartier watch and her shoes were Jimmy Choo. She talked about popular culture – *Star Wars* and *The Hunger Games* – but I noticed her reading Franz Kafka. The playlist on her iPhone included Björk and Madonna, but finding a piano in the rehearsal room, she sat down and played the first bars of a Bach prelude. I was quite sure there was something she wasn't telling us.

That left Tirian Kirke, playing Mark Styler. He had come in late, replacing the actor who had decided that five months on the road was enough for him, and I'm afraid he was the only cast member I didn't warm to . . . but then he and I had history.

A couple of years older than Sky, Tirian had made many appearances on TV, playing a junior case officer in *Spooks*, a police constable in *Line of Duty* and, for three seasons, a footman or some sort of under-butler in *Downton Abbey*. He wasn't quite a household name, but he was well on his way to becoming one, so I had been very pleased when he was cast in a show I'd written called *Injustice*. This was a five-part legal drama starring James Purefoy, screened by ITV in 2011. It was also, coincidentally, the show where I first met Hawthorne. He was our technical adviser.

Tirian was going to play a young offender who falls foul of the prison system and eventually ends up taking his own life. It was a really good role. The character had four or five hefty scenes, plenty of screen time and a memorable death.

He'd done a great audition and had been offered the part almost at once. He had accepted. The contract had been drawn up. But then, at the last minute, he had changed his mind. According to his agent, he had decided that the script wasn't good enough, which hardly endeared him to me. The part was eventually played by Joe Cole, who did a brilliant job and went on to become a major star – but that didn't change my feelings about Tirian. He'd wasted time and money. He'd let us down.

So I was nervous when Ewan told me that he had been cast as Mark Styler. Firstly, I was afraid that my earlier experience might repeat itself, but more to the point, Tirian came across as rather too pleased with himself to play the part, too self-conscious, with his carefully groomed hair, his designer clothes and the Ducati motorbike he drove to rehearsals. I had to remind myself that all of this had come with success and that he was, at heart, a very good actor and we were lucky to have him. The first time I saw him reading the part, he even looked exactly how I had imagined the character: slim and bony, with dark eyes and an unusual, angular face. He had a crooked nose and a lazy, roguish smile, far removed from the anodyne good looks of many young British actors. He was the sort of actor you couldn't help noticing – and this was exactly what had happened. He had come to the attention of the Hollywood director Christopher Nolan, who had cast him in a big-budget production – *Tenet* – which was due to start shooting later in the year.

Tirian was going to be famous, which might be useful for the London production. Unfortunately, he knew he was going to be famous. This did not make him especially popular. He was actively disliked by Jordan Williams, who had got on much better with the actor he had replaced. Jordan frequently complained about Tirian not knowing his lines, upstaging him, refusing to give him eyelines, and Tirian would snap back, accusing the older actor of grandstanding. Sky stayed out of it, keeping herself to herself.

At any event, this was the team that moved into the Vaudeville Theatre in the first week of April. I didn't go to the tech run-throughs or the dress rehearsals. There was nothing more for me to do by then and I was becoming increasingly nervous. It was strange. This was my ambition. This was what I had always wanted. As I arrived at the theatre for the first night with my wife, my sister and my two sons, I should have been more excited. There was my name in lights! (Well, not all of it. The 't' in Anthony had fused.) But I wasn't excited at all. I was feeling sick.

It's going to be OK, I told myself. It's going to be fine. Audiences loved it in York and Southampton. Why shouldn't they love it here?

'Are you all right?' my wife asked.

'Yes,' I lied.

We went in.

3

First Night

The Vaudeville is such a beautiful theatre. The Victorians really wanted you to enjoy your evening so they went crazy with the gilt and the red plush, the mirrors and the chandeliers, making sure that the sense of drama would begin long before you sat down. It's strange that they were less concerned about leg room, sight lines and toilets, but I suppose you can't have everything.

The lobby was already packed with people milling about in different directions: to the stalls, the circles, the bar, the box office to pick up their tickets. It was a tortuous process, making our way through the labyrinth that the foyer had become, but as we continued, step by step, I made out a few familiar faces. There was Ahmet, wearing a black double-fronted jacket with loops instead of buttons. As always, Maureen was with him, weighed down with costume jewellery and with some long-dead animal draped around her neck. Ahmet had never mentioned having a wife or family and I had often wondered if he and Maureen had a relationship that extended beyond the office.

There were a couple of actors I knew but whose names I couldn't remember: they were presumably friends of the director or the cast. I glimpsed Ewan Lloyd disappearing down the staircase to the stalls. He seemed to be on his own. I continued to look through the crowd and although I wouldn't have wanted to admit it, I was wondering if Hawthorne might surprise me and turn up after all. He wasn't there.

We made our way down to the auditorium, where we had seats in the middle of the stalls, and as we squeezed past the people who had arrived before us, I had the strange sensation that I was, briefly, the centre of attention. It wasn't true, of course. I doubt if many people had recognised me, but at the same time, I felt trapped. The theatre was going to be full tonight: almost seven hundred people on three levels. I could see them all around me, many of them in the shadows, diminished by the distance between us. They were no longer individuals. They were an audience . . . perhaps even a jury. My stomach was still churning. I felt like the condemned man.

And then I saw them: my real judges.

The critics.

They were scattered across the stalls, easily recognisable by their blank faces and, in some cases, the notebooks they were already balancing on their knees. Michael Billington from the *Guardian*, Henry Hitchings, the *Standard*, Libby Purves, *The Times*, Harriet Throsby, the *Sunday Times*, Dominic Cavendish, the *Telegraph*. Many of them were familiar to me from my time at the Old Vic, where I had recently joined the board. They had been deliberately placed apart from each other and seemed to be avoiding each other's eyes. They weren't exactly rivals but nor, I thought, were they friends. They sat alone.

Was I afraid of them?

Yes.

I have never worried about the critics who write about books and TV. They can be harsh, but it's open to question how much influence they have over what people watch or read. And anyway, they can't hurt me. They're reviewing something I wrote a long time ago – in the case of a TV drama it could be years – and I've signed my next contract. I'm employed on a new project. They can tell the whole world I'm useless, but it's already too late.

These critics were different. Here they were, some of them in the same row as me. Their reviews could, quite simply, shut us down. Sitting there with the curtain about to rise, I began to have second thoughts about what I'd written. Would they find that joke funny? What would they make of the attack on Nurse Plimpton at the end of the first act? Had it been a mistake, raising the question of Dr Farquhar's sexuality? A moment ago, I had been worrying about the first-night audience. But they weren't the ones who mattered, and anyway, they were on my side. Most of them had been given free tickets, for heaven's sake! It was the critics who held my fate in their hands.

My wife touched my arm. 'It's starting late,' she said.

I looked at my watch and my heart missed a couple of beats. She was right. Seven thirty-five. So what had happened? Had Tirian failed to turn up? Was somebody ill? I looked around me. So far so good. Nobody else seemed to have noticed. I waited, sweatily, for the play to begin.

At last, the house lights dimmed. I took a deep breath. The curtain went up.

ACT I

The action of the play takes place in the office of Dr Alex Farquhar at Fairfields, an experimental hospital for the criminally insane. The office is cosy and old-fashioned. It seems to belong to the sixties, perhaps to the world of Hammer Horror.

A large, cluttered desk dominates the room. A window looks out onto fields, trees and a low wall. On the other side, a door opens into a cupboard. Incongruously, a complete human skeleton stands on a frame in one corner.

Sitting in the chair in front of the desk is Mark Styler, a writer in his early thirties. Casually dressed, his face is pale and his haircut is a little odd … otherwise he's the archetypal 'expert', as seen on TV.

He's been kept waiting. He looks at his watch, then takes out a digital recorder and switches it on. He records.

STYLER: Recording. Six fifteen. Thursday. July twenty-second.

And so it began.

I'm not sure I breathed during Styler's opening monologue, watching him walk around the office, recording his thoughts as he had done a hundred times before. I knew what I was waiting for. *Mindgame* is, at least in part, a comedy. It had to sell itself as such to the audience and my experience on the road had taught me that the first laugh was crucial. After that, everyone could relax.

It came when Styler moved away from the window and examined the bookshelves.

STYLER: Dr Farquhar arranges his books in alphabetical order. I wonder if I can trust him?

It wasn't a particularly funny line but for some reason it had always hit the spot with the audience and it did the same now. I heard the ripple of laughter spread through the darkness and something pricked at the back of my neck. I thought, for the first time that evening, that it was going to be all right.

The next hour sped past and it seemed to me that the play went as well as it possibly could. Nobody fluffed their lines.

The set worked. The laughs arrived more frequently, and as the action became darker, I could feel the tension in the house. Nurse Plimpton was attacked. Mark Styler was tricked into putting on a straitjacket. Dr Farquhar walked towards him with a scalpel. Curtain. Applause. Interval.

I went outside once the house lights had come up. There was no point hanging around in the bar as, this being a first night, people would largely be keeping their opinions to themselves, so there would be nothing to overhear. And if anyone did say anything memorable, my family would pick it up and report back to me. After the tension of the opening moments, I needed some fresh air. It was an unpleasant night. Although this was April, a wintery breeze was blowing down the Strand and there was a sheen of rain making the pavements gleam. I noticed Ewan Lloyd had come out too. He was standing at the corner of the theatre, dressed in a black astrakhan coat buttoned up to the neck, and I went over to him.

'How do you think it's going?' I asked him.

He grimaced. 'Tirian missed out two lines in the first scene,' he said. 'And the bloody projector got stuck again.'

The projector was used to make the picture on the wall change from one image to another during the performance, but it had to happen slowly so the audience didn't notice. It had seemed fine to me, and I hadn't noticed the missing lines. It struck me that Ewan was even more nervous than I was, but then this was his first London production for some time.

'Otherwise it's OK,' he went on. 'I think they're enjoying it.'

'The critics?'

'I mean the audience. You can never tell with the critics, sitting there, making notes. Did you see that Harriet Throsby from the *Sunday Times* is in the house?' I was surprised by the hatred in his voice.

'Is that so surprising?'

'I'd have thought she'd have sent an assistant rather than coming herself. We're an out-of-town production.'

'Maybe that's a good thing.' I was thinking we might get a more prominent review if she wrote it herself.

'Nothing about that woman is good. Nothing! She's a complete bitch, and you might as well know that I've never had a good review from her.' Ewan hadn't raised his voice. His anger was all the more striking for being expressed in such a subdued way. He stared out at the rain, which was falling harder now. 'Some of the stuff she writes is pure vitriol,' he went on. 'She chooses her words carefully, rancid opinions carefully laced with deeply personal insults. They say she started life as a journalist but wanted more power. That's what it's all about. I don't think she even likes theatre.'

'Well, there are plenty of other critics.'

'She's the most influential. People read her because she's so vile. It's like watching a car crash.'

'She might be enjoying the play.'

He sniffed. 'What she thinks is one thing. What she writes is another.'

I remembered this conversation as the second act began and as a result, I wasn't able to enjoy even a minute of it. All the doubts and misgivings that had been at the back of my mind suddenly came rushing to the fore and I remembered that audiences in the provinces and audiences in the capital are noticeably different. Expectations are considerably higher in London. So are the seat prices. Outside London, people tend to be more forgiving, more determined to enjoy themselves. Could we pass muster as a West End show? It suddenly struck me that the set was looking shabby and fragile after months on the road followed by several weeks stacked up in a warehouse in Slough. The second half was too long. I couldn't stop myself glancing at Harriet Throsby, her face in the light reflected from the stage. She was wearing glasses that hid her eyes, but I could see that she wasn't smiling. She wasn't showing any emotion at all. Was she my enemy? She certainly seemed to be Ewan's.

I felt a surge of relief when the curtain fell and then rose again for the cast to take their bows. I noticed Jordan Williams point in my direction and smile. He had spotted me in the audience and I was grateful for the gesture. The applause was loud and sustained, but was it sincere? It was impossible to tell on a first night. The audience was on our side. They wanted us to succeed. But they might be acting too.

I made my way out into the street, shaking hands with people I'd never met, surrounded by smiles and congratulations. Out of the corner of my eye, I saw the critics slipping away and tried to put them out of my mind. It was over. It had gone well. Now it was time for the first-night party and I was determined to enjoy myself. I would drink too much. This was my moment.

The Vaudeville Theatre was almost opposite the Savoy Hotel with its gorgeous cocktail bars and Grill Room, but Ahmet hadn't been able to stretch quite that far. Instead, he had taken over a Turkish restaurant called Topkapi, on the edge of Covent Garden, which happened to be owned by his cousin. It was a small place, just off the piazza, with a wooden front decorated to look vaguely Byzantine and an outstretched canopy that was catching the rain. There was a bar as you entered and tables beyond, lots of mirrors, and lights that were a little too bright. As I walked in, I heard music playing and saw a three-man band in traditional costumes, sitting cross-legged on a square of carpet: lute, violin and drums. Waiters in tight-fitting black trousers and waistcoats were circulating with glasses of sparkling wine. The food – dolmas, borek and koftas – was spread out on the bar.

Ahmet, standing beside the door, greeted me with an embrace. 'My dear friend! I am bursting with happiness. You heard the applause? One minute, thirty-two seconds. I timed it on my watch.' He pointed to what was, I suspected, a fake Rolex. 'We have a success. I know it.'

Standing beside him, Maureen looked less convinced.

Ahmet snapped his fingers at one of the waiters. 'A glass of Yaşasin for the author!' He beamed at me. 'Or maybe you would prefer the Çalkarasi rosé? It's excellent. The best.'

There were about a hundred people in the room, their numbers doubled by the floor-to-ceiling mirrors. The cast hadn't arrived yet – it was a tradition that they would come in late – but the entire production team was here, along with the actors I had noticed at the theatre. They were chatting to my sister, who seemed to know them well.

Meanwhile, Ahmet and Maureen had moved further into the room and were talking to a nervous-looking man – tall and slender, wearing a suit. I wasn't sure why he was nervous. Perhaps he was one of our backers. I remembered him because he had been sitting exactly behind me during the play and I'd noticed him as I sat down. He hadn't been looking too happy then either. I took a sip of the sparkling wine I had been given. It was too sweet for my taste, but at least it was cold. I was beginning to think that maybe I wouldn't stay here long. I was walking distance from my flat in Clerkenwell. I'd go home with my family and celebrate there.

But then the cast arrived: Tirian, Jordan and Sky, all three of them smartly dressed, smiling and confident, Sky in a pink puffball dress, Tirian wearing what looked like a very expensive black leather bomber jacket. Their appearance brought the party to life. Suddenly the crowd became more relaxed and cheerful. The music rose in volume and everyone had to talk more loudly to make themselves heard. More silver platters of food came out of the kitchen. Even the waiters picked up their pace.

And that was when I saw something so extraordinary that I had to look twice, and even then I didn't quite believe it and had to look again.

The *Sunday Times* critic, Harriet Throsby, had come through the front door of the restaurant, accompanied by a younger woman who might have been her assistant or perhaps her daughter. What was going on? Had she decided to go for a Turkish meal after the play and wandered in without realising that this was where the party was taking place? No. As I watched, she helped herself to a glass of wine, sniffing the contents disapprovingly. The younger woman didn't look happy to be here and Harriet muttered a few words into her ear. Ahmet had seen them both. He went over to them and bowed, gesturing towards the food. They were expected. They had been invited.

But that was impossible, wasn't it? Critics never attended first-night parties. It was completely inappropriate and might even be seen as unethical. I couldn't imagine what she was thinking, coming here. Could it be that she was a friend of one of the actors? That was extremely unlikely, given what Ewan had told me, and anyway, it would still have been wrong. Her job was to go home and write whatever she was going to write. She wasn't part of the production and for all

Ahmet's smiles, she couldn't be welcome here – particularly if she hadn't liked the play.

I watched Ahmet leaning towards her, speaking earnestly. It was impossible to hear what he was saying with all the noise. For her part, Harriet was already bored and looking past him. I saw her eyes settle on the man Ahmet had just been talking to – the thin man in the suit. Brushing past Ahmet, she went over to him, smiling as if he was an old friend. The thin man stared at her, appalled. Harriet said something and he replied. Again, the words were lost in the crowd.

As the two of them continued their conversation, I pushed my way through about a dozen people and found Ewan, who was standing next to Tirian Kirke and Sky Palmer. 'Have you seen?' I asked.

'What?'

'Harriet Throsby!'

Ewan grimaced. 'Didn't Ahmet warn you she'd be here?' he said. 'She always comes to first-night parties. She expects to be invited . . . in fact, she insists upon it. Whatever you do, don't ask her about the play – and I mean the writing, the performances, the scenery . . . anything. Just don't go there. She won't tell you what she thinks. She never does.'

'Then why is she here?' Tirian asked. He was as surprised as I was.

'God knows. It doesn't make any difference to what she's going to write, but I think it gives her a sense of power. She knows we're all scared of her.'

'I'm not scared of her,' Tirian said.

'Then she's probably never given you a bad review.'

Tirian thought for a moment. 'I haven't done much theatre – and I don't care what she thinks. I've already got my next job and there's nothing she can say that can change that.'

'*Tenet*,' Sky said.

'Yes. We're going to be shooting in Paris. I've never been to France, so I can't wait. And we might be going to Denmark and Italy too.'

'Who are you playing?' I asked.

'A spy. The character doesn't have a name. In fact, he doesn't even have a character. They sent me the script last week and the truth is, it's completely insane. There are bullets that travel backwards in time, something called the Algorithm that's going to either destroy the world or save it – I don't know – and doors between dimensions. It's total nonsense. Christopher Nolan may be a big-shot director, but he's got his head right up his arse. Not that I care. Eleven weeks shooting. A ton of money. And I go to France.'

'Shh . . . !' Sky warned.

It was too late. Harriet Throsby had made her way over to us and had heard what he was saying. It certainly wasn't the best way Tirian could have described his big breakthrough, and he was startled when he saw her standing behind him. She glanced at him and I saw a spark of malevolence in her eyes. Tirian twisted away awkwardly.

'Good evening, Harriet,' Ewan said, with no enthusiasm.

The *Sunday Times* critic stopped and examined us, measuring us up as if she was intending to review the party as well as the play. For the first time, I was able to examine her properly.

She was not large but she certainly had presence, expensively dressed in a cut-off jacket with a faux-fur collar and pearls. She was wearing horn-rimmed glasses that might have been deliberately chosen to make her look antagonistic, and she had a bulky black leather handbag – big enough to hold a laptop – looped over her arm. Her hair was obviously dyed, which was odd because it was an unpleasant colour, somewhere between brown and ginger. She had cut it short with a fringe, like a flapper girl from the twenties, which was exactly what she wasn't. It didn't suit her at all. I guessed she was about fifty. Her skin was pale and her make-up – the rouge, the lipstick, the eyeshadow – was so pronounced that it concealed her face rather than highlighted it. She could have been wearing a mask.

The girl who had arrived with her had followed her across and I decided that I was right and that she must be Harriet's daughter. She also had short hair, the same eyes and turned-up nose, although in almost every other respect the two women could not have been more different. She looked downtrodden, miserable. She had deliberately chosen to dress down for the occasion with a denim jacket and a loose-fitting T-shirt printed with a photograph of Kristen Stewart in her role as the star of *Twilight*. Nor did she make any attempt to connect with the people in the room. Everything about her appearance and her manner suggested an archetypal stroppy teenager, dominated by a mother she didn't like. The trouble was, she was actually quite a bit older, probably in her early twenties.

'How nice to see you, Ewan,' Harriet said brightly and even in that greeting and the cold smile that accompanied it, I got a sense of the game she was playing. She was enjoying herself, watching us squirm. I thought there was an American twang to her voice, but maybe it was just her extreme self-confidence, the way she targeted her words. 'How have you been keeping?'

'I'm very well, thank you, Harriet,' Ewan said, his eyes blinking more rapidly than ever.

'What a delightful idea to have a party in a Turkish restaurant, although I have to say I'm not a big fan of foreign food. Olivia and I had half an hour in the Savoy. Excellent cocktails, although those big hotels don't exactly light my fire. And they're shockingly expensive too.' She changed the subject without pausing. 'I hear Sheffield have their new artistic director. I thought you might have been in the running.'

'No. I wasn't interested.'

'Really? You do surprise me. So, you're trying your hand at comedy thrillers. Very hard to get right. I saw . . . who was it? . . . in *Deathtrap* a few years ago. Simon Russell Beale, of course! I never forget a face! I thought he was excellent, although the play had rather dated. Ira Levin. I used to like his novels. As a matter of fact, I recently read one of yours.' It took me a moment to realise that Harriet was now addressing me. She had a strange way of avoiding my eye while she spoke, looking over my shoulder as if hoping someone more interesting had come into the room.

'Thank you,' I said.

'I've always been a fan of crime fiction. I used to write about crime. Non-fiction. I didn't find it entirely satisfying, though. Criminals are so boring. Not all of them – but most of them. What was the one I read? I can't remember now. But Olivia used to read your books too. Didn't you, dear!'

'Alex Rider.' The girl looked embarrassed.

'You used to like them. They were stories about a young assassin.'

'He's not really an assassin,' I said. 'He's a spy.'

'He did kill people,' Olivia contradicted me.

Her mother leered at me. 'And now you're writing for the theatre.'

'Yes.' I couldn't stop myself. 'Did you enjoy the play?' Ewan glared at me. Tirian and Sky looked embarrassed. It was the one thing I'd been told not to do but I'd gone ahead and done it.

Harriet ignored me. It was as if I hadn't spoken. 'So, you've been cast in a big film,' she said. Now she was talking to Tirian. 'Personally, I have to say that I think it's a shame, all our young talent going over the Atlantic.'

'I'm only crossing the Channel,' Tirian replied. 'We're shooting in Paris.'

'You know what I mean, dear. I suppose the Americans pay so much better, but what does that do for our own theatre and television?' Again, that malicious gleam.

There was an uncomfortable silence. None of us wanted to talk to Harriet Throsby. I think we were all hoping she'd go away.

Sky broke the silence. 'It's nice to see you, Olivia,' she said.

'Oh. Hello, Sky.'

'Do you two know each other?' Harriet asked.

Olivia said nothing, so Sky explained. 'We met at the first-night party for *The Crucible* at the Barbican. I played Mercy Lewis.'

'Yes. I remember you.'

'You didn't like the production.'

Harriet shrugged. 'It had its moments. Unfortunately, as I recall, they were too few and far between.' She turned back to me, although once again her eyes refused to meet mine, as if she was trying to remind me that I meant nothing to her. 'I'm glad I spotted you. What a lovely party! So unusual to have it Turkish-themed. Come on, Olivia. Our car's waiting for us . . .'

And then the two of them were gone, crossing the restaurant to the exit and disappearing into the rain. I watched the door swing shut. The four of us were left trying to work out what had just occurred.

'I need a large whisky,' Ewan said. He put down his glass. 'This Turkish wine tastes like cat's piss.'

'I've got a bottle of vodka in my dressing room,' Sky said.

'I've got some Scotch,' Tirian added.

'Then why don't we go back?' Ewan suggested.

None of us wanted to be at the party any more. Harriet Throsby hadn't said anything mean or vindictive about the play but she had nonetheless spoiled it for all of us, which was exactly what she had intended.

Ewan looked at his watch. 'I'll go and get Jordan. Let's meet there in ten . . .'

I shouldn't have gone. I wish I'd listened to my earlier instincts and gone home with my family. Everything would have been so different. But, of course, you never know these things at the time. That's why life is so different to fiction. Every day is a single page and you have no chance to thumb forward and see what lies ahead.

4
The First Review

Going backstage at the theatre is always a bizarre experience. It's like stepping into a secret world.

All the comforts that the audience enjoys and expects disappear the moment you step through the stage door. Backstage, everything is relentlessly old-fashioned and utilitarian, as if the architects have deliberately set out to remind the actors and the crew that they are only the servants and matter less than the paying guests. The Vaudeville was built in the Romanesque style back in the late nineteenth century. Henry Irving had his first noticeable success there. I've described the luxuriousness of the lobby and the auditorium. But the corridors and dressing rooms on the other side of the mirror were quite another matter. Here, the flooring was covered by linoleum. Pipes and cables snaked willy-nilly along the walls, twisting between fire extinguishers, alarm boxes and overbright naked light bulbs. I was fascinated by the pieces of defunct machinery that had been screwed into place a century ago and then forgotten. Even the noticeboard with its tatty cards and clippings could have come from a police station or a failing secondary school. I found it all rather alluring. The backstage area of any London theatre would make a great set. One glance and you'd know exactly where you were.

It was pelting with rain when I made my way back to Maiden Lane, the little backstreet in which the stage door of the Vaudeville was located. Normally, the theatre would have closed by ten o'clock, but Keith, the deputy stage-door manager, had agreed we could hang out there until midnight. Sky Palmer had arrived ahead of me and was shaking water out of a Gucci umbrella. It had the trademark diamond-shaped pattern and logo and, unlike Ahmet's watch, I didn't think it was fake. I was quite surprised she had agreed to come. She didn't often socialise with the rest of the company, but perhaps, on the first night, she felt she couldn't let the others down.

I had barely spoken to her at the party and congratulated her on her performance. 'I thought you were great tonight.'

'Did you? I don't know . . .'

Why did she have to be so unenthusiastic? 'I think the audience enjoyed it.'

'Maybe.' She didn't sound convinced.

Fortunately, we were rescued by Keith, who stepped out of his cramped, awkwardly shaped office carrying a white box. 'This came for you,' he said. He handed it to me.

It was a first-night present with a label wishing me good luck, signed by Ahmet. Sky was looking at it dubiously but I have to say I was rather touched. I opened and took out an object tightly wrapped in tissue paper. I tore off the paper to reveal, of all things, an ornamental dagger, about twenty centimetres long, in a black leather sheath. The blade was silver and very sharp. The handle was wooden, embossed with a circular metallic medallion decorated with what might have been Celtic knotwork. It looked like an old Scottish dirk, although it was obviously a reproduction and not very well made. The medallion wobbled when I touched it.

'Oh . . . look at that,' I said, showing it to Sky. At the same time, I couldn't help thinking that it was also rather odd. 'I don't know what it's got to do with the play,' I added. It was true. *Mindgame* is violent, but nobody is killed – and certainly not with a dirk.

'You have to look at the blade,' Sky said.

I did as she suggested and saw four words engraved in the metal: *Is this a dagger . . . ?*

'He did *Macbeth* last year,' she went on in a matter-of-fact way. I was surprised that, unlike most actors, she wasn't superstitious about naming what most of them would call 'the Scottish play'. It reinforced my impression that she wasn't completely committed to the acting world. 'He put it on in the ruins of a castle in Yorkshire, but it didn't last very long. It poured with rain for the first three performances,

Banquo slipped over in the mud, and it closed at the end of the week. He had these made for the cast.'

'And he's giving the ones that were left over to us?'

'That's right. I've got mine in my dressing room. I don't know what I'm going to do with it.'

'Well,' I tried, 'I suppose it's the thought that counts.'

'Yes. He thought we wouldn't notice he's a complete cheapskate.'

We signed our names and added the time in the register that was kept in the corridor, then went through the swing doors and past the first dressing room. Jordan Williams came out and laughed when he saw me with water trickling down my face. Unlike Sky, I hadn't had an umbrella.

'You look like a drowned rat!' he exclaimed, enunciating every word as if they'd been rehearsed. He handed me a towel. At the same time, he noticed the knife. 'I see you've picked up your opening-night prezzie.' He produced his own and waved it at me. 'Touché'. He was evidently in a good mood. As far as he was concerned, the performance had gone well and he'd already had plenty to drink. 'Shall we go down?'

The Vaudeville is unusual among London's Victorian theatres in that it has a green room where the actors can meet and relax. We went down the stairs and along the corridor to a door that opened into a small, square space where Ewan and Tirian were already waiting for us. As promised, Tirian had opened a bottle of Scotch. He was sitting at a table with a half-filled glass in front of him and a backpack resting against his chair. Sky had popped into her dressing room, which was next door, and returned with a bottle of vodka and a chocolate cake – both of them gifts from friends. Jordan, in the dressing gown that he always wore between performances and still holding his dagger, threw himself into an armchair with his leg lolling over one side. Ewan poured him a glass of whisky, spilling a few drops onto the carpet and adding to the stains from a hundred first nights, a liquid history of the Vaudeville. The room would have been shabby in any other context but here it seemed homely, with a battered table, chairs and a worn-out sofa. There was a sink on one side and an old fridge. The rain was hammering at the window, but inside it was warm and cosy, with a two-bar heater turned on full and a CD of Noel Coward playing in the background. Everyone was relaxed. Even Jordan and Tirian seemed at ease with one another.

When I look back on the London production of *Mindgame*, I think this was my only truly happy night. It represented the brief interval between believing that the play might have succeeded and knowing that it hadn't. For that one hour in the green room, I was part of the company and during that time all the tension and the hostility that had accompanied the rehearsal process evaporated – as if we had accepted that whatever happened, we were all in this together. We had given it our best shot. We might as well get drunk and enjoy ourselves. We talked. We laughed. We retold some of the stories from rehearsals and the road. Tirian did an imitation of Ewan that actually caught him remarkably well. Jordan used his Scottish dagger to cut slices of cake.

At about half past eleven, Ahmet turned up with two bottles of Turkish champagne and – no surprise – Maureen accompanied him. She had dressed very smartly for the first night. Along with the fur and the jewellery, she'd had her hair permed so ferociously that it looked like one of those balls of wire you use to scrub pans. Ahmet was in an ebullient mood, smoking a foul-smelling cigarette even though it wasn't allowed backstage. He had come from the party with compliments ringing in his ears. He was certain the play was a success and grabbed me with both hands.

'You are a genius!' he exclaimed. 'A great genius!' He sounded almost relieved. As if he had never believed it until now.

Everyone picked up their glasses and drank a toast to me. By now we'd all had too much to drink.

It couldn't last long. And it didn't.

It was at exactly twelve o'clock midnight when Sky suddenly looked up from her phone.

'There's a review online!' she exclaimed.

'That's a bit early,' Ewan said. He didn't look pleased. 'Who's it by?'

'Harriet Throsby.' She gazed at the screen and we all saw the look that came over her face. 'I can't read this,' she said, in a low voice.

'Let's see it.' Tirian snatched the phone from her and laid it on the table. We all crowded round. This is what we read:

MINDGAME AT THE VAUDEVILLE

by Harriet Throsby

Is there any torment greater than the comedy thriller that is neither comedic nor thrilling? It's so easy to fall between the two stools … and what you might call a theatrical stool, in quite another sense, will inevitably result. That, I'm afraid, is what Anthony Horowitz provides at the Vaudeville Theatre. Known for his Alex Rider series of books, which, to be fair, have encouraged a generation of boys to read, his talents fall lamentably short of what is required for an entertaining evening in the more adult arena of the West End and he must take much of the blame for what ensues. Having said that, I have to ask what it was that drew so much talent to this painful farrago.

We can dispense with the story fairly quickly. A journalist, Mark Styler (Tirian Kirke), arrives at a lunatic asylum to interview one of the inmates, a serial killer by the name of Easterman. But first he has to persuade the asylum's director, Dr Farquhar (Jordan Williams), to allow him access. We quickly realise that things are not as they should be. Why is there a skeleton in Dr Farquhar's office? What are the strange screams coming from B Wing? Why is Nurse Plimpton (Sky Palmer) terrified?

The lunatics have taken over the asylum, that's why. Nothing is what it seems, and as the identities of the main players are shuffled around like playing cards before a particularly feeble magic trick, even the set joins in. A door opens into a cupboard one minute and into a corridor the next. A picture on the wall changes slowly. It may be that these special effects are meant to say something about madness and sanity, about how we can't trust our perception. But sadly, the production has been so cheaply mounted that they aren't very special at all and tell us only that we should have gone somewhere else.

As the play continues, the gratuitous violence mounts. It turns out that Easterman, the killer, is free and in control of the action ... which becomes ever more distasteful as Nurse Plimpton is tied to a chair and threatened with immolation. By this point, I myself was tempted to punch an usher and make a break for the exit. The casual use of a woman as a would-be victim of male-inflicted aggression is particularly displeasing. Sky Palmer is a talented actress who struggles with a part that demeans and devalues her at every turn. By contrast, Jordan Williams seems to be having a good time as Dr Farquhar, but has failed to notice that nobody else is. Mr Williams is becoming increasingly grandiloquent with age and gives the impression that he is only performing to entertain himself. In this, he may well be right. One really must wonder how many more bad career choices he can make before he realises that he no longer has a choice or, indeed, a career.

Most disappointing for me is Tirian Kirke, whom I recognised from the first time I saw him as one of the most promising actors of his generation. It's a promise broken. His performance is quite childish and, surprisingly, he is completely unconvincing when things turn violent. Kirke was so very good in *Line of Duty* on TV, but has failed to make a successful debut on the stage. He has been poorly assisted by Ewan Lloyd, who seems to be directing on autopilot. In his hands, the play never really catches fire, limping to a conclusion I had guessed long before the interval.

My advice to Mr Horowitz would be to stick to children's books, where, perhaps, he will find a less discerning audience and one that will put up with his somewhat jejune ideas. And my advice to the audience? I'd say you should run to get tickets for this one – if you really want to see it. I suspect it won't be around for long.

There was a long silence once everyone had read it.

It was Ewan who spoke first. 'Well, at least she's given us a quote,' he said. '"Run to get tickets"! We can put that outside the theatre.'

I didn't know if he was joking or not.

It was a gut punch; there could be no denying it. The fact that it was the first review – and out so quickly – only made it worse. Would other critics read it? Was this to be the opening volley in an onslaught? Almost every person in the room had been insulted by Harriet Throsby and I could imagine each one of them obsessing about the parts of the review that referred to them. Ewan Lloyd on autopilot.

Jordan Williams grandiloquent. Tirian Kirke childish. Only Sky Palmer had got off relatively lightly. She was a talented actress undermined by the idiot writer. And what of me? Harriet had devoted more words to me than to anyone else, cheerfully apportioning me 'much of the blame'. Of course, I would have to pretend that I didn't mind, that it was just one review, that she didn't know what she was talking about, but I was already overwhelmed by a sense of failure that had fallen on me like a huge wave, dashing away any chance of a long West End run, a transfer to Broadway, the film of the play, the sequel. What struck me more than anything was the malice that ran through the review, the sense that she had enjoyed thinking up her little bons mots and spitting them in my direction. That joke about the stool, for example. Did she really have to do that?

'What is "jejune"?' Ahmet asked. There was a suggestion of hopefulness in his voice. Perhaps he was thinking that it might be a compliment.

'It doesn't matter,' Maureen said. She was standing right next to him, white-faced, her lips pressed tightly together.

'The bitch!' Jordan had not raised his voice, but the words exploded out of him. His eyes were staring, his face filled with fury. 'This isn't a review. This is a filthy piece of slander! And it's the third time she's done this to me. Everything I do – every time – she has it in for me. I'll kill her. I swear to you . . .!' He was holding the dagger that Ahmet had given him. He slammed it down into what was left of the cake.

'It's just one review.' Ewan was echoing exactly what I had been thinking, doing his job as director, trying to hold us all together. He took off his glasses and rubbed his eyes. 'This is just her opinion,' he went on, tiredly. 'The other critics often disagree with her. It was the same when I directed *Antigone*.'

'Someone should put a knife in her!' Jordan hadn't finished yet. 'She's a monster. She shouldn't get away with it.'

'How did she manage to write it so quickly?' I asked. 'The curtain only came down a couple of hours ago.'

'She starts her reviews before the play's finished,' Ewan explained. 'She's famous for it. She writes about the first half during the interval and does the rest on her way home.'

'She lives in the back end of Paddington,' Sky said. 'She's got a place near the canal. She probably finished it in the back of a taxi.'

'But why has she posted it?' I went on. 'Couldn't she wait until Sunday?'

'She must have wanted to get ahead of the pack.' Sky hastily turned off her phone and slid it into her pocket. 'I'm sorry. I wish I hadn't opened it now.'

Ahmet was sitting with his shoulders slumped, his face darker than ever. His hair was still wet from the rain and stuck to his skull like paint. He snatched up his cigarettes and lit one, then threw the packet down. 'What this woman says is all lies,' he announced. 'In Bath, in Reading, in Windsor, people liked the play. I was there! I saw them. What she writes here . . . this is shit.'

'She's disgusting,' Maureen said quietly.

Tirian hadn't spoken for a while. He seemed to have shrunk inside his expensive clothes, as if he – rather than they – had just come out of the washing machine, and right then he looked a bit like a teenager, sullen and scrawny, biting his lower lip as if he'd been told off for talking in class. 'Sod her!' he said. 'I'm going home. I've had enough to drink anyway.' He collected his few belongings, snatched up his backpack and hurried out of the room.

We all wanted to leave, but to end the party immediately would be to admit that we'd been defeated by Harriet Throsby's review, proving her power over us. So the six of us who were left talked for a few more minutes and drank some more vodka and whisky. But our hearts weren't in it. Sky was the next to go. It may have been that she was more miserable than any of us – but then she was the one who had spoiled the evening by showing us the review. I followed her.

I couldn't wait to get out. I wanted to go home, to put the Vaudeville behind me, to forget the play had happened. I knew I was being childish. It was only a bad review. But there isn't a writer in the world who hasn't felt that sense of anger, shame, resentfulness and sheer misery that comes when a critic lets loose. It's just that some of us hide it better than others.

The rain had eased off, but I was still damp and shivering by the time I got back to my flat in Clerkenwell. It was one o'clock in the morning and I was worn out. I went to bed in the spare room and fell asleep almost immediately. Not surprisingly, I dreamed of Harriet Throsby. Once again, I saw those horn-rimmed glasses she'd been wearing and heard the brittle edge to her voice. Jordan Williams was also there, stabbing the cake, and I heard him too: *'Someone should put a knife in her!'* That was when I woke up.

I looked at my watch. It was twenty past eleven. I don't know how I'd managed to sleep in so late, but the pounding in my head told me that a mixture of whisky, vodka and Turkish wine had probably helped. The moment I padded out to the kitchen in my bare feet, I knew the flat was empty. Jill would have gone to work hours ago. Sure enough, there was a Post-it note from her stuck to the fridge. *Quite a good review in The Times. Hope others are OK. Back at 6 p.m. Don't forget laundry.* Quite good. I knew Jill too well. We'd worked together for years in television and we both knew that 'quite good' was never good enough.

I wasted the rest of the morning. I was tempted to go out and get the newspapers or check them out online, but that's something I never do any more. Why rush out in search of a self-inflicted wound? I imagined Ewan or Ahmet would call me with the bad news. It was always possible that Throsby had turned out to be the lone voice of dissent. Throsby and *The Times*. Maybe some of the other critics had loved the play. I decided that, for a few hours more, I would live in hope.

So I made myself breakfast. I had a bath and listened to music. I fiddled with the next book I was about to start writing – *Moonflower Murders* – but although I liked the idea of forward motion, moving on to the next project, anything that wasn't a play, the words wouldn't come. I stared out of the window at the Shard and St Paul's Cathedral and vaguely wondered if it would be possible to hang-glide from one to the other. As it turned out, this was something Alex Rider would do in his next adventure. I drank two mugs of tea and ate too many chocolate digestive biscuits.

At ten past four, the doorbell rang.

I went to the intercom, assuming it would be a delivery. Living six floors up and with no video camera, I seldom saw anyone's face. My day was punctuated by disembodied voices. 'Yes?'

'Mr Horowitz?'

'Who is this?'

'It's the police. Can we come in?'

My first thought was that something had happened to Jill or to one of my sons. I hurried down six flights of stairs and over to the double set of doors at the end of the hallway. I was still in my bedroom slippers and I had forgotten my keys, so I had to wedge the inner door behind me with one foot whilst stretching awkwardly to push open the outer one. And that was how I was, strangely contorted, as I took in the two figures standing on the pavement and realised that

I knew them and that they were really the last people in the world I wanted to see.

The bulky frame of Detective Inspector Cara Grunshaw was blocking my view of Cowcross Street with an expression on her face that brilliantly amalgamated a scowl and a smile. Her assistant, DC Mills, was behind her.

'Hello, Anthony,' she said. 'I wonder if we could have a word?'

5

Daggers Drawn

I knew Detective Inspector Cara Grunshaw very well. When Hawthorne was investigating the murder of the Hampstead divorce lawyer Richard Pryce, she had been the officer in charge of the case and she hadn't been amused when he arrived at the truth ahead of her. That wasn't the worst of it. I had inadvertently given her false information that had led her to arrest the wrong man – much to Hawthorne's amusement. He'd even suggested she might lose her job. Well, that clearly hadn't happened. Here she was, waiting to come in, with her equally unfriendly assistant, Detective Constable Derek Mills, standing beside her, both of them gazing at me like hyenas who have stumbled across a fresh carcass. I knew I was in trouble even if I had no idea what that trouble might be.

'What's this all about?' I asked, innocently.

'We'd prefer to talk inside, if you don't mind.'

'Do I have to let you in?'

Cara exchanged a knowing glance with her deputy. 'We could throw you in the car and take you down to the police station if you prefer,' she said.

This might not have been true, but I decided not to argue. I've always had a fear of authority figures that goes back to my schooldays, and Cara somehow encapsulated the maths, French and history teachers who had terrified me when I was eight. She was a round, solid woman with an overbearing presence defined by muscular arms and broad shoulders that would have served her well in a scrum. She wore heavy plastic spectacles that seemed to be sinking into the bridge of her nose. In fact, her whole face had a soft, pliable quality as if she had been created out of playdough. Her eyes, popped in as a last-minute afterthought, were small and hostile. What I most remembered about her was her jet-black hair, which didn't look real. The strands swept down on both sides like miniature curtains that had been pulled back to give a view of her face. She was wearing a well-tailored, dark olive suit and a roll-neck jersey. No jewellery.

She elbowed her way past me and into the entrance hall, followed by Mills, who could have concealed himself in her shadow. He was smaller and lighter than her, with thinning hair that he never bothered to brush. He was wearing the same leather jacket as the first time I'd met him, though with more food stains. He eyed me briefly as he came in, making sure that I had registered his complete contempt for me, for my home, for the entire neighbourhood.

'Which floor?' Cara asked.

'I'm at the top,' I said.

She looked at the stairs. 'Do you have a lift?'

'I'm afraid it's out of order.' This wasn't true, but the lift was tiny and slow and I couldn't bear to think of myself trapped inside it with the two of them.

We walked up and into the main living room, with the seating area on one side, a dining table in the middle and a kitchen at the back. The flat had been a meat warehouse a hundred years before and it still had an industrial feel with high ceilings, exposed brickwork and lots of empty space. I saw Cara taking in her surroundings and felt strangely violated, having her here. She hadn't been invited. She had invaded.

'Would you like to sit down?' I gestured at the table. I wanted this to be businesslike and the sofas didn't feel appropriate. Nor did I offer her coffee or tea. I still had no idea what had brought her here but I wanted her and her assistant out as soon as possible.

They sat at the table. 'Nice place,' Cara said.

'Thank you.' There was a long silence. I was standing by the grand piano – which I had inherited from my mother and which I played every day – and I realised that Cara was waiting for me to join them. I walked over and took my place at the end of the table, as far away from them as I could. 'So . . . ?' I asked.

'I wonder if you could tell us where you were last night?'

It was a line I would never have used in a television drama – it's such an old chestnut – but that was really how she began.

'I was in bed,' I said.

'Before that.'

'I was at the theatre.'

Mills had already been scribbling my answers down in his notebook, but somehow he picked up the fact that he'd been given his cue. 'It was the first night of your play,' he said.

'If you knew that, why did you ask me?'

He ignored me. '*Mindgame* at the Vaudeville,' he went on. He twitched his moustache without seeming to move his upper lip. It was a neat trick. 'It hasn't had very good reviews,' he went on. 'The *Guardian* said it was pretentious.'

'I don't look at the reviews,' I muttered.

'The critic from the *Daily Mail* said it was the worst play he'd ever seen. *The Times* wasn't sure. *Variety* said: "It's so goofy it's almost fun."' He looked at me sadly. 'Almost,' he repeated.

I felt the familiar sickness in my stomach. 'It's very nice of you to come and tell me what the newspapers think of my play,' I said. 'But wouldn't you say that's a slight waste of police time?'

'And Harriet Throsby was the worst of all,' Mills went on. 'She really tore it apart. I imagine they'll publish her review posthumously in the *Sunday Times*. Maybe they'll frame it in a black border. That would be a nice touch, wouldn't you say, ma'am?'

These last words had been addressed to Grunshaw. She nodded slowly.

'Sort of a . . . final curtain,' Mills added.

'What are you saying?' I cut in. 'Is Harriet Throsby . . . ?' I couldn't finish the sentence. Not because I was shocked. It just seemed so unlikely.

'Did you meet her at the theatre?' Cara asked, ignoring my question.

'Yes, briefly.'

'And did you read her review?'

'Yes. We all did. It was on Sky's phone.'

'That would be Sky Palmer.'

'She played Nurse Plimpton.' I wondered why I'd used the past tense. Perhaps it was because I knew that my play was dead too.

'There was a party backstage at the theatre, is that right? Can you remember what time you left?'

Suddenly I was angry. 'Look, I'm not going to answer any of your questions until you tell me what's happened. Has Harriet Throsby been murdered?'

Cara looked shocked. 'Whatever gave you that idea, Anthony?'

'You said she'd written her last review. You said it would be published posthumously.'

'She could have had a heart attack. She could have fallen under a bus.'

'Then what are you doing here?'

Cara conceded the point. She let Mills tell me. 'Harriet Throsby was stabbed to death in her home sometime around ten o'clock this morning. Can you tell us where you were at that time?'

'I was in bed.'

'Still in bed?' Mills sounded disbelieving.

'I went to bed late. I got up late.'

'Could your wife verify that?'

For a moment I was confused as various thoughts crossed my mind at the same time. 'No,' I admitted. 'She'd gone to work.'

'When did she go to work?'

'I can't tell you that. I was asleep.'

Mills wrote down my answer, presumably word for word. He underlined something not once but twice. He was making it clear that he doubted what I was saying.

Cara took over. 'Do you own an ornamental dagger?' she asked.

'No,' I said. She had caught me unawares and looked at me sadly, as if I had just given myself away. She was waiting for me to continue and I realised the mistake I had made. 'Actually, I do have a sort of dagger,' I said. 'Ahmet gave it to me last night.'

'You're referring to Ahmet Yurdakul, the producer of *Mindgame*?'

'Yes. It was a first-night present. He gave one to everyone.' I stared. 'Are you saying that Harriet was stabbed with one of the daggers?'

Again, I received no answer. That was Cara's technique. She wanted me to know that she was in control. 'Can you describe the dagger?' she asked, sweetly.

'All the daggers were the same. They were silver. About this long . . .' I showed her with two fingers. 'And there were some words on the blade. "*Is this a dagger . . .?*"'

'I would have thought that was pretty obvious,' Mills said.

'It's a quotation from *Macbeth*,' I explained. '"*Is this a dagger which I see before me?*" Ahmet had produced the play in a castle somewhere in Yorkshire and he had some left over.'

'I don't suppose your dagger had any distinguishing features?' Cara asked. She sounded completely reasonable and it should have warned me that she had constructed a trap into which she was gently leading me.

'No,' I said. 'I explained to you. The knives were identical.' Then I remembered. 'Actually, there was one thing. My dagger had a sort of decoration on the hilt. A round disc. It was loose.'

Cara raised her eyebrows as if to say that this was what she had been expecting. 'And where is your dagger?' she asked.

I was ahead of her. From the moment she'd mentioned the dagger, I'd been wondering what I'd done with the bloody thing. I remembered opening the package at the stage door and talking about it with Sky Palmer. I'd certainly had it with me when I went into the green room. But after that, things were a bit hazier. I'd had a lot to drink, both at the formal cast party and afterwards. Then there had been the bombshell of the review and the whole evening had disintegrated. All I'd wanted to do was go home. I was sure, though, that I'd brought it with me. I could see it in my hand as I walked the short distance up the Strand and across to Clerkenwell. What could I have done with it when I got in? I tried to reconstruct my movements. I hadn't wanted to disturb Jill, so I'd used the downstairs bathroom. I'd left my clothes on the piano.

But I had gone – briefly – into my office on the top floor! I remembered that now. I'd wanted to check my emails to see if any of my friends had said anything nice about the play. And I'd put the dagger on my desk beside the computer. I must have done.

'It's upstairs,' I said.

'Would you mind getting it for us?'

'Not at all. I'll just be a minute.'

I didn't like leaving them there. I didn't want them going through my things. But I had to get this over with and so I ran up to my office, which was right at the top of the flat, and went straight to the computer. And the knife, of course, wasn't there.

It's been the same ever since I turned fifty. I spend hours every day looking for glasses, my wallet, my phone, the letter I need, the shopping list I've been given. I hate the idea of getting old, but that's how I feel when I go into a room to get something and forget what it is I've come for before I can even begin looking. And then there are the false memories. The pen that I definitely put in my pocket. The watch that I'm sure I left by the bath. Except I didn't – and they're not there. That was how it was now. I quickly searched my office but I knew that I wouldn't find the dagger. It seemed likely that I'd never brought it home in the first place.

I went back down.

'It's not there,' I said, trying to sound casual. 'I must have left it in the theatre.'

'We've been to the theatre,' Cara said, barely able to keep the triumph out of her voice. 'It wasn't there.'

'Well, I'm not sure what I've done with it.' I forced a smile to my lips, fighting the strange sensation that I was acting a part, that nothing I said or did was real any more. I had this extraordinary urge to confess, to say 'I killed her!' even though I hadn't.

'Perhaps we can help you,' Cara said. She nodded at Mills.

'We retrieved an ornamental dagger from the home of the deceased,' Mills intoned, effortlessly slipping into the stilted language so loved by police officers. 'And we can confirm it has a medallion with a silver design on the grip. That said medallion has come loose.'

'Well, the daggers were cheap,' I exclaimed. 'They were all faulty!'

Cara shook her head. 'We've already spoken to the other recipients,' she told me. 'Ewan Lloyd, the director. Sky Palmer, Jordan Williams and Tirian Kirke in the cast. They all have their daggers and we've been able to examine them. None of them have any loose parts. We've also contacted Ahmet Yurdakul, who assures us that there were only the five daggers given out at the London premiere.'

'The dagger that killed Harriet Throsby is your dagger,' Mills said.

'No. That's not possible.'

'Then where is it?'

'I just told you. I was very tired last night. It was late. I must have forgotten it and left it behind at the theatre.'

'That's not what you said a moment ago.' Cara Grunshaw was merciless. 'You told us it was upstairs.'

'I thought it was.'

'You lied to us.'

'That's ridiculous. Get out of my flat. I'm not talking to you without a lawyer.'

'It's a bit late for that, Anthony.' Cara was enjoying herself. It was always possible that she really believed I had killed Harriet Throsby, but that didn't matter. The identity of the killer was almost irrelevant. This was revenge for what I had done to her, feeding her the false story that had led to her humiliation.

She left the honours to Mills.

'Anthony Horowitz,' he said, 'I am now arresting you on suspicion of the murder of Harriet Throsby at 27 Palgrove Gardens, W9. You do not have to say anything. But it may harm your defence if . . .'

You must know the words. I've written them enough times in enough books and police dramas. But I zoned out as he pronounced the formal police caution. I saw his lips moving but I didn't hear anything. I was being arrested! No! That was insane.

And what was it, echoing in my brain, ricocheting around my skull, the one thing that could save me, the one person I needed to see right now?

Hawthorne.

6
One Phone Call

After he had arrested me, Mills went out to the car, leaving me alone with his boss. I was completely dazed. Perhaps I was even in shock. In all my time on the planet all I'd ever managed was a speeding ticket and now I was being arrested for murder? I couldn't get my head around it. I asked her if I could make a phone call.

'You can do that from the station,' she said.

'But I've got a phone here.'

She scowled at me but in a way that suggested she was enjoying every minute of this. 'Did you really kill her because she gave you a bad review?' she asked.

'I didn't kill anyone!' I tried to appeal to her human side. 'Look, if you're annoyed with me because of what happened the last time we met, that really wasn't my fault. I mean, I didn't do it on purpose—'

'It'll go easier for you if you come clean,' she interrupted.

She had no human side. For the next few minutes, she said nothing, sitting at my table like some sort of malevolent Buddha, unmoving and imperious, letting me sweat it out as I wondered what was going to happen next.

Then Mills returned. Cara got up and let him in – she wouldn't even allow me to answer my own door phone and I marvelled at the way that, when the police take control of you, they assume almost total power. Mills was carrying a pile of oversized plastic bags, which he placed on the table. 'You're going to have to get changed,' he said.

'What?' I was wearing a T-shirt and the same jeans I'd had on the night before. 'Why?'

'We need your clothes.' He searched in the pile and pulled out a pale blue onesie with a zip up the front. It was made of a very thin fabric, like paper.

'I'm not putting that on!' I protested.

'Yes, you are,' Mills assured me.

'I'll leave you two men together,' Cara said and left the room with a half-concealed smirk. She didn't go far, though. I could still feel her presence out in the hallway. She was probably watching through the crack in the door.

Mills made me strip off and put on the jumpsuit. He put plastic bags over my hands. 'Where's your bedroom?' he asked.

We went up together and he made me show him the clothes I'd worn the night before. All of these went into the plastic bags, which he carefully labelled and sealed. After what had happened the last time we met, he wasn't going to make any mistakes. Finally, the three of us left together. I was feeling ridiculous in the outfit they'd given me. It rustled as I walked. But from the research I'd been doing half my life, and, indeed, from what Hawthorne had told me when I was writing *Injustice*, I knew they weren't doing all this just to humiliate me. They were keeping the evidence clean, preventing any fibres transferring themselves from me to their police car and vice versa. My humiliation was just an enjoyable extra.

Their car was parked outside – not a police car but a tatty Ford Escort. I asked them where we were going, but of course they didn't tell me, and once again I felt the whisper of terror that comes from having handed over all choice, all control to representatives of the state. I was a parcel in their hands and they could deliver me where they liked.

That turned out to be Islington, a couple of miles away. We drove past Marks and Spencer and the Vue Cinema, then turned off into a series of streets I had never visited. Another left turn brought us to a surprisingly handsome low-rise building that might have been a council office designed for the more upmarket residents of the borough. My two arresting officers made no comment and there was no sign of any police activity outside. We slowed down and stopped in front of a rather more menacing wall that abutted the building, topped with spikes and razor wire. A gate opened and we drove into a car park filled with police vehicles, gravel, security cameras and despair. As the gate swung shut behind me, I felt utterly cut off from my own life. I can't quite describe my sense of emptiness, a sense of disbelief that wrenched me from the world I had always known.

A side door led into the custody office, which was small and utilitarian, painted in drab shades of grey and white with official forms pinned to every wall. It reminded me of an old-fashioned bank or building society on a particularly bad day. There were three uniformed officers sitting behind desks with plexiglass screens and computers. I was placed on a stool opposite. But I wasn't here to take out money. In fact, I was the one being deposited.

'Name?' the custody sergeant asked, sweetly. She was in uniform, very neat and well presented, and it struck me that in another life she would have done well as a receptionist, perhaps at the Savoy.

I was about to reply, but then realised she had not expected me to answer for myself. Why should I when I was nothing more than an object to be processed? She had been addressing Cara Grunshaw.

'This is Anthony Horowitz,' Grunshaw said. 'He has been arrested on suspicion of the murder of Harriet Throsby. It is necessary for him to be held in custody in order to interview him and secure evidence.'

They were lines that could have come out of the world's worst-written play, delivered by actors who had never learned to act. Of all the languages in the world, officialese is the grimmest, lacking any sense of humanity. And the custody sergeant, for all her smiles, was no better. 'I have heard the reason for the arrest and the need to detain you,' she told me, once Grunshaw had finished. Her voice mangled the lines, as if she couldn't quite believe she was saying them. 'You will be held here to secure and preserve evidence and to obtain evidence by questioning. Is there anything you wish to say at this stage?'

What could I possibly say?

'I would like to assert and to place on record the possibility that, as evidenced from the two previous statements, you and your colleagues have absolutely no idea what you're doing. You're all idiots. This is completely crazy. And if you don't let me go, I'm going to sue the whole lot of you . . .'

But I didn't say that. This probably wasn't a good place to make enemies.

'You're making a mistake,' I said.

They all smiled. They'd never heard that one before.

'Would you like someone informed you are here?'

Oh God! That was a difficult question. Of course I had to tell my wife. But at the same time, I couldn't. It wasn't as if there was anything she could do and what was the point of worrying her when, surely to goodness, I'd be out of here before she noticed I was missing. Hilda Starke? My agent hadn't come to the first night of *Mindgame*: she was on holiday in Barbados. I wasn't even sure what the time was over there. She might be in bed or, worse still, sunning herself on the beach. She wouldn't appreciate being interrupted and anyway, I wasn't sure how she could help. The only lawyers I knew were the ones who had helped me buy my flat and I wasn't even sure they had a criminal division. Hawthorne? No, not yet. He was the ace up my sleeve. There was still a chance this would sort itself out. I would only use him when I had to.

What would happen if all this got into the press? I don't know why I asked myself that question just then, but suddenly I could see it: the headline. ALEX RIDER AUTHOR ON MURDER CHARGE. My children's books would collapse. On the other hand, it might help my crime-fiction sales. I couldn't believe I'd had that thought. This wasn't, under any circumstances, the sort of publicity I wanted. I was still clinging to the hope that the police would hold me for a few hours and then let me go.

'Not for the moment, thank you,' I said.

The process continued, everything done by the book. I was made to stand on a yellow mat (the words SEARCH MAT were helpfully written on the surface) and searched with a metal detector, even though I wasn't wearing my own clothes and had no pockets. I was escorted to a second room and photographed. After that, images of my fingerprints were taken. I was quietly disappointed that this was done not with an inkpad, but digitally against a glass panel, although I really should have known. Meanwhile, a middle-aged woman in a stretch-cotton tracksuit had been brought in and was being processed alongside me, a torrent of swear words pouring out of her mouth. As the shock of my arrest wore off, I found myself feeling increasingly uncomfortable. I don't think I'm a snob. But the criminal class was one I'd never wished to join.

Cara Grunshaw and Derek Mills had retreated to a distance, but whenever I looked at them, they were staring in my direction, watching me being processed like an oven-ready chicken and clearly relishing the entire business. Worse than that, they were waiting for me to be delivered back to them. All this was being done for their pleasure. Eventually, I would be placed in their hands, the door would slam . . . and what then? I wondered how long they could keep me. When they finally realised their mistake, as surely they would, how would they make up for it? Could I sue them for wrongful arrest? That, at least, was a pleasant thought.

I was taken down a narrow corridor and into a third room. I call it that, but it had no walls, no door, no obvious shape. It had the feel of a storage area. There was another police officer sitting at a table, surrounded by cardboard boxes. Bizarrely, this turned out to be the surgery. The officer pulled the bags off my hands and used a wooden paddle to scrape some of the detritus from under my fingernails. I assumed they were hoping for traces of Harriet Throsby's blood and that thought cheered me up a little as I knew they wouldn't find any. Next, the officer used a swab to take some cell samples from the inside of my mouth and it was while he was setting about this intimate process that I realised he hadn't so much as said hello to me. I hoped a rectal examination wasn't about to follow.

In fact, it was almost over. The officer plucked a few hairs off my head and carefully deposited them in a plastic bag. He now had different bits of my DNA in a whole variety of containers and each one of them would prove that I was innocent. That was all that mattered.

I was escorted back to the custody sergeant.

'You are entitled to free legal advice,' she told me.

'No, thanks.' I hadn't done anything wrong. That was what I told myself. Somehow this would sort itself out. I didn't need a lawyer yet.

'Would you like to read a book called *The Code of Practice*, which explains all our police powers and procedures?'

I was tempted. It didn't sound like a smash-hit bestseller, but I had nothing else to read. 'No, thank you,' I said.

'You can now make a phone call, if you wish. You will only be permitted to make one phone call so please consider carefully who you would like to speak to.'

I had been thinking of nothing else. This was the reason why I didn't need my agent or a lawyer or even my wife. There was only one person in the world who could get me out of this mess and all along I'd been waiting for the opportunity to make the call. 'I have a friend . . .' I said.

The custody sergeant had a desk telephone and slipped the receiver under the plexiglass screen. I gave her the number and she dialled.

On the third ring, Hawthorne answered.

'Hawthorne!' I said.

'Tony!'

For once, I didn't correct him. 'I need your help.'

'What's happened, mate?'

'I've been arrested.'

'What for?'

'Murder!'

He didn't speak for a moment and I heard what sounded like a station announcement in the background. 'Are you still there?' I asked.

He was still there. 'Who did you kill?'

How could he ask that? 'I didn't kill anyone!' I almost shouted. I had to control myself. This was the only call I was allowed. I took a deep breath. 'Harriet Throsby has been stabbed,' I explained. 'She's a critic. She gave my play a bad review.'

'It's had a lot of bad reviews,' Hawthorne said. 'I've seen the newspapers.' He paused. 'Have any of the other critics been murdered?'

I ignored this. 'You've got to get me out of here.'

'Where are you?'

'In Islington. Tolpuddle Street.'

'There's not much I can do, mate. They can keep you for ninety-six hours.'

'Ninety-six!' Somehow, with my brain whirling, I managed to do the maths. 'That's four days!'

'They'll need to see a superintendent to get permission to keep hold of you after the first twenty-four. Who's the arresting officer?'

'That's the thing. It's Cara Grunshaw.'

The custody officer was gesturing at me. My time was up.

'Say hello from me!' Hawthorne said.

'Hawthorne – she hates you,' I hissed into the phone. 'And she hates me even more.'

'Yeah, you've got a point there. That's not good news.'

Was he doing this on purpose? Then I remembered. I'd refused to work on the fourth book. We'd had an argument. I should have known he would leave me in the lurch. 'Can you do anything to help?' I asked, suddenly miserable.

'Not really. I'm on the tube.'

'Can you talk to Detective Inspector Grunshaw?'

'I doubt she'd listen to me.'

'I shouldn't have rung you, should I.'

'Not really. This is what I'd do if I were you—'

I almost heard the tube train as it plunged into a tunnel. I certainly felt the darkness close in on me. The phone went dead. I handed the receiver back to the custody sergeant. I was on my own.

Cara Grunshaw stepped up to me. 'We'll talk tomorrow,' she said.

I watched as she and Mills walked out through a door that opened for them but wouldn't do the same for me.

A few minutes later, an older man – a police sergeant, I think – came for me and led me through a quite different door that took me further into the building. There was a barred gate on the other side and I could see a short corridor with eight cells. Now I could hear the woman who had been arrested at the same time as me. She was still screaming swear words. In another cell, a man was cackling with laughter. The air smelled dreadful: a mixture of sweat, urine, detergent and cheap microwaved food. The sergeant unlocked the cell and led me through.

'I've put you in at the end,' he said. 'It's a bit quieter there.' He was trying to be kind, but he could have been the ferryman taking me to hell. 'My son's read your books,' he added as we continued on our way.

'Has he?'

'He used to read them when he was small. He's twenty-eight now, but he'll be amazed when I tell him I met you here.'

'What does he do?' I asked, hoping he wouldn't tell anyone else.

'He's a journalist.'

We reached the door and he opened it with another key. 'I'll bring you in some supper in half an hour. Do you have any allergies?'

'I'm not hungry.'

'Well, I'll bring it anyway. I'm sure I can trust you not to throw it at the wall. Honestly, some of the people we get in here!'

My cell.

It was rectangular with a concrete floor, a bed moulded into the wall and, behind a screen, a metal toilet with a push-button flush and no seat. There was a barred window with milky glass so that it allowed no view, but that didn't matter because it was too high up to look through anyway. I could make out the glare of a sodium light and I got the feeling that the evening had arrived and it was already dark. I had no watch. A CCTV camera looked down at me from the corner. I wondered if Mills and Grunshaw were examining me at this very minute.

I sat on the bed. It had a blue plastic mattress, a scrubby blanket and a pillow that had played host to too many heads.

'Are you going to be all right?' the sergeant asked.

'I'm fine, thank you,' I said, but without conviction.

'You can change out of that jumpsuit now. We've left you some clothes you'll find more comfortable.'

I noticed the clothes for the first time, piled neatly at the end of the bed. A pair of grey tracksuit trousers, a grey sweatshirt, elasticated shoes . . . poor cousins to trainers.

The sergeant left and with the clank of the key turning in the lock came the awful realisation of what had happened to me. My freedom had been taken away from me. I was going to be forced to stay in this horrible place for possibly ninety-six hours. I could still hear the laughing man and the screaming woman. There were other sounds too: hollow echoes, more doors slamming, the buzz of an electric switch. Of course prison is horrible. I'd visited enough of them to know that for myself. But I had never experienced what it meant to be a prisoner, and that was much worse. I had never felt more alone. I almost wanted to cry.

I curled up on the bed, feeling the plastic crackle beneath me. I dragged the pillow towards me, then threw it away once I'd smelled it. I drew up my legs, closed my eyes and waited for sleep to come.

7
The Custody Clock

'So, how are you feeling?' Cara Grunshaw asked, managing to load that normally innocent question with an extraordinary amount of malevolence.

Beside her, Derek Mills smiled unpleasantly.

It was the following day, and I was sitting in yet another horrible room, this one designed for interrogations. It was soundproofed, with a two-tone wall – brown on grey – the two dreary shades separated by a black panic strip. I was being video-recorded, sitting on one side of a metal table with the two of them opposite. All of this was predictable. But what had surprised me was how long my arresting officers had left me on my own before calling me in for this interview. The custody clock was ticking. Ninety-six hours! That was how long they could keep me, according to Hawthorne. He'd also told me they would have to get authorisation from a superintendent after twenty-four.

I glanced at my phone. It was already eleven o'clock. I'd been twiddling my thumbs all morning, but finally I could see a way out of this nightmare. Unless the superintendent was as mad as they were, he or she would understand that I was completely blameless and that Cara Grunshaw was pursuing a personal vendetta. Apart from the murder weapon, there was no evidence whatsoever to implicate me. Ahmet had handed out at least five of those absurd, cheaply made daggers, and for all I knew, he could have a dozen more at home. And did she really think I would murder Harriet Throsby simply because she had given me a bad review? It's critics who kill writers, never the other way round.

'I'm fine, thank you,' I said.

It might have given Cara some measure of satisfaction, leaving me here the whole morning. But I could put up with it because I was counting the hours before I walked out of here. I was sure of it. I would get a taxi home. I would have a bath and put all this behind me.

So why was Mills still smiling?

Cara Grunshaw produced a sealed bag. Inside it I saw one of the *Macbeth* knives, coated in blood that had turned brown and smeared itself across the plastic. Seeing it like this only reminded me what an absurd gift it had been in the first place. It wasn't even as though it was simply an ornament. It was actually lethal!

'This is the dagger that killed Harriet Throsby,' Cara said. 'It's your dagger. We have examined all the others and this is the only one that has a faulty design. More to the point, your dagger is the only one that's unaccounted for. How do you explain that?'

'I left it in the green room,' I said. 'Anyone could have picked it up.'

'You told us you took it home,' Mills remarked, with evident satisfaction.

'I thought I had. I must have made a mistake.'

'You lied to us.'

'No. It was a mistake.'

'We found a set of fingerprints on this dagger,' Cara told me. She was holding the bag in front of her as if she could actually see them. 'They are your fingerprints, Anthony. They're a perfect match.'

'I held the dagger when I was at the Vaudeville. I'm not denying that.'

'And you're saying someone stole it. But there are no other fingerprints on the hilt, which means that they would have had to handle it very carefully. Do you think they were deliberately trying to incriminate you?'

'I suppose that's possible.'

'Payback for writing such a crap play,' Mills sneered.

'Do you know where Harriet Throsby lived?' Grunshaw asked.

I sighed. 'Yes. Twenty-seven Palgrove Gardens, Little Venice.'

Her eyes widened at this admission. 'How did you know that?' she demanded.

'You told me when you arrested me.'

Cara thought back. I saw the calculation in her eyes. 'I didn't mention Little Venice.'

'You said W9. Anyway, I know where Palgrove Gardens is. I often walk my dog along the Regent's Canal and it's close to the tunnel.'

Was I deliberately digging my own grave? Mills leapt on me. 'So you admit you know the vicinity.'

'I didn't know Harriet lived there,' I replied. 'Until you told me.'

'But you could have known. There was a feature on her in *House & Garden* magazine in January – three months ago. "A Great Place to Live". It didn't give the address, but they mentioned the area where she lived and they were stupid enough to show the front of the house, along with the number. So it wouldn't have taken you long to track it down.'

'Except that I've never read *House & Garden*.'

'Did you have any contact with Harriet Throsby when she came to the Vaudeville?' Cara asked. I should have recognised her technique. She was deliberately and very quickly changing the subject, giving me no time to think.

'No.'

'You didn't shake hands – or embrace?'

'No!'

'Forensics found a hair on her blouse . . . the blouse she was wearing when she was killed. We've sent it for tests, but on first examination, it's the same colour and length as yours.'

'It can't be mine,' I said. 'I never went anywhere near her. And I was nowhere near her house.'

'You can say that now,' Cara said. 'But once we have a DNA match, it'll all be over. And there's something else. Show him, Derek.'

'Yes, ma'am.' Mills presented his next magic trick. This time I found myself looking at a black-and-white photograph of a man walking along the towpath next to the canal. The picture was taken by a CCTV camera and from behind, but I saw at once that the man had a very similar height and build to me. He was also wearing a grey puffer jacket with the hood up. I had a piece of clothing just like that.

'This was taken at half past nine yesterday morning, approximately thirty minutes before Harriet Throsby was stabbed to death. The camera was positioned round the corner from where Ms Throsby resided, close to the Maida Hill Tunnel. Do you recognise the man in the picture?'

'No.'

'It looks very much like you.'

'It can't be me. At half past nine yesterday morning, I was in bed.'

'But you have no witnesses to that. We only have your word for it.'

I had a sense of the clouds closing in and suddenly that twenty-four hours was looking more like twenty-four years. The weapon was mine. It had my fingerprints on it. A man very similar to me had been photographed in the area at the time of the murder. My hair was on the body. I had a motive: the bad review.

'It will make this a lot easier for you if you confess,' Cara Grunshaw said.

'And the judge will take it into account too,' Mills added.

They both sounded so reasonable.

'Go to hell,' I said. There was no point antagonising them, but I couldn't stop myself. I'd had enough.

After that, I was taken back to the custody cell. I knew what was going happen next. Cara was waiting until the DNA on the stray hair had been analysed by the laboratory and then, assuming there was a match with mine, she would charge me with murder. Was there any way one of my hairs could have ended up on the dead body of a theatre critic in Little Venice? It was impossible. I hadn't come into contact with her at the theatre. And even if someone had set out to frame me, as Cara had suggested, there was surely no way they could have plucked it out of my head without my knowing.

The next few hours passed very slowly. The laughing man and the screaming woman had gone, but I had a new neighbour who made up for their absence by sobbing, chanting and slamming something – perhaps his head – against the wall. I'd had very little sleep the night before, but somehow I must have managed to nod off because the next thing I knew, the door had banged open and Cara Grunshaw and Derek Mills had marched in, the custody sergeant lingering behind. I knew at once that something had gone wrong . . . at least, as far as they were concerned. Cara was holding a pile of my own clothes.

'We're letting you go,' she announced.

'So you know I'm innocent,' I said.

'We know you did it. The motive, the murder weapon, the opportunity . . . they all point to you, and the DNA result will screw you once and for all. But it seems you've had a bit of luck. We've got a computer problem at the Metropolitan Police Forensic Science Laboratory in Lambeth. We're not going to get your results until the end of play tomorrow and the superintendent has decided you're not a flight risk, so we don't need to hold you.'

'You still have to surrender your passport,' Mills added, nastily.

'And there's someone here to see you.'

They waited outside while I got changed. Already feeling more human, I followed them out of the cell, back down the corridor, then through the barred gate and, finally, the metal door into the room where I had first been processed.

Hawthorne was waiting for me.

I felt a sense of something close to affection. Right then, I almost wanted to throw my arms around his shoulders and hug him – something that would have been unthinkable in normal circumstances. I didn't understand how he came to be there and at that moment it didn't occur to me that he might have had anything to do with my release. All I could think was that I had called him and, eventually, he had come.

'How are you doing, Tony, mate?' he enquired, cheerfully.

'I've been better,' I growled.

'I thought you might like a lift out of here.'

'Have you got a car?'

'I've got a cab.'

As usual, of course, I'd pay.

'You two enjoy yourselves,' Grunshaw muttered. 'And just remember, "Tony", we can rearrest you at any time.'

'Come off it, Detective Inspector!' Hawthorne looked amused. 'You know as well as I do that Tony had nothing to do with the death of Harriet Throsby, whatever evidence you've managed to cobble together against him. First of all, he could never hurt anyone. Look at him! The only thing he's ever hit in his life is a computer keyboard. He writes about murder but I've seen him get queasy at the sight of blood. And if he killed every critic who had something bad to say about his work, there'd be hundreds of corpses littered across the country.'

'Why don't you say something nice about me?' I muttered.

'Well, if he didn't do it, who did?' Cara asked.

'I suppose that's what I'm going to have to find out for you, like I did last time. And maybe you should think about that. Another false arrest coming so soon after the last one isn't going to look too good on your CV, is it!'

'There is no one else, Hawthorne,' Cara sneered. 'You can investigate if you want to, but you'd better make it quick because as soon as we have the DNA evidence, I'm going to fall on him like a ton of bricks.'

'You've definitely got the physique for it, Cara.'

'Get out of here. Both of you.'

There was a taxi waiting for us outside the custody centre. I expected we'd be going back to Farringdon, but to my surprise it took us past my flat and on to Hawthorne's place at Riverside View. I used the journey to tell him what had happened in the last few days – at least, from my own perspective. What I described was pretty much everything I have written so far here. Hawthorne said little. He was looking away from me, gazing out of the window, and I wondered if he was even listening. But that was his way. When he interrogated people, he often seemed to be distracted, although there was never a single word, not even a nuance, that he missed.

We sat down in the kitchen where we had met a few days ago and he made me a cup of coffee. It felt very good to be sitting there, in spotless surroundings, in my own clothes, acting normally, with nobody screaming or praying next door. Better still, Hawthorne was on my side. At least, he seemed to be.

He brought the coffee over. 'You OK?' he asked.

'I'm much better,' I admitted. 'Thanks for coming to Tolpuddle Street.'

'I couldn't leave you in there on your own. It's not a nice place, is it!'

'You can say that again. Have you got a biscuit?'

'No.'

I'd barely eaten for a day and a half.

Hawthorne was sitting opposite me and I felt him examining me, his eyes boring into mine. 'What is it?' I asked.

'There's something I've got to know,' he said. He grimaced. 'Did you do it? Did you kill Harriet Throsby?'

'What?' I almost choked on my coffee.

'I hate to ask you, mate. I mean, I don't want to be nasty about this, but it'll be a waste of both our time if it turns out you did actually stick in the knife.'

'How can you possibly think that!' I struggled to find the words. 'After what you said to Grunshaw . . .'

'I had to say that to get you out of there. I had to make it sound like I believed you. But the truth is, I wouldn't blame you. Harriet was really nasty about your play.' He shook his head. 'Maybe in future you should stick to books.'

'I didn't go near her.'

'You may say that – but the trouble is, Grunshaw's got enough evidence to hang you out to dry. And when the DNA results come in . . .'

'It's not my hair. It can't be. I never went near her.'

'That's where you're wrong, mate. I've already seen the analysis. It's a definite match – 99.999 per cent probability.'

'That's impossible! Wait a minute . . .' There were so many different thoughts in my head that they could have been having a massive punch-up, trying to get my attention. I played back what he had said. 'How do you know that?' I asked. 'Cara hadn't even seen the lab report. Do you know someone who works there?'

'Not exactly . . .' Hawthorne was being coy. There was something he didn't want to tell me.

The answer arrived a moment later.

I noticed a movement at the door and, unannounced, Kevin Chakraborty came in. He was the teenager who lived with his mother in a flat one floor below. He was steering himself in the motorised wheelchair he was forced to use: he had been born with Duchenne muscular dystrophy, which, inch by inch, was stealing away his muscles and his ability to move. But as helpless as he might look to some, he was actually a brilliant computer hacker – whether it was my phone, the Police National Computer or the five million CCTV cameras across the UK. It would have been quite wrong to think of Kevin as disabled. He was one of the most spectacularly enabled people I had ever met.

'Hello, Mr Hawthorne,' he said. 'I heard you arrive.'

'No, you didn't, Kevin. You've connected yourself to the video entry system and you watched us come in.' Hawthorne was pleased to see him. 'We were talking about you. Or I think we were about to.'

'Kevin . . .' I'd worked out exactly what had happened. 'Have you hacked into the Metropolitan Police Forensic Science Laboratory in Lambeth?' I demanded. I could have been a parent telling off a naughty boy.

'It's nice to see you, Anthony.' Kevin was ignoring my question. He pushed the lever on his wheelchair and rolled towards me. 'Mr Hawthorne told me you'd been arrested. I must say, I was jolly surprised. I never thought you had it in you to kill anyone.'

'He says he's innocent,' Hawthorne said.

'I got the DNA results,' Kevin went on. 'It's a definite match. It's your fingerprints too. I've got a photograph of them.' The thing about Kevin was that he had a boyish enthusiasm for what he was doing and seemingly no awareness that it was a criminal offence. This, combined with his Bollywood good looks and, I suppose, the wheelchair, made it easy to forget how dangerous he was.

'How long have we got?' Hawthorne asked.

'I took down their servers with a general denial-of-service attack,' Kevin replied. 'It means they've got the information, but they can't access or share it—'

'Wait a minute!' I interrupted. 'What exactly are you talking about?' Then I remembered. 'Cara said she had a computer problem. Was that you? What's a denial-of-service attack?'

Kevin glanced at Hawthorne as if asking his permission to reply. Hawthorne nodded. 'We had to buy you time,' he explained. 'So I hacked into the system and installed a bot. The bot made all the computers come together in a botnet, which then flooded the servers with, like, millions of connection requests: spam, porn, the complete works of

Shakespeare . . . that sort of thing. It's called a DDoS attack. It's crude but effective.'

'You brought down the police computer!'

'They'll get it sorted eventually. They've already called in a DDoS mitigation company and they'll be scrubbing all the inbound traffic, sorting out the load balancers, firewalls and routers—'

'How long?' Hawthorne repeated.

'Twenty-four hours, definitely. Probably forty-eight.'

'Thank you, Kevin.'

'A pleasure, Mr Hawthorne.' Before Kevin left, he turned to me. 'I really liked *The Word Is Murder*,' he said. 'Am I going to be in the next one?'

'Not unless you want to end up in jail,' I replied.

'Maybe best not, then.' He pushed the electronic control and, with a gentle whirring sound, propelled himself out of the room.

'I hope you realise he's stuck his neck out for you,' Hawthorne said, once he'd gone.

'I'm very grateful,' I replied. And I was.

'So we'd better get moving then.' Hawthorne was already on his feet, reaching for his cigarettes and front-door keys.

'Where are we going?'

'You heard what Kevin said. He's bought you forty-eight hours maximum before Cara rearrests you. If you didn't murder Harriet Throsby, that's how long we've got to find out who did.'

8
Palgrove Gardens

Little Venice is one of the more secretive corners of London, tucked away between Paddington Station and Regent's Park and unknown to almost everyone except the people who live there – and who wouldn't want to live anywhere else. The traffic roars past along the Marylebone Road, heading for Heathrow Airport and the west, unaware that there's this quiet enclave of handsome, expensive houses, eclectic shops and attractive cafés, almost a village in its own right, lurking just out of sight. The Regent's Canal skirts round Lord's Cricket Ground and London Zoo, then continues through the middle of it before passing through the Maida Hill Tunnel. The closer you are to the water's edge, the more you are likely to pay. Harriet Throsby had lived a few minutes away from the canal. If I had killed her, I could have followed the canal path virtually from my flat to hers. It wouldn't have taken me much more than an hour.

And here I was, supposedly returning to the scene of the crime. For some reason, Hawthorne hadn't given the driver the house number and we were cruising slowly along an elegant crescent, looking for the right address. The houses were very similar, Victorian, tall and narrow, with bay windows looking out over private parking bays, and expensive loft conversions above. Japanese cherry trees sprouted out of the pavement, one for every two or three houses, looking a little sad in the damp April weather.

'Which house is number 27?' Hawthorne asked.

'I don't know . . .' We continued on our way until, suddenly, it occurred to me. 'You asked me that on purpose!' I exclaimed.

He looked at me innocently.

'Yes, you did. You wanted to know if I'd already been to her house. Do you really think I'm stupid enough to fall for that?'

'Well . . .'

'And you're still ready to believe I could have killed her!'

'I'm trying to keep an open mind.'

I pointed. 'There it is, over there. I may be wrong, but I'd guess it's the one with the policeman standing outside.'

The taxi drew in. We got out, I paid and then together we walked up to the front door. There were two bells. Hawthorne rang the lower one – marked *Throsby*. I thought the policeman might stop us from entering, but he had barely acknowledged us as we approached. Maybe Hawthorne had a certain authority about him. After all, he had visited enough crime scenes.

Harriet's husband opened the door.

It had to be him. He had the blank, exhausted look of someone whose life has been turned upside down. We were two more strangers entering his house to ask yet more questions and he looked at us with sad resignation.

'Yes?' he asked, incuriously.

'Mr Throsby?'

'I'm Arthur Throsby, yes.'

'My name is Daniel Hawthorne. I'm very sorry for your loss. I'm helping the police with their inquiries. Can we come in?'

Hawthorne was lying. In fact, he had lied twice. He wasn't officially helping anyone except me. And he wasn't sorry at all.

Throsby looked puzzled. 'I've already spoken to Detective Inspector Grunshaw,' he said. 'I've made a full statement.'

'Yes. There were a couple of things she wanted to follow up on.'

'I thought we'd covered everything. She didn't say anyone else would be coming.'

'Mr Throsby, we're trying to find out who killed Harriet. You can phone DI Grunshaw if you like. But I think it's fair to say that every minute we waste is a minute the trail gets cold. It's up to you.'

He was bluffing, of course, but it worked.

'No. It's all right. I'm . . . well, I'm sure you understand.' Throsby stepped back to allow us in. This was something I'd learned after three investigations with Hawthorne. When someone was murdered, people expected to be asked questions. It was as if they'd seen so many murder stories on television, they knew the part they had to play and didn't ask too many questions themselves.

We stepped through the front door and found ourselves in a narrow communal area with two further doors facing each other at angles. Harriet Throsby had lived with her husband and daughter in the ground-floor and basement of the building, with access to the garden, while a second flat had been carved out above. The door on the right was open, showing a brightly lit, airy space with a wide corridor leading into an open-plan kitchen and living room with French windows at the end. The taste was simple, on the edge of chintzy: floral wallpaper, lots of brightly coloured vases and original theatre posters hanging in frames. The wooden floor, what I could see of it, was original, but we were standing in an area that had been covered by translucent plastic sheeting with numbered tags underneath.

'She was found out here, next to the entrance?' Hawthorne asked.

Arthur nodded. 'The police were in the flat all day and much of the evening. They took samples and covered the whole place in fingerprint powder. They asked me a lot of questions – and my daughter too, as if she had anything to do with it. Neither of us were even here! And now, I suppose, you want me to go over it all again.'

'That would be helpful,' Hawthorne said. 'I know it may seem like a waste of time, but when you repeat things, you can often remember details you might have forgotten the first time round. Anyway, I prefer to hear it straight from you, if you don't mind.'

'Let's go into the kitchen. Do you want a coffee?'

'No, thank you.' Hawthorne answered for both of us.

We walked down the corridor, passing a half-open door that gave me a glimpse of an untidy room with an unmade bed, clothes everywhere, a *Lord of the Rings* poster on the wall.

'That's Olivia's room,' Arthur said. He had noticed me staring in and pulled the door shut.

We went into the kitchen. There was a pine table and a breakfast bar. Between the scattered coffee mugs, the unpaid bills, the theatre programmes, the day's newspapers still open at the obituary columns and the unwashed plates piled up in the sink, it gave me a pretty good insight into life before and after Harriet Throsby. She hadn't been gone forty-eight hours and her memories were everywhere. But the mess, I suspected, was Arthur's. I glanced through the windows at a small, well-tended garden and I wondered how long it would be before it went to seed.

We sat down.

'Nice place,' I said, breaking the silence.

'Do you think so?' Arthur Throsby didn't look so sure. 'Harriet wanted to move. She'd been talking about it for a while, but I suppose I'll stay here now that she's—' He broke off. 'Where do you want me to start?'

He was exactly the sort of man I'd expected to be married to someone like Harriet. She had been dominating, assertive. He was softly spoken, downtrodden, with thinning hair and a face that was mournful now for good reason but which might have been the same since the day he got married. He hadn't shaved and the clothes he was wearing looked old and unironed. He made himself a coffee without once looking at his hands, almost robotically. He didn't want the coffee. It was just something to do.

'Why don't you tell us your movements on the morning of your wife's death?' Hawthorne suggested.

'All right.' He stirred his coffee and brought it over to us. It sat there, steaming gently in front of him. 'Harriet was still in bed when I got up. That was at seven fifteen. I don't set the alarm because she didn't like being disturbed, but I always wake up on the dot. I made myself breakfast and squeezed some fresh orange juice for her to have later. She wouldn't drink it if it wasn't fresh. I tiptoed in and left it by the bed, then I set off for work shortly after eight.'

'Where do you work?'

'I teach history at the Harris Academy in St John's Wood. I usually go there by bike. It's about twenty minutes away. Otherwise, I take the tube from Paddington.'

'Did you go by tube or bike yesterday?'

'I took the bike. Olivia saw me leave. We spoke a few words. Nothing of any interest.'

'Your daughter went to the theatre with your wife, but you didn't,' Hawthorne said. I'd told him that I'd met Olivia at the party and that she was a friend of Sky Palmer, the actress who played Nurse Plimpton.

'That's right.'

'Why was that?'

Arthur shrugged as if the answer was obvious. 'I don't much like theatre. Anyway, Harriet preferred it if I didn't come. I have a slight problem with asthma and she used to say the sound of my breathing put her off.'

'So when was the last time you spoke to your wife?'

'I called her from school. That was a few minutes before ten o'clock, between lessons. She was already up and at work by then.'

'How did you know?' I asked.

Hawthorne wasn't pleased. He never liked it when I chipped in and perhaps it was a bit inappropriate, me being the main suspect.

'I FaceTimed,' Arthur replied. 'I could see her. She was sitting in her study.' He pointed at a door leading off from the kitchen. 'It's the dining room, but we never used it for eating. We never had guests. That was where she worked.'

'Can we see it?'

'If you want.' He got up, leaving his coffee behind.

Harriet's office could be accessed directly from both the kitchen and the corridor: there was a second door opposite Olivia's bedroom. It was a rectangular space, running to the bay window I had seen as I approached the house. Most of the area was dominated by a dining table, which was evidently where she had worked. It was piled up with notepads, files, newspaper clippings and theatre programmes. There were about a dozen pens spilling out of a *Book of Mormon* mug, a half-empty bottle of wine and a glass decorated with a lipstick smear that must have been made by Harriet, the last mark she had left in this world. I glanced at the bookshelves. I wasn't surprised to see play texts, actors' and directors' biographies, histories of different theatres. She also had a strong interest in crime and I remembered her telling me that it was something she had written about. I hadn't realised she had meant books, though. I noticed three of them spread out on the table with her name on the covers, placed there as if to impress.

'This is her room,' Arthur said. 'It doesn't get enough light . . . she was never happy with it. That's the trouble having a house that's north-facing.' He looked around him. 'Your lot have taken her computer and some of her papers,' he went on. 'But otherwise this is more or less how she left it.'

Hawthorne peered out of the window. 'She could see whoever was at the front door,' he said. 'So it's quite likely she knew the person who killed her.'

'Unless he was dressed as a postman,' I said.

Hawthorne ignored this. 'Why did you call your wife?' he asked.

'She liked me to ring her every morning around then. She would tell me if she wanted any shopping done.'

'And did she?'

'She wanted some avocados. There were avocados in the fridge, but they were too hard.' He shook his head sadly. 'She was always going on about that fridge. She hated the temperature control. We could never get it right.'

'Anything else?'

Arthur thought for a minute and shook his head. 'I can't think of anything that might be relevant.'

'How long had you been married, Mr Throsby?'

'Twenty-five years.' He pointed to an ornamental silver candlestick at the end of the table. 'I bought her that as a wedding-anniversary present. She didn't much like it, though. She didn't see the point.'

'I think it's very nice,' Hawthorne said.

'Thank you.'

Hawthorne hesitated. 'Would you say you were happily married, Mr Throsby?'

Arthur had to think about that. 'Well, she wasn't an easy woman. I'll be honest with you. She could be . . .' He searched for the word.

'Critical?' Hawthorne suggested.

'Yes. I suppose you could say that. Perhaps it went with the territory.' Astonishingly, he was talking as if it had never occurred to him before. 'She could be quite judgemental.'

'You never lost your temper with her?'

'Certainly not. You're not suggesting . . .' Arthur blushed. 'I was nowhere near the house when she was attacked, and I can assure you, there were dozens of witnesses who saw me at school. You think I would do anything to harm her? The mother of my child?' He looked genuinely pained. 'I loved Harriet! I knew the two of us were going to be together the day I met her. She was a very attractive young woman and a terrific journalist. I'd never met anyone so ambitious, so determined.'

'Where did you meet?'

'We were both journalists – at the Bristol *Argus*. I wrote about politics and education. She was crime.'

'Not theatre?'

He shook his head. 'Not to start with. No. She was their senior crime reporter and she was very good at it. She got an honourable mention from the Bevins Trust and she was the Best Regional Journalist at the British Press Awards in 1997.' His eyes fell on the dining table. 'She was a published author too.'

Hawthorne spread out the three books. *No Regrets: The Strange World of Dr Robert Thirkell*. *Lady Killer: The Crimes of Sophie Comninos*. And *Bad Boys: Life and Death in an English Village*. I noticed that the titles followed the same pattern, almost like crossword clues with the answers printed next to them. The covers were also similar: black-and-white photographs snatched from old newspapers with gaudy lettering for the title and the author. The books looked determinedly old-fashioned; somehow stuck in the worlds they described.

'Robert Thirkell was a doctor working in Bristol,' Arthur explained. 'He killed off half a dozen elderly patients . . . put rat poison in their tea. He thought he was doing them a favour. Harriet managed to get close to him before he was arrested and the two of them became good friends. That was how she got the material for the book. Sophie Comninos was a hotshot TV executive until she murdered her Greek husband. She smashed a bottle of pink wine over his head after losing at a game of backgammon and then she killed two more people trying to cover it up.'

'What about this one?' Hawthorne had picked up *Life and Death in an English Village*.

'She got into a lot of trouble with that,' Arthur said. 'It was about Trevor and Annabel Longhurst. You may remember them? Their son came under the influence of an older boy and the end result was that he got involved in the death of a teacher at a local primary school. They were living in a village near Chippenham – Moxham Heath – and they weren't popular. They were very rich. Incomers. Champagne socialists, you might say. They were both of them into politics, big time. Harriet was accused of doing a hatchet job.'

With everything I had learned about Harriet Throsby, that didn't surprise me.

'These were all stories she'd covered for the *Argus*,' Arthur went on. 'The books didn't sell a lot of copies, but the advances helped pay for this place. Anyway, her heart wasn't in it. Crime, I mean. When I first met her, she was already thinking about moving on.'

Once again, I saw Harriet as she had been, alive and opinionated, at the Turkish restaurant after the play. What was it she had said? *'I didn't find it entirely satisfying. Criminals are so boring.'* Her husband might have been blind to her failings, but it seemed he was telling the truth.

'What did she want to do instead?' Hawthorne said.

'She was very good friends with the drama critic at the *Argus* . . . a chap called Frank Heywood. She'd go with him to the theatre whenever she could and she'd tell me all about it afterwards. How bad it was, how the lead actor should never have got the part.' The ghost of a smile shimmered across his face. 'I think she actually preferred the plays if they were no good. Anyway, she was always reading Frank's articles and then, after he died, she went straight round to the editor and asked if she could take over.'

'How did he die?'

'Food poisoning. Harriet had dinner with him that night and she was very ill too. But Frank had a weak heart and that was the end of him. The editor – his name was Adrian Wells – didn't want to give her the job. It would mean losing his best crime reporter. But she threatened to walk out if he didn't do what she wanted, so that was what happened.' Arthur sighed. 'She only stayed at the *Argus* for a couple of years and then she moved up to London. She wrote for *The Stage* to begin with. After that, she worked on various papers until she got the top job at the *Sunday Times*.'

'What about you?' Arthur looked puzzled, so Hawthorne went on. 'You said you were a journalist. Now you're a teacher.'

'Oh. Well . . . Harriet always said I was wasting my time, and perhaps she was right. There wasn't a lot happening in Bristol and she used to say my stuff was boring. Council elections. The new one-way system. The annual Ofsted reports. We had a nice little house down there – a view of the docks – but I didn't mind selling it, I suppose. When we came up here, I fished around for a bit, but then I got fed up with it and trained as a teacher. I'd written about education, so it seemed a natural move.'

'You'll forgive me for saying this, Mr Throsby . . .' I always knew when Hawthorne was going to turn on someone. He could be friendly one moment, ferocious the next. 'But you don't seem too put out by the death of your wife.'

'You can think that if you like, Mr Hawthorne. But you don't know me and you never met Harriet, as far as I'm aware. She wasn't the easiest of people to get along with, but we were happy together. And just because I'm not standing here tearing out my hair or whatever it is you'd like me to do, it doesn't mean I'm not deeply upset.'

He didn't sound deeply upset.

'Harriet wasn't perfect, but I never wished her any harm and what happened to her is horrible. I'm not going to put on a show for you and your friend and if you haven't got any more questions, I'd like to be left on my own.'

In his own quiet way, Arthur was angry and I was thinking it was probably time for us to make an exit when the door opened and Olivia came in. She was dressed to go out – in a glittery jacket and T-shirt, carrying a leather bag on a chain. Her hair was still damp from the shower. 'Dad, I'm on my way—' she began, then stopped when she saw me and Hawthorne. 'What are you doing here?' she demanded.

'These are police officers,' her father told her.

Olivia looked at me petulantly. 'No, he's not,' she replied. 'He wrote the play. The one that I went to with Mum.'

'What?' Arthur turned on me. 'You told me—'

'I didn't say anything,' I said.

'I'm a private detective,' Hawthorne cut in. He was addressing Olivia and just for once he seemed to be on my side. 'I sometimes help the police and that's why I'm here. Tony works with me – and if you'll give us a few minutes of your time, maybe the two of us can find out who killed your mother.'

'I don't care who killed her,' Olivia said.

'Olivia!' Either Arthur was a brilliant actor or he was genuinely shocked by his daughter's attitude.

'Oh, come on, Dad,' Olivia insisted. 'What difference does it make? Knowing who killed her won't bring her back, and don't pretend you're going to miss her. You know what she was like.'

'Olivia! I can't believe you're saying these things. You know I'll miss her. I already do!'

'She was always criticising you. She never stopped! She was driving you out of your mind.'

'You're wrong, dear. You're quite wrong. It's never easy . . . relationships, marriage! It's a balancing act. There are ups and there are downs—'

'She's gone, Dad. She was a total cow and she ruined our lives. Neither of us has to pretend any more.'

Olivia went over to him and rested a hand on his arm, and in that brief moment I was aware of a real affection between them. What had it really been like living with Harriet all these years? The two of them were survivors.

Hawthorne was less impressed. 'You don't seem to have many fond memories of your mum,' he observed.

'You don't need to answer any of his questions.' Arthur put an arm around his daughter, protecting her. 'These gentlemen were leaving anyway.' He pointed a finger at me. 'And you had no right to be here in the first place!'

Olivia glared at Hawthorne. 'I'll answer anything you like,' she said, defiantly. 'I've got nothing to hide.'

Hawthorne smiled. 'So when was the last time you saw her?'

'We came home in a taxi from the theatre.' She glanced at me. 'She really hated your play, by the way. She finished writing her review when we were in the Savoy and I could tell she was ripping into it from the way she typed.' She turned back to Hawthorne. 'I didn't see her the next morning. I had to be at work by nine.'

'Where do you work?'

'Near Paddington Station. I've got a job at Starbucks.'

'And you were there until when?'

'Until the middle of the afternoon. Three o'clock.'

'How far is the Starbucks from here?'

'Five minutes.'

'Ten minutes there and back.' Hawthorne looked at her, the obvious question hanging in the air.

'You think I popped home and killed Mum?' Olivia smiled unpleasantly. 'I couldn't leave work. Someone would have seen me. And anyway, I know exactly what you're doing. You're only accusing me because you know who really did it.'

'And who was that?' Hawthorne asked.

'Him!'

Him? I glanced left and right, but there could be no avoiding it. She meant me!

'What are you talking about . . . ?' I began.

'You threatened her!'

'That's nonsense. That's absolutely untrue.' I could feel the blood draining from my face. Or possibly rushing into it. 'We chatted at the party in the Turkish restaurant. That was all. I didn't say anything!'

'You asked her what she thought of your play.'

'Well, yes . . .'

'It was the way you asked her. She felt threatened by you. She said so on the way home.'

'It was a reasonable question!'

'She didn't think so. You frightened her!'

'Did she say that?' Hawthorne asked.

'She didn't need to. I could tell just by looking at her.'

'I think you should leave,' Arthur said, again.

Hawthorne nodded and, much to my relief, we did. It was only when we were out in the street that he asked me: 'Is it true . . . what Olivia said?'

I couldn't believe what I was hearing. 'Hawthorne,' I said. 'You can't be serious. All I did was ask Harriet Throsby what she thought of the play. We hardly spoke otherwise. I didn't threaten her! There were lots of people there. Ask them!'

The policeman who was still standing there, on duty, overheard us. 'Are you the writer?' he asked.

'Yes.'

'My son really likes your books.'

'Thank you.'

'He'll be very sorry to hear what you did, sir. I can understand you being angry, being criticised that way. But I think you've let down all your readers.'

I'd had enough. I stormed down the street. I looked back and saw Hawthorne hadn't moved. 'We're going back to the theatre,' he called out to me.

Right. The Vaudeville was near Charing Cross. We could get there from Warwick Avenue Station on the Bakerloo line – but that was at the other end of the street.

I turned round and stormed off that way.

9

Seven Suspects

It was a very different experience returning to the Vaudeville Theatre that evening. Two nights before, I had been nervous almost to the point of feeling sick – but it was clear to me now that I'd got things out of proportion. The failure or success of *Mindgame* was rather less significant than the prospect of twenty years in jail, and although I knew I hadn't gone anywhere near Harriet Throsby, I could see the evidence inexorably piling up against me with two malignant police officers bulldozing their way to a false conviction. Why had Olivia been so malicious? She knew I hadn't threatened her mother. Worse still, why had Hawthorne been so ready to believe her? His lack of faith was almost as dispiriting as the accusation itself, and although it was true that he'd managed to delay the police investigation – with Kevin's help – that was all he'd done so far. Couldn't he at least have been a bit more worried about me? Weren't we supposed to be friends?

I was also aware that time was trickling away. Hawthorne had said that we had forty-eight hours to solve the crime and two of those had already gone. Fighting my way into the station, getting stuck behind a woman searching for her Oyster card, waiting for the next train, which, the departure board told me, was going to take an infuriating seven minutes to arrive, stopping at a red signal with the driver refusing to announce when we would be moving . . . all this played havoc with my nervous system. I'm the sort of person who gets panic attacks about the average-speed cameras on a motorway. Having Grunshaw and Mills lumbering up in the fast lane behind me, flashing their lights and shouting 'Murder', terrified me. It was something that had never happened to me before.

But Hawthorne was in no hurry as we climbed back up to street level at Charing Cross Station. I saw him take out his cigarettes and knew what he wanted. 'Fancy a coffee?' he asked.

'Not really,' I said. I looked at my watch. 'The play begins in an hour.'

'I've already seen it.'

'I wasn't suggesting we go in and see it, Hawthorne. I mean—' I played back what he had said. 'You've seen it? When?'

'I went to the Wednesday matinée. I was on my way home when you called from the custody centre.'

'What did you think of it?' After everything that had happened in the last two days, was that really the question I'd just asked? But it was out of my mouth before I could stop it. It really mattered to me.

'I thought it was very good. Very witty. William enjoyed it too.'

'You took your son?'

Hawthorne nodded. 'His school closed early for staff training and the kids had the afternoon off.'

'He didn't think it was too violent?'

'You should see his school!' Hawthorne lit a cigarette before I could stop him. 'He didn't get some of it, but nor did I – and that gave us something to talk about afterwards.'

I felt an unusual sense of warmth towards Hawthorne and I was annoyed with myself for what I'd just been thinking. 'You should have let me buy the tickets,' I said. 'I could have got them half-price.'

'That's OK, Tony. They were selling them two for the price of one anyway.'

The theatre was right in front of us. The pavement outside the main entrance was deserted. Not a good sign.

'I suppose we're here to see the actors,' I said. 'They'll be onstage in an hour.'

'Plenty of time, mate. Lucky it's a small cast!'

We ducked round the side and went up Lumley Court, one of those old, forgotten alleyways that London does so well. On one side, the wall was topped with razor wire. On the other, a set of double doors provided an emergency exit from the theatre itself. Hawthorne tested the doors – he did it without thinking – and seemed to be pleased that they were firmly secured. We then climbed a short flight of concrete steps that led up to Maiden Lane and the stage door.

I remembered coming here after the first-night party when I was still hoping the play would be a success. It felt like a lifetime ago . . . and someone else's life.

The back of the theatre felt even more deserted than the front, but, as always, Keith was perched at his desk, surrounded by old-fashioned telephones with large punch buttons and four small TV screens. I have described him as the deputy stage-door manager, but he'd only been at the theatre for a short while and it was unclear if he was temporary or permanent. He was only in his thirties – most of the stage-door managers I'd met had been much older than that and very much the cornerstone of the buildings they guarded. Keith was more wayward, sitting with his legs stretched out, displaying grubby jeans and trainers. Whenever I went past him, he seemed to be rolling a cigarette, although I'd never actually seen him smoke one.

'Good evening, Keith,' I said.

'Oh, hello, Anthony! How are you doing?' One thing that he'd definitely got right was that he was always cheerful. Bad reviews, poor audiences, murder . . . he took them all in his stride.

'I'm OK, thanks, Keith.' He had never told me his surname. 'How are we doing?'

He had a rash on his neck and he scratched it. 'We've taken a knock with some of those reviews,' he admitted. 'Critics can be bastards. But we've got a decent audience. Not too bad for midweek.'

It was actually Thursday.

'It'll pick up at the weekend,' he went on. 'These days it's all about word of mouth. You'll see.'

Meanwhile, Hawthorne had been examining the television screens. There were only four of them, but they showed six different views of the theatre, the fuzzy black-and-white images shifting as one camera took over from another. I saw the main entrance to the foyer with a few early arrivals trickling in, the stage door and a stretch of Maiden Lane, the stairs leading down to the dressing rooms, the entire length of Lumley Court looking down to the Strand, the auditorium – with row upon row of empty seats waiting, perhaps forlornly, to be filled – and the stage itself, with a stagehand sweeping the floor. 'Do these just show you what's happening, or do they also record?' he asked.

'This is Daniel Hawthorne,' I explained. 'He's a detective. He's looking into the murder of Harriet Throsby.'

'Oh, yes.' Keith's face fell. 'I've had it up to here with that, to be honest with you. We had the police in and out all day yesterday, asking all sorts of stupid questions. Did I see Harriet Throsby arrive? Of course I did!' He pointed at the screen showing the front entrance. 'That's what I'm here for! They went on and on about those bloody knives. I didn't buy them! I just handed them over. And they've only gone and closed the green room. Why would they do that? She wasn't murdered there! They still haven't told me if I'm allowed to open it . . .'

'You saw her arrive,' Hawthorne said, repeating what Keith had just told him.

'That's right.'

'How did you recognise her?'

'You get to know all the critics, working in this job.' Keith eyed Hawthorne suspiciously, as if he resented this further interrogation. 'I was at the Lyric before I came here and there was a picture of her in the laundry room.' He smirked. 'Complete with Hitler moustache.'

'How long have you been at the Vaudeville?'

'Two months.'

'Do you enjoy it?'

'It's all right. I used to work in hospitality. Barman at the Best Western in Avonmouth. Night manager at the Bristol Marriott. This is a lot more interesting. We had Emily Blunt in this morning!'

'Did she buy tickets?' I asked.

'No. It was the wrong theatre. She was looking for the Aldwych.'

Hawthorne cut in. 'So, do the cameras record?'

'You've got to be kidding!' Keith shook his head disdainfully. 'All this equipment is rubbish. It's years out of date. I'm meant to see everything and if there's anything funny going on, I call Pranav, the stage manager. That's if the phones are working, but half the time the line's down!'

'Did you see anything unusual on Tuesday night?'

'I already told the police – that fat one and her ratty assistant. It was a first night. Everyone was a bit tense and there was a lot of movement at the stage door. Flowers arriving. Champagne. The weather wasn't too good, so no one was hanging around. It was a full house, of course. Lots of people milling around at the front . . .'

'What about after the play?'

'I don't know what you're on about, Mr Hawthorne. You can't think that anyone working here had anything to do with it. I mean, she was a critic. She didn't like the play. But there's no way an actor would ever have wished her harm.'

'Or a writer,' I added.

Hawthorne ignored both of us. 'You were here all evening,' he continued.

'That's right. Yes. I'm always the last to leave. Make sure everything's secure, lock up and home by midnight, except when it's Shakespeare and then it seems to go on half the bloody night.' He sighed. 'The curtain came down at nine forty-five, but there was a party and then the cast came back for drinks downstairs, so it was almost one o'clock before I got away.'

'Do you know what time they all left?'

'We have a book.' He pointed at the table behind us. 'Everyone has to sign in and sign out. The management is very strict about that.'

Hawthorne swung the book round and turned back a couple of pages. Sure enough, everyone who had been in the green room had left a record of their visit.

Name	**Time In**	**Time Out**
Ewan Lloyd	*10.20 pm*	*12.45 am*
Tirian Kirke	*10.20*	*12.25*
Jordan Williams	*10.30 pm*	*00.50 am*
Sky Palmer	*10.45*	*12.35*
Anthony Horowitz	*10.50 pm*	*12.40 am*
Ahmet Yurdakul	*11.25*	*12.55*
Maureen Bates	*23.25*	*00.55 am*

The times accorded with what I already knew. Ewan and Tirian had been drinking in the green room when I arrived at the theatre and went down. Jordan had met me. He was still upstairs in his dressing room. Sky had arrived moments ahead of me. I had caught up with her outside as she shook off her umbrella.

At the end of the evening, after reading the review that had brought the party to a close, Tirian had been the first to leave, followed by Sky. I had been the third out of the door and remembered looking at my watch and scribbling the time in the book. Ahmet and Maureen, it turned out, had been the last to depart, shortly after Jordan. I couldn't help wondering what they'd got up to in those last few minutes.

'So you saw everyone on the way out.'

'That's right.'

'Did you talk to any of them?'

'None of them were in the mood for a chat after that review. Tirian mentioned it – but only briefly. He was catching the last train to Blackheath and he only had ten minutes to get down to Charing Cross.'

'He didn't have his motorbike?' I asked.

'He'd have been mad to get on that fancy bike of his after the amount you lot had had to drink. I cleared away the bottles! Sky had a cab waiting for her. Mr Lloyd called an Uber.' Keith frowned. 'I'm not sure if I saw you, Anthony. Maybe you slipped out while my back was turned!' He said this as if I had done something wrong. 'I didn't see Jordan either, but I checked you'd both signed the book before I locked up. I spoke to Mr Yurdakul for quite a few minutes. He was the last to leave. He wasn't at all happy.'

'According to this, he was with his assistant, Maureen Bates,' Hawthorne said.

'Yes. She was with him. She was holding on to his arm. He didn't look well.'

After one bad review? Wasn't that a bit of an overreaction?

'Can we get into the green room?' Hawthorne asked.

Keith thought for a moment. 'You can do what you like,' he said. 'It's no skin off my nose. The police haven't said anything more to me and we can't keep it locked up for ever. It's not as if anything happened there – and anyway,

I cleared up after everyone left, so if there were any clues or whatever it is you're looking for, I'd have got rid of them, I'm afraid.'

'When you say you cleared up, what do you mean?'

'Well, they'd had a cake. I put what was left of it in the fridge. I suppose it's still there. I did the washing-up, which didn't take a minute. Like I said, I cleared away the bottles. There was some sparkling wine, which I put on the side, and I threw away a couple of empties . . . whisky and vodka, I think. That was it.'

'Did you find an ornamental knife? A dagger?'

'You mean from the producer? They all got one . . . I know because when they were delivered, I had to take them in. There were five of them, stacked up in the office . . . first-night presents. And the answer to your question is yes. One of them was left behind in the green room. Someone had stuck it in the cake.'

That was Jordan Williams's knife. I remembered him stabbing the cake after Sky had read the review. It was something I would never forget.

'What did you do with it?' Hawthorne asked.

'I washed it and left it in the sink.'

'Were there any other daggers in the room?'

'There may have been. I didn't really look.' Keith frowned. He had suddenly remembered something. 'And there was the broken glass!' he exclaimed. 'I cleaned that up too.'

'What broken glass?'

'I should have mentioned it to you earlier. You asked me if I'd seen anything unusual. But I didn't see it exactly. I heard it.' He paused. 'It was twenty past twelve and I was just thinking of going downstairs to tell everyone it was time to get moving. They weren't meant to be there after midnight. That was what we'd agreed and it wasn't as if I was being paid extra to stay here. Anyway, that's when I heard the sound of breaking glass – on the other side of those doors.'

He pointed at the double swing doors that led into the backstage corridor.

'Did you find out what it was?' Hawthorne asked.

'Yeah. It was really strange. It turned out that one of the light bulbs had exploded. I can't imagine how that happened because there was nobody around. I had to get a dustpan and brush and look here . . . !' He held out his hand, showing us a cut on his finger. 'I did that picking up the pieces. I was looking for a plaster when Tirian came up and told me about the review and the party finishing. Maybe the light bulb was a bad omen!'

'Does that happen often? Electrical appliances blowing up?'

'Well, I haven't been here very long so I can't say. But a lot of the fittings in this theatre are very old. Maybe it's haunted? I don't know.'

Keith handed over the key to the green room – an old, prison-style key on a wooden block – and we passed through the swing doors. It seemed strange to me that he'd recognised Harriet Throsby. He'd seen a photograph of her in another theatre – and one that had been defaced. It surely wouldn't have been easy to pick her out in a crowd, the image projected onto a blurry black-and-white TV.

I said as much to Hawthorne.

'She had quite distinctive looks,' he said. 'You recognised her too.'

'I'd seen her at the Old Vic,' I countered, back on the defensive.

We reached the staircase. Looking around me, I noticed that both upstairs and downstairs, the backstage area was brightly lit. 'Do you think someone broke the bulb deliberately?' I asked.

'It's possible.'

'Maybe they were trying to hide something,' I suggested. 'There was something they didn't want Keith to see too clearly.'

'That's possible too.'

Hawthorne had nothing more to add. We continued downstairs, past the dressing rooms and back underneath the stage-door manager's office. The green room was in front of us. Hawthorne unlocked the door and we went in.

I wasn't sure what he expected to find, but the room was exactly as I remembered it: warm and secluded, a refuge from difficult audiences and bad reviews. It had been dark and raining when we had gathered here on the first night.

Now it was early evening and the weather had improved – not that either of these things made much difference. The glass in the window was frosted and even if we'd been able to look out, the alleyway wouldn't have allowed much light to penetrate. I thought I could smell alcohol, but that was probably the carpet. Instinctively, I ran my eyes over the various surfaces, hoping to see the dagger I had been given and which, after all, I might have forgotten and left behind. Of course it wasn't there. The last time I'd seen it, it had been in Cara Grunshaw's evidence bag.

It should have been obvious all along, but I'm afraid the truth of my situation only occurred to me at that moment. Somebody had taken my dagger. They had done it quite purposefully, using a towel or a plastic bag to make sure that they didn't add their fingerprints to my own. In other words, long before Harriet Throsby was killed, they had decided to frame me. Somebody hated me. And it could only be one of seven people.

Six of them had been in the green room with me that night: Ewan, Tirian, Jordan, Sky, Ahmet and Maureen. The seventh was Keith, and although I couldn't think of an earthly reason why the deputy stage-door manager would want to do Harriet Throsby harm, he had been the last person to enter the green room and he could easily have picked up the dagger belonging to me, so it seemed only reasonable to add him to the list. It was an unpleasant thought that one of them had been lying from the start, smiling at me and jollying me along while, all the time, they were planning to send me to jail. But the cloud had one silver lining. Seven suspects! That made it easy. Hawthorne would have solved the whole thing before breakfast.

I watched him as he went over to the dustbin and pulled out two empty bottles: Sky's vodka and the whisky that Tirian had brought. He glanced at it and was about to put it back in again when he noticed something else. He leaned down and took out a crumpled packet of cigarettes. I saw the branding – L&M – the white letters printed sideways on a bright red background. I recognised them immediately. 'Those are Ahmet's,' I said.

Hawthorne opened the packet. 'He left three inside.'

I looked more closely. It was true. There were three cigarettes inside the package. They had been broken up when the carton was crumpled. 'Why would he do that?'

'What makes you think it was him?' Hawthorne asked.

'That's definitely his brand. And he was smoking them after the party.' I tried to come up with an answer. 'Maybe he decided to give up.'

'A bit of a strange time to make a decision like that, mate.' He slipped the pack and the broken cigarettes into his pocket.

'Listen, Hawthorne . . .' I was excited to share what I had just worked out. 'My knife was taken from this room. I'm sure of it. It only had my fingerprints on it. That means someone deliberately set out to frame me!'

'You think so?' He sounded surprised.

'How else could one of my hairs have ended up on Harriet's body? The killer must have done that too.'

'Can you remember anyone pulling a hair out of the back of your neck?'

'No!' Was he being deliberately facetious? 'But I told you. I never went near her. So it follows that someone must have put it there.'

Hawthorne considered what I'd just said. 'Then the question is, who hated you enough to want to do that?'

'I don't know . . .'

'They were all probably a bit pissed off with you. After all, you'd written the play.'

'They all liked the play,' I said. 'That's why they agreed to do it. Nobody could blame me for the bad reviews.'

'Harriet Throsby did: " . . . *his talents fall lamentably short of what is required for an entertaining evening in the more adult arena of the West End and he must take much of the blame for what ensues.*" That's what she wrote. Maybe there was someone else in the cast who agreed.'

Had Hawthorne really learned the whole bloody review, word for word?

'I don't know what the reason was for killing her,' I said. 'But it's crystal clear. Whoever did it wanted to make sure I got the blame.'

'It's definitely a possibility.'

And yet the way he said it made it sound unlikely.

I heard the bang of a door somewhere above and a deep voice making inarticulate sounds. It was Jordan Williams. He had signed in at the stage door and was making his way to his dressing room, doing some sort of voice exercise.

Hawthorne looked up. 'Seven suspects,' he said. 'And it looks as if the first is right next door.'

10

Dressing Room 5

All the dressing rooms at the Vaudeville Theatre were more or less identical, dominated by a make-up table and recessed mirror with a wardrobe, a sofa, a fridge and a desk. But they were important to the actors in different ways. This was where they relaxed, prepared themselves for the performances, greeted friends. Hid.

Jordan Williams had the only one situated on the upper floor, closest to the light and (since all the windows in the building seemed to be nailed shut) to fresh air. It was just past the stage-door manager's office, on the other side of the swing doors that you passed through when you came in from the street. I had met Jordan here on the opening night, but I had never been inside and crossing the threshold now, I almost felt as if I was trespassing.

Ewan had mentioned to me that Jordan had refused to sign his contract unless he could have Dressing Room 5 and I had to wonder if it had been worth the fight. It might have been a couple of square metres larger than the others. Instead of a sofa it had a daybed. But otherwise, the furniture was just as tatty, the carpet equally worn. The room was quite cluttered. His wardrobe was open and I was surprised how many clothes he'd managed to pack in, along with the suit he wore during the play. A battered suitcase stood against one wall and there were more old clothes in a plastic laundry basket on the floor. A variety of bottles were squeezed together on the fridge, and books and magazines were piled up everywhere else. As well as the flowers and good luck cards, I noticed a large, silver-framed photograph of Jordan embracing a fair-haired woman – he in a suit, she in white silk – the two of them posing in front of what looked like a registry office. A wedding photograph? It struck me as rather endearing that he should have brought it here. It would be the last thing he saw before he went onstage.

He was not pleased to see us.

'Anthony – this isn't a very good time. I like to be alone before a performance. This is a very important time for me. It's the journey from where I am to where I need to be, from me to my character.' Jordan often talked like this. He could be jovial – as he had been when I'd shown him my dagger on the first night. But he also took himself very seriously and this was reflected in his choice of language, which was often a little self-important.

I introduced Hawthorne and explained why we were there. 'We just need a few minutes,' I assured him.

'Well, take a seat. You'll forgive me talking with my back to you, but I'm doing my make-up.' He reached for a pad of cotton wool. 'So, you're here about poor Harriet, are you?' He grimaced. I saw the reflection in the mirror. 'I really shouldn't say this, but I think someone has done the world a favour. She won't be missed.'

'She had a husband and a daughter,' Hawthorne reminded him.

'So did Lucrezia Borgia. Forgive me, Mr Hawthorne. If you expect me to feel sorry for her, you're wasting your time.' He glanced at me over his shoulder. 'Did you read the other reviews? The *Telegraph* was excellent. The *Guardian* didn't get it at all – but that's typical. We had a very good audience last night. They thoroughly enjoyed it.'

'Did you kill her?' Hawthorne asked.

Jordan stopped with the cotton pad halfway down the long slope of his nose. 'I beg your pardon?'

'It's just that I understand you called her a monster and threatened to put a knife in her.' Hawthorne paused just long enough for the words to sink in. 'And that's exactly what occurred.'

Jordan scowled. The cotton pad completed its journey. He threw it down and turned round. 'I hope you haven't been breaking the confidentialities of the green room, Anthony,' he exclaimed, and for the first time I heard a trace of an

American accent in his voice. It was because he was annoyed. 'What goes on tour, stays on tour. I thought you'd understand that.'

'This is a murder investigation,' Hawthorne said.

'Well, I won't deny what I said. But if we're being direct with each other, I might as well tell you that I wasn't alone. Anthony, for one, was all for it.'

'I didn't say anything!' I exclaimed.

'You nodded.'

'No, I didn't!'

'You can ask the others. They all saw you. I said what I said and I may not have meant it, but you nodded your head in total agreement.'

'You think Anthony killed her?' Hawthorne asked.

'I'm not saying that. Not at all. I'm just pointing out that he had as much motive as any of us. She really hated his play!'

'You know that she was killed with a dagger,' Hawthorne said.

'So the police informed me. I spoke to two of them yesterday in this very room. A lady by the name of Cara Grunshaw and her rather kickable sidekick. They were particularly interested in the murder weapon.' He leaned forward and grabbed the dagger he had been given by Ahmet. He waved it in our direction. 'As you can see, I still have it. Not the murder weapon! Mine is unsullied! It wasn't the most generous first-night present in my opinion. Quite tacky and irrelevant to the play. But much as I like Ahmet – and in many ways he is a decent enough chap – he doesn't have much sense of style.'

'So why did you agree to appear?' Hawthorne asked.

That surprised him. 'For the same reason that I agree to do anything. The script, dear boy, the script. I thought *Mindgame* was a genuinely interesting piece of work. That's why I was so angered by Harriet Throsby's intervention. And a comedy thriller! Why not? I've always believed it's the mission of the actor to spread one's wings. Shakespeare, Molière in the original French, Mamet, O'Neill. I spent two years on Broadway . . . in *Sweeney Todd*, Sondheim's masterpiece.'

'Who did you play?' I asked.

'I was the lead.'

The Demon Barber of Fleet Street. Another killer.

'In fact, the first part I took when I came to this country was also in a musical. *Cats*. I took over as Mr Mistoffelees at the London theatre. It was a wonderful experience.'

'So how did you become an actor?' Hawthorne asked.

'Why do you want to know?'

'I'm a big fan. I very much enjoyed your performance as Dr Farquhar. I remember seeing you as King Lear at the Hampstead Theatre. And I watched *Dick Turpin* with my son.'

It was remarkable how easily Hawthorne lied. Those were exactly the two productions I had mentioned to him. But it did the trick. There are very few actors who don't warm to someone who admires their work. Jordan put down the weapon and reached for some blusher instead.

'I have been very fortunate to find my inner spirit,' he began. 'You could say that I began my life with nothing. I had no family. I had no background. Everything I held dear was taken away from me.'

'You were born in America?'

'Yes. In South Dakota. I'm sure Anthony will have acquainted you with my heritage, Mr Hawthorne. I never knew my parents, which is to say, I was taken from them when I was just three years old. They were members of the Sicangu Tribe, good people I believe, but victims of a cruel system about which the world knows very little and cares even less.'

There was a protracted silence while he carefully smoothed out the shadows beneath his cheekbones.

'I would imagine you have never heard of the Indian boarding schools that were prevalent across the United States from the end of the nineteenth century,' he went on. 'The Carlisle Indian Industrial School will mean nothing to you, even though a hundred and eighty Native children are buried there. It was all in the name of assimilation. Do you know what the motto was at Carlisle? "Kill the Indian, save the man." I never went to the school. It had closed down long before I was born, but even so, that, in a nutshell, was what happened to me. That was the beginning of my life experience.'

He turned round to face us.

'Until I was three years old, I lived with my mother in Rosebud, one of the poorest reservations in America. I wish

I could tell you something about that time, but I don't have any memories at all. I'm not sure if we even had running water or electricity, but I believe, in my heart, that we were a happy family . . . or at least, I would like to think so. All I know for certain is that my older brother got into some sort of trouble. He stole a car. As a result of this, my parents were deemed "unsuitable guardians" and a week later, two social workers turned up, removed me and my three sisters and took us all to foster homes. Separate foster homes. We never saw each other again.

'Don't think for a minute that my experience was unique. The state was allowed to remove children who were considered to be in danger and the social services acted with complete immunity. There were even cases of children being taken from school, snatched on the way to class. You or I would call it kidnap, but they believed they were saving us. Oh, and since the state received a thousand dollars in federal funds for every child taken into custody, it was a nice little earner too.

'I suppose I was fortunate. Some of those children suffered terrible abuse, but I was adopted by a couple from California, Harry and Lisbeth Williams. They wanted only the best for me and I was brought up in a caring and supportive household in Pomona, to the east of Los Angeles. My adoptive father worked for a large casting agency in Hollywood and therein lies the answer to your question, Mr Hawthorne. Our table talk was often about feature films and actors and it was hardly surprising that before I was even in my teens, I should have decided to join the profession. In a way, my entire life was a performance. I was playing the part of the all-American boy, even though I experienced almost daily reminders that this was far from the case.'

'You experienced racism?'

'In high school, the other children made jokes about me being Lakota. They called me "Chief". They would make tomahawk gestures . . . that sort of thing. I had to get used to being stopped quite unnecessarily by the police and there was an occasion when I was accused, falsely, of shoplifting. Later on, when I started work as an actor, I found I was treading a thin line between being stereotyped and being excluded. How many Indigenous actors can you actually name? Only one has ever won an Academy Award.* I'm not complaining! I consider myself in many ways to be very fortunate. But that is how it is.'

'Have you ever gone back to Rosebud?' I asked. 'Did you find your birth parents?'

Jordan frowned. 'No. I'm very disconnected from my tribe. Jayne, my wife, was born in Huddersfield. I have two children with British passports. And in all this, I have had to consider the feelings of my adoptive parents. It may be that they felt a residue of guilt when they considered what they had done. When I was fifteen, Congress passed the Indian Child Welfare Act, which was designed to

* That figure has now risen to three, with Taika Waititi and Wes Studi (both in 2019).

prevent any further adoptions such as mine – not, incidentally, that it succeeded. They never said as much, but I could tell that they were unhappy about my looking back, searching for my roots, as it were. They discouraged me from visiting the Rosebud Reservation. I have never been there. There are some who might criticise me for this, but I owe Harry and Lisbeth a great deal. Despite the distance between us, we are still very close. They're elderly now . . . both in their late eighties. I have honoured them by trying to be what they want me to be, even if that is not entirely what I am.'

He stopped and turned back to the mirror, as if he was aware that he had been talking too much.

'Did you find *Mindgame* easy to do?' Hawthorne asked.

'Acting is never easy, Mr Hawthorne. I always say that if it's easy, something is very much amiss. It's an act of self-sacrifice, pulling the character from inside you. It can be painful. But that is how it should be.'

'I was thinking about the violence at the end of Act One. And in most of Act Two.'

'It's not real. You surely can't believe that it in any way connects me with what happened to Harriet Throsby.'

'People can be violent without knowing what they're doing.' Hawthorne paused. 'For example, during rehearsals I understand you hurt Sky Palmer.'

'Did she tell you that?'

'It's no secret.'

Of course, I was the one who'd told Hawthorne what I'd seen. Just for once, he'd been considerate enough not to name me.

Jordan drew in a breath and I saw his hand, which had been lying flat on the make-up table, curl into a fist. 'I am not a violent person, Mr Hawthorne, despite what you may have heard. That business with the cake, for example. I was just letting off steam. I had just read an unpleasant review and I overreacted. I do that sometimes. But if you really think I was planning to kill her, do you think I would have announced it in front of the entire company?'

Hawthorne didn't reply.

'As for Sky, that happened at the end of a long and tiring day. I had things on my mind. I'll admit that there are times when I don't know my own strength. We were rehearsing the scene where Styler and I have to tie the nurse to a chair. I had done it many, many times on the road without any issues, but just for once I suppose I lost concentration. I gripped her too tightly and I left bruises on her arms. Of course, I was mortified. Sometimes, the role, the created truth, can consume the actor. Have you read Stanislavski? That's what happened for just a few brief seconds.'

'You're lucky it wasn't *Julius Caesar*. There'd have been blood everywhere.'

Jordan ignored this. 'I wrote her a note and I brought her flowers. I thought the incident had been forgiven and forgotten. I'm sorry to hear otherwise.'

'Nobody's complained about you, Jordan,' I said hastily.

'I'm glad to hear that. I've enjoyed my experience with *Mindgame* and from the start I've considered this to be a very happy company.'

'Tell us about the others.' Hawthorne had moved on. He was being positively genial now. 'I'd be interested to know what you think of them.'

'You mean – the other actors?'

'Yes.'

'As performers?'

'As potential killers.'

'That's ridiculous.' Jordan was more certain of himself now. 'Sky Palmer is a dear, sweet girl. Tirian is a bit of a cold fish, but then he only joined the company for the London run and I haven't had a chance to get to know him well.'

'I'm told there were difficulties between you.'

'Someone has been doing a lot of telling where this production is concerned.' Jordan turned to the mirror and his reflection glanced accusingly at me. 'Tirian Kirke is a young actor who is just finding his feet and I think it's significant that he's had no formal training – which is to say, he did not attend drama school.'

'What difference does that make?'

'It makes a great deal of difference, although I would find it difficult to explain to someone who is not in the profession, particularly . . .' he looked at his watch '. . . as we have so little time. Let us just say that he is not entirely giving as a performer. Movement on the stage is a symphony. One actor has to be aware of the others. It's all about eye contact, about empathy, about heart. Tirian will learn in time, I'm sure, but he still has a long way to go.'

'He's just got a part in a big Hollywood movie.'

'We all know about that, Mr Hawthorne. He never tires of telling us.'

'Do you get on with Ewan Lloyd?'

'I have enormous respect for Ewan. I remember his production of *Much Ado About Nothing* in Stratford years ago. He set the whole thing in 1930s Sicily. Don John and Don Pedro were Mafiosi. Dogberry was FBI. I have very much enjoyed working with him.'

He stood up and went over to the wardrobe. He took out the suit that he wore as Dr Farquhar. 'And now, if you don't mind, I need to get changed.'

Hawthorne and I both stood up. I thought we were going to leave, but as we moved towards the door, Hawthorne stopped in front of the photograph that I had noticed. 'Your wife?' he asked.

'Yes.'

The monosyllable was heavy, inviting no further questions, but Hawthorne went on anyway. 'Does she still work as a make-up artist?'

Jordan was taken aback. 'Why do you want to know?'

'You are still married.'

'Most certainly.'

'I was just surprised she wasn't in the audience at the first night.'

How had Hawthorne known that? He hadn't been there and I was sure I hadn't mentioned it – if, indeed, I'd even noticed.

Jordan Williams didn't move. His eyes met Hawthorne's. 'She was out of London,' he said. 'She's working on a BBC drama in Leeds.'

'But you saw her after the party?' Hawthorne asked. 'When you went home?'

'It was well after midnight. She was asleep.'

Hawthorne shook his head a little sadly. '"*Men were deceivers ever,*"' he muttered. '"*One foot in sea and one on shore, to one thing constant never.*"'

'What are you talking about?' Jordan asked.

'That's *Much Ado About Nothing*. You mentioned it a moment ago.'

'I think I've told you everything I want to tell you, Mr Hawthorne.' Jordan got up and snatched the photograph. Without stopping, he turned it face down. It was unintentional, but the movement was so violent that the glass broke and when Jordan lifted his hand, there was a bead of blood on the side of his index finger.

'Now look what you've made me do,' he said, dully.

We left him sucking his finger. The blood stained his lip.

11

Star Quality

I turned on Hawthorne the moment we were back in the corridor. 'You didn't believe him?' I demanded.

'About his wife?'

'About me!' Before he could answer, I went on. 'We were all upset by that review. We'd had a lot to drink and nobody was expecting it . . . not so soon, anyway. But he was the one who went crazy. He put a knife in the cake! Like he was stabbing it, not slicing it. And I didn't nod. I was actually quite shocked.'

Did I think Jordan had killed Harriet Throsby? Despite what had happened that night, I thought it unlikely. He was a method actor. He'd mentioned Stanislavski. It seemed that some of the violence of the part had spilled over into his real life. But the murder had taken place at ten o'clock in the morning, long after the party had ended. I could see Jordan lashing out in a fit of anger, in much the same way that he had managed to hurt Sky, but premeditated murder was something else. It just didn't fit with what I knew of his character. And there was another question. The killer had attempted to frame me. Why would Jordan have done that? We'd become quite friendly during the rehearsals and the out-of-town run. I was quite put out by what he'd just said.

It was as if Hawthorne had been reading my mind. He looked at me with those muddy, innocent eyes. 'Don't worry about Jordan Williams, mate. I'm on your side.'

'I'm glad to hear it.'

'We'll ask everyone who was in the room what they saw. And then we'll know the truth.'

Well, I thought, that's a vote of confidence.

We went downstairs. Dressing Room 6 was the first one we came to, a short way down a brightly lit corridor. The door was half-open and I could hear someone moving on the other side. I looked in to see Tirian Kirke wearing a sweatshirt but no trousers, getting into his costume for the performance, which was now about thirty minutes away. He saw me and smiled, unembarrassed. 'Hi! I didn't expect to see you tonight.'

'I'm sorry to interrupt you, Tirian. Can we come in? This is Hawthorne. He's a detective. He's looking into what happened to Harriet Throsby.'

'I don't suppose he's going to find anything here.' Tirian grabbed Mark Styler's trousers and pulled them on. 'But sure. Come on in. I can make you some tea if you like.'

We made our way in and closed the door behind us.

The room was a little smaller than Jordan's, but it was much less cluttered, which gave an impression of space. I noticed that Tirian had received just three good luck cards and a single bunch of flowers – much less than the older actor. These first-night offerings were looking a little sad, arranged on a single table with nothing else around them. Everything was very neat and tidy. No dirty clothes or dog-eared paperbacks here. The cushions on his sofa had been arranged at exact intervals and I noticed the towels beside the sink hanging with almost military precision.

As we sat down, he pulled off his sweatshirt, exposing a well-toned chest and shoulders that suggested a lot of time spent in the gym. There was something about him right then that reminded me of James Dean, who had become a cultural icon when he was just twenty-four and who had died the same year. Tirian had the same careless good looks combined with a sense of disengagement, the rebel without a cause. I was reminded that he had just been cast in a major Hollywood picture that might make him a household name and I could already see that he was halfway there. Star quality is hard to define, but I've met many young actors before they've become famous and they've all had it. It's not exactly physical. It's not even a force of personality. It's just a sense of being different; the prescience that one day, quite soon, they're going to be loved.

'I couldn't believe it when I heard about Harriet,' he said. 'It's the most terrible thing to have happened. That poor woman . . .'

'You feel sorry for her?' Hawthorne sounded surprised.

'Well, of course I do! She's been killed!' He stopped himself. 'I know she said bad things about the play, and I have a suspicion she wasn't exactly sweetness and light in real life either, but murder is murder and for what it's worth, she was actually quite nice about me. She said I was one of the most promising actors of my generation.' He couldn't resist an approving glance in the make-up mirror. 'You don't think one of us did it, do you?' he went on. 'Is that why you're here?'

'It's a possibility,' Hawthorne replied.

'Well, I think you're barking up the wrong tree, if you don't mind me saying so. I mean . . .' he held up his hand and began to count the various names off on his thumb and four fingers '. . . Sky. She couldn't have been kinder to me when I joined the company and she clearly doesn't have a bad bone in her. Ahmet and Maureen. They're just a joke. Do you think they're having it away? I do. They really are the world's worst producers, as witness those ridiculous daggers they gave us on the first night. I still have mine, by the way. The police came round to my place asking to see it. It was lucky I hadn't put it in the skip. Funny, isn't it. So many murder weapons. All identical.'

'Not very funny,' I muttered.

He touched another finger.

'Ewan hated her. I get the feeling that the two of them have history, although he never talks about it. You saw how angry he was!' This was addressed to me. 'But I really can't imagine him going round there and doing her in. He's much too civilised. You should have seen him when he was having one of his hissy fits in rehearsals. Sometimes I was afraid he might stab me with his spectacles, but that's about as far as it ever went.

'Then there's Keith on the door.' Tirian counted him on his little finger. 'He was here that night and I have a feeling he's out of his head on dope half the time, but what reason would he have had to kill her? Revenge because she panned *Mindgame*?' He sniffed. 'If we close tomorrow, another play will open the next day. It makes no difference to him.'

He lowered his hand.

'You've missed out Jordan Williams,' Hawthorne said.

'Oh. Yes. You're right.' Tirian's face fell. 'Well, we all heard what he said that night, so I'd imagine that makes him the prime suspect.'

'He said she deserved to die.'

'That's right.'

'Did anyone else in the room seem to agree?'

I could see where Hawthorne was going with that one, but to my relief, Tirian wasn't having it. 'I don't think so. Nobody said anything. It was all a bit embarrassing.' He shook his head, dismissing the thought. 'It's no secret that Jordan and I don't get along. But – hand on heart – I don't think he had anything to do with Harriet's death. The thing about him is that he's always sounding off. It was the same during rehearsals. But it was all just a lot of hot air.'

'Why did he have a problem with you, do you think?'

'Why don't you ask him?'

'It's your perspective that interests me.'

'All right. But let me start by saying that I don't dislike Jordan. My rule in life is to try and get on with everyone. Why not? You're only in this world once, so you've got to make the best of it.' Satisfied that he had made this clear, he continued. 'I think he was jealous. That's the only way to explain it. From the moment I joined the show, he was on my case. I haven't learned my lines. I'm upstaging him. I'm not giving him what he needs when he's doing his big soliloquies . . . you know, like I should be hanging on every word.'

'He'd heard about your part in *Tenet*?'

'Oh, yes. I don't know why it pissed him off so much. I mean, he had some big parts in American TV before he came here. He could have stayed and had a Hollywood career. Maybe it's just because I'm so much younger than him. Some of the old-school actors are like that. They think you've got to spend years doing walk-on parts in the provinces and bit parts on TV before you get your big break. It's happened to me faster, that's all. And he doesn't like it.'

'You didn't go to drama school.' This was something that Jordan had told Hawthorne. He certainly hadn't been happy about that.

'Actually, you're right. That's definitely something Jordan resented. I never "learned my craft". But it wasn't my fault! I never even wanted to go into acting. The whole thing was as big a surprise to me as anyone else.' Tirian had a little travel alarm clock on the table beside him and he twisted it round to check the time. 'It happened when I was twenty-two. It's funny, really. I just walked into it.'

'Tirian is a Welsh name . . .' Hawthorne said. It was one of his habits, throwing in observations that seemingly came from nowhere.

Tirian smiled. 'Yes. I was born in Chepstow, in Monmouthshire. My mother called me Tirian because it means "kind", which is what I always try to be.'

'She must be very proud of you.'

His face fell. 'She's dead. I lost both my parents when I was very small. They were in a car accident. Their car was hit by a delivery truck just outside London.'

'I'm sorry.'

'I was only five years old. I hardly even remember them really. I moved up to Harrogate in North Yorkshire. I was brought up by an aunt.'

That explained the sense of otherness I'd felt when I was with Tirian, and perhaps the absence of many cards or flowers in his dressing room. He had no family and I'd never seen him go out with friends.

'My parents were very ordinary people. My father was a doctor. My mother worked in the same surgery – she was the receptionist. I was an only child and they weren't sure what to do with me after the accident. I'd probably have ended up in an orphanage or something except that my dad had an aunt, my great-aunt May, and she stepped in and said I could live with her. She was on her own and she was quite well off. She was everything to me growing up. She's still close to me now.'

He reached out and picked up one of the three cards he had been sent. It showed a cartoon of a man reaching down to pick up a four-leaf clover . . . just missing an old-fashioned safe that was plummeting down from a building behind him. The words GOOD LUCK were printed in silver foil. Hawthorne opened it and we read the message, written in a cramped, almost childish hand. *Hope the first night goes well. All my love. AM.*

'Nice of her to remember,' I said.

'She's got dementia,' Tirian replied. 'She's in a care home now and the nurses will have helped her with the card because she doesn't remember anything very much.' For a moment he was sad, but then he smiled. 'I had a wonderful time living with her. She had a beautiful house, a two-up-two-down on Otley Road . . . just opposite the tennis club. I used to go there all the time. I wasn't crazy about the sport, but mixed doubles was definitely my thing. That's where I had my first kiss. And my first cigarette.'

'Did you go to school in Harrogate?'

'Yeah. I got into Harrogate Grammar School. It was only five minutes away from where I lived. I was there until I was sixteen. Funnily enough, there was a teacher there – Miss Havergill – who was always trying to get me interested in drama. She put me in *The Pied Piper*, playing the king of the rats. I enjoyed that. Maybe it should have told me something, but I was a lazy little sod. I didn't do A levels. I couldn't wait to start work.'

'What did you want to do?'

'I didn't really care. I just wanted to have enough money to have my own place, a fast car, travel . . . that sort of thing. Aunt May managed to get me a job with the National Trust in York. I started as a programmes manager in the event-management department. Twelve thousand pounds a year – that was my first salary. It was pretty boring, to be honest with you, and I wouldn't have stuck it very long, but then one of those weird coincidences happened and it sort of changed my life.'

He was talking faster now, aware of time ticking away.

'They were shooting a TV series called *Heartbeat* in one of our properties near Leeds. You must remember it. It was a cop show set in the sixties. I was sent down there to act as a liaison officer – to make sure that everything went all right – and they asked me if I'd like to be an extra, just for a lark. I ended up playing a stable boy. The episode was about a farmer who shoots someone's dog or something. Anyway, I was up to my knees in mud, hanging on to a horse, which terrified me because I'd never been near one before, and I loved every minute of it.

'I can't explain it to you, really. The moment I went on the set I felt I'd sort of arrived. I'd never realised that so much work and so many people went into the making of an hour's TV. I was amazed by all the equipment – the cameras and the dollies, the catering trucks, the lights. It was massive. And then there were the stars. There was no "them and us". They were really nice. I watched them doing their stuff, not once but lots of times, doing the same scene from lots of different angles, and I thought – I can do that! Maybe I remembered doing that play with Miss Havergill. I wanted to do it. She'd been right. I had it inside me. I was an actor!

'And what happened that first day was really amazing. As it happened, the casting director happened to be on set. He was a guy called Malcolm Drury and after we finished filming, I went over and asked him if he could help me . . . you know, get into the business. I was actually quite nervous, but he couldn't have been nicer.'

The strange thing was, I'd met Malcolm Drury myself. He'd worked on a TV play for children that I'd written at the end of the eighties. I'd liked him too.

'We had a long chat. I was freezing cold and stinking of horses, but he took a liking to me and said he'd let me know if anything came up – and he was as good as his word. I got a few lines in *Spooks* and *Little Dorrit* – more horses – and after that I packed in the National Trust and got an agent and it all took off. There are lots of people who are a bit snooty, like Jordan, because I never went to drama school or anything like that, but I love what I'm doing and it seems I got lucky.' He stopped. 'I'm afraid I haven't helped you very much, have I – and now I've got to get ready. I didn't kill Harriet Throsby and I hope you find out who did. Let me know! But if you don't mind . . .'

Hawthorne and I stood up.

'Can I ask you one thing?' I asked. Hawthorne glanced warily in my direction. He was always warning me not to intrude. But there'd been something on my mind from the moment I'd met Tirian and although this probably wasn't the best time to mention it, I might not get another opportunity. 'Do you remember a TV show called *Injustice*?' I asked.

'A cop show, wasn't it? About a lawyer . . .'

'I wrote it. You were going to play Alan Stewart, the young man who takes his own life in jail. You'd agreed but at the last minute you backed out. I've always wondered why.' Even as I spoke, I realised that I was being ridiculous. I was in the middle of a murder investigation! But it was too late now. 'I just wondered . . .' I added, apologetically.

'Yes. I remember that.' Tirian looked uncomfortable. 'It wasn't my decision. I thought the part was great. It was my agent who advised against it. There were lots of offers on the table and she didn't think it was right for my career at the time. I know that sounds a bit rubbish, but I always listened to what she said and she just didn't think it was right. I'm sorry.'

*

'I think he killed Harriet Throsby,' I said, as soon as we were outside.

Hawthorne looked at me curiously. 'Really?'

'Why didn't you ask him where he was on Tuesday morning when she was killed?' It was the first time I had ever challenged Hawthorne, but I was tired and irritable. I'd had no sleep the night before and I'd been on my feet almost the whole day. I'd been in prison! My nerves were in shreds.

'There was no point, mate.' To my surprise, Hawthorne hadn't taken offence. He sounded completely reasonable. 'He's an actor. He got home late. He was probably in bed until mid-morning.' He paused. 'Like you.'

'Well, he was definitely lying.'

'How do you work that one out?'

'When he said his agent didn't want him to do *Injustice* – I know for a fact that's not true. He had the same agent as one of the other actors and I met her quite a few times. She was really angry he turned the part down. It was the exact opposite of what he just said. She told me she thought it was perfect for him.'

'Maybe she was the one who was lying.'

'I don't think so. She dropped him a short while later . . . or maybe he dropped her. Either way, she would have told me the truth.' Hawthorne didn't seem convinced so I went on. 'I know this isn't about my work, and I'm not angry with him because he didn't want to do my series. I'm just saying that you shouldn't believe everything he says.'

'I never believe everything anyone says.'

'Including me?'

He smiled. 'Why would I believe someone who spends his entire life making stuff up?'

I had an answer for that, I was sure. But before I could come up with it, he had already set off down the corridor, on his way to the third and last dressing room. Shaking my head, I fell in behind.

12

Another Knife

'Why do I have to talk to you? I've already spoken to the police. I haven't got anything else to say.'

Sky Palmer sucked on her vaping device and for a brief moment the end glowed an angry red. She hadn't been happy from the moment I'd introduced her to Hawthorne, as if a murder investigation was nothing more than an inconvenience added to her busy diary. She threw down the vape and picked up her hairbrush, scratching at hair, which had gone from pink to her natural colour . . . a very light blonde.

'I'm going on stage any minute,' she went on. 'I'm still doing my make-up. And I don't really like to talk to anyone before I start. It messes with my head. I have to think about my character.'

From the first time I'd met her, I'd found Sky difficult to pin down: that mixture of youth and self-assurance, shyness and arrogance. It was even harder now, seeing her sitting there dressed as Nurse Plimpton. Her costume had been designed to turn her into a caricature. It was deliberately tight-fitting around her breasts and hips, with a tear in her black tights . . . one of the critics had even mentioned it. Tucked under her blouse, there was a plastic bag of fake blood – Kensington Gore – which would burst when she was stabbed (with a scalpel) at the end of Act I. It was all very *Rocky Horror Picture Show* and she carried it off perfectly on the stage. In the dressing room, though, it was disconcerting. She was trapped between the two characters and I wasn't sure which was which.

I had to remind myself that Sky was very young, no more than twenty-five. Strolling into rehearsals in her leggings and boas, knee-high boots, gloves with the fingers cut off and every day a different piece of antique jewellery that she might have inherited from a wealthy aunt, she seemed to be modelling herself on Sally Bowles in *Cabaret*. Maybe that was how she saw herself, skating along the surface of life, admired by all. Hawthorne was looking at her dubiously. He wasn't impressed.

Her rose-gold telephone rang and without a glance in our direction, she picked it up and answered it.

'Yeah . . . Yeah . . . No, I can't talk to you right now. I'm about to go on and I've got someone with me. No . . .'

But although she didn't talk, she listened, holding the phone with her little finger pointing in the air.

I took in the rest of the dressing room while I waited for her, wondering what Hawthorne would make of it all. Somehow, I didn't think he would find it too difficult to work out Sky Palmer's background, her family history and everything she'd done in the last ten years, given the multiple clues scattered around.

There was barely a surface that wasn't crowded out. She had been sent so many flowers she could have opened a shop – or perhaps a funeral parlour – including a huge bunch of roses that had been shoved into a single vase and were struggling to survive. Most of her good luck cards were expensive: handmade rather than mass-market. I'd already noticed Sky's Gucci umbrella and Cartier watch. The luxury brand names continued with crystal flasks of perfume, hand cream in porcelain tubs, Fortnum & Mason biscuits and loose-leaf tea in fancy tins, liqueur chocolates, soap and scent diffusers, those weird stick things that poke out of a jar of oil, dispensing, to my mind, no scent at all. Three bottles of champagne and a bottle of gin had been lined up on one shelf and there were a dozen glasses that didn't appear to have been washed.

None of this connected with what I knew of her. She had spent three years appearing as a barmaid in *EastEnders*, and during rehearsals she'd always spoken with an Estuary English accent, although dismissing us just now, she had been much more Cheltenham Ladies' College. I thought I'd had a good understanding of everyone I'd met so far – Tirian,

Jordan, Arthur and Olivia Throsby. But Sky was something else. A mystery within a mystery.

'*This is a fifteen-minute call for members of the* Mindgame *company. You have fifteen minutes to curtain up. Thank you.*'

It was a disembodied voice that I presumed belonged to Pranav, the stage manager. It came over the intercom system and for the first time I noticed the speaker set high up in a corner of the room. Sky heard it. 'I've gotta go! Bye!' She disconnected the telephone and set it down, then turned to us. 'I'm really sorry. I have to get ready.'

'Come on, darling. I've seen the play. You're not on for the first fifteen pages.' When Hawthorne was annoyed, he often slipped into language that I would not have used myself. Perhaps he did it deliberately, to show he didn't care. 'We need to ask you a few questions about Harriet Throsby,' he added.

'I told you. I've got nothing to say. I hardly knew her.'

'Did you know where she lived?'

'Why are you even asking me that? Are you accusing me of something? Yes, I knew where she lived. We all did.' She looked directly at me. 'You showed me that article in the magazine.'

'What?'

Once again, I felt the ground opening up beneath my feet. How many more ways could I be found guilty of this crime?

'*House & Garden*. You showed it to me during the first week of rehearsals. There was a picture of her house. The article said she lived next to the canal . . . near a tunnel.'

'I have no idea what you're talking about!' I exclaimed. 'I never saw the magazine. I didn't know her address . . .'

'Are you calling me a liar?'

I turned to Hawthorne for help. He glanced at me and shook his head a little sadly – but his attention was still fixed on Sky. 'No one's calling you anything,' he said. He waited until she had calmed down. 'Tell me what happened in the green room, when you all got together after the first performance.'

'You mean . . . the party?'

'I'm talking about the review.'

That shook her. 'Yes. I wish I hadn't mentioned it now. But Tirian snatched my phone before I could stop him and he showed it to everyone. I had no idea it was going to be so cruel,' she added, defensively.

'It certainly put a crimp in the evening,' Hawthorne agreed.

'But it didn't have anything to do with Harriet being killed!' Sky stared at Hawthorne. 'Do you seriously think she was murdered because she didn't like the play? That's ridiculous. And I'm not going to be held responsible. If there was someone in the room who was crazy enough to kill her, they'd have killed her at the weekend when what she'd written was published in the newspaper, so telling everyone what she'd written wouldn't have made any difference.'

Hawthorne wasn't giving up. 'We can't be sure of that, Sky. It had been a long day. A lot of alcohol. A late night. Maybe you inadvertently triggered something. You saw what happened for yourself.'

Her phone pinged. She glanced at the screen and I could see that she wanted to pick it up and respond. She turned it face down.

'Are you talking about Jordan?' she asked. 'Maybe you should be talking to him, not me. He's the one with the temper. Fighting with Tirian. Him and his wife . . . always shouting at her down the phone. And what he did to me during rehearsals! Have you heard about that? You should have seen the bruises.' She rubbed her arm, realising that she'd said too much. 'But that thing with the knife was just stupid,' she went on. 'He wouldn't kill anyone. He doesn't have it in him. I quite like him, really. When he isn't going on about his boring stagecraft or boasting about his career – *American House of Horror* and all the rest of it – he can be all right. He bought me flowers. And he wasn't the only one who was upset that night. Harriet slagged Ewan off too and he was just as angry.'

'He didn't seem that upset to me,' I remarked. I was still reeling from what she had said about the magazine. I thought back to the rehearsals in Dalston and the tech run-through here at the Vaudeville. I had absolutely no memory of handing her anything. 'He made a joke about it. He didn't seem to care about the review at all.'

'You don't know him,' Sky said. 'He never likes people to know what he's thinking, but it's all happening inside his head. He's the complete opposite of Jordan.'

'How well do you know Ewan Lloyd?' Hawthorne cut in.

'This is the second time I've worked with him. He's OK. I did *Macbeth* with him in Yorkshire.'

'What did you play?'

'There were only six of us in the cast. I played Lady Macbeth, Lady Macduff, Fleance, the Porter and all three witches.'

'Was that a good experience?'

'Not really. It never stopped raining and nobody came.'

'*This is your ten-minute call. Ten minutes to curtain up. Thank you.*'

'There's one thing I don't quite understand.' Hawthorne spoke softly . . . always a dangerous sign. 'Where exactly did you find the review?'

'It was on my phone.'

'That's not what I mean.' He looked at her sadly. 'I've searched the internet and it's not there. It's not anywhere. And when you think about it, it doesn't make much sense, does it. Why would Harriet Throsby have posted her review on social media if she was being paid by the *Sunday Times*? They've got a paywall. They wouldn't want it leaking out. The only way you could have read what she'd written was if you'd had access to her computer.' He paused. 'Or knew someone who did.'

There was a pause. For the first time, Sky looked vulnerable.

'You're wrong,' she said. 'There was a website . . .'

'What website?'

'I didn't look.'

Another pause. Hawthorne waited. Sky said nothing.

'I think you need to remember that this is a murder investigation,' he reminded her. As always, he leaned heavily on the first part of the word 'murder', as if he was relishing it. 'You can explain yourself to me or you can talk to the police. It's your choice.'

'I'm not talking to you.'

Hawthorne smiled. 'Then we'll do it the other way. I'll put you in touch with Cara Grunshaw. It may not work out too well for you, though. Obstructing a murder investigation is never a good idea. I hope you've got an understudy ready to take over your part. You can go to prison for that.'

He got up, as if to leave.

'Wait,' Sky said. I could see her weighing up her options. It didn't take her long to realise that she didn't have any. 'Olivia sent it to me,' she said.

'Harriet's daughter!' I muttered.

'Yes.'

Hawthorne sat down again. 'Why would she do that? Do the two of you know each other?'

Sky's shoulders slumped. 'We've met a couple of times.'

'Where?'

'The first time was at the Barbican Theatre. It was a production of *The Crucible*. As usual, Harriet barged her way into the first-night party. Why did she do that? She must have known that nobody wanted her there. Olivia was dragged along too. I could see she was embarrassed. We got talking and we sort of hit it off. We had a lot in common.'

'Like what?'

'Well, a mother we couldn't stand, for a start. A stepmother in my case. If you want to make friends with someone, that's a good place to begin. We kept in touch on Facebook. We met up for a drink a couple of times. It was no big deal. I didn't even ask her to send me that review. She just thought I'd like to see it.'

'She hacked into her mum's computer?' Hawthorne sounded shocked, as if he had somehow forgotten that only that morning he'd raided the Police National Computer and shut down their forensic laboratory in Lambeth.

'She didn't hack into anything,' Sky protested. 'She knows the password. She just wanted to let me know that her mum hadn't slagged me off. And she didn't, incidentally. She was quite nice about me. The mistake I made was telling everyone that I had it. That was stupid of me. When the police told me what had happened, I couldn't believe it at first . . . that Harriet was dead and that someone had killed her. But it never even occurred to me that it might be one of us, despite what Jordan had said. It just didn't seem possible.'

Her phone pinged a second time – but whoever was trying to reach Sky was concealed from us.

'The police came to your house?' Hawthorne asked.

'Yes.'

'Where is that?'

'Victoria Park.'

'You were there all Wednesday morning? Around ten o'clock, for example?'

She looked down. 'That's when it happened,' she said quietly. When she met Hawthorne's eyes again, she was defiant. 'I was at home all day. I was on my own. Why don't you check the CCTV cameras? There are loads of them down my street, and all around the canal where Harriet lived, for that matter. I didn't go anywhere.'

'You live alone?'

'Yes.'

'Renting?'

Sky hesitated. She was embarrassed, but there was no point lying. 'It's my own place,' she admitted.

'Acting doing well for you, then,' Hawthorne remarked.

'My dad helped me buy it.'

'And who is your dad?'

She didn't want to tell him but she had no choice. The police would have probably found out all about her. She was, after all, a suspect in a murder case . . . or had been until I'd been arrested. I wondered if Hawthorne already knew the answer to his question. It wouldn't have surprised me.

Sky's father was the lead singer of one of the UK's biggest rock groups. Even I recognised the name when she told us. Immediately, everything about her made sense: all the luxury goods, owning a house in her twenties, her ambiguity about the play. She didn't need to work. She had quite possibly drifted into acting because of her father's connections in showbiz. It would have been that or some sort of PR or work in a posh Mayfair art gallery. I also remembered his divorce, which had been all over the papers. He had left his wife for a model not all that much older than his daughter.

'He didn't come to the first night,' Hawthorne said. He knew that because it would have been obvious if he'd been at the theatre. Keith would have told us. There would have been paparazzi crowding around the entrance.

'He didn't even know it was happening. He's on tour.'

She looked at us defiantly, but there were tears in her eyes. In a few words she had told us everything we needed to know about her relationship with her father.

'*This is your five-minute call, ladies and gentlemen. Five minutes to curtain.*'

'Can you go now? I really do need to get ready.'

There was nothing more to be said and we did as she asked. I felt a little sorry for Sky as we left the room. I've met a few young people with famous parents and it's often the case that the problems outweigh the privileges.

We went out through the fire escape that led into Lumley Court. The door opened with a push-bar mechanism and didn't set off any alarms. We hadn't signed in when we arrived, so there was no need to go back past the stage-door manager's office. As soon as we were outside, I turned on Hawthorne. 'I've got to explain to you about that magazine—' I began.

Hawthorne shook his head. 'You should have told me earlier, Tony.'

'I'd forgotten all about it. It must have happened during the rehearsals in Dalston. There were loads of things on my mind. Maybe someone passed me a magazine and I passed it to her, but I didn't look inside. I didn't even look at the cover.' I realised I was burbling. 'I had no idea where Harriet lived until Cara told me,' I concluded, feebly.

'I believe you, mate.' Hawthorne considered. 'It might not be so easy to persuade them in court, but maybe the jury will take pity on you. I mean, you've certainly stacked up the evidence against yourself.'

We walked on in silence, making our way back to the Strand. The front of the theatre was deserted now, but it was exactly seven thirty and the first act would have begun. I glanced inside and saw the box-office manager, sitting on his own. He didn't look happy.

'Hawthorne . . .' I'd had a thought while I was in the dressing room and I expressed it now. 'Sky Palmer was in *Macbeth*.'

'I heard.'

'But you must realise what it means! She must have been given one of the original daggers. Ahmet had a whole lot made for the cast in Edinburgh.' I thought back to what she had said. 'And Ewan Lloyd directed it. So he must have a second dagger too.'

'I'd sort of figured that one out, Tony. The trouble is, it doesn't really help us.'

'Why not?'

'Your producer could have had another dozen knives made. Friends, sponsors, costume designer, front-of-house manager and so on. But you've lost yours. And the one that killed Harriet Throsby had your fingerprints on it.'

I felt deflated. 'That's true.'

Hawthorne looked at his watch. 'Ahmet's waiting for us in his office. I said we'd call in tonight.'

'Can't it wait until tomorrow?' I was exhausted. I'd had no sleep the night before, I'd spent half the day in jail and we'd visited one suspect after another, including – in the past hour – the entire cast of *Mindgame*.

'It's up to you, mate. But the clock's still ticking. The DNA results could come in any time. And if you want to head back to Tolpuddle Street . . .'

The custody centre. Cara Grunshaw. Suddenly I was awake again. 'No. Let's go.'

We continued past the front of the theatre. I could imagine Tirian Kirke onstage, describing Dr Farquhar's office. Would the line about the books have got a laugh? I noticed my name in lights. Another letter had fused. I'd been reduced to ANONY. One more short circuit and I'd be completely anon. Which, given the reviews, was probably what I deserved.

Hawthorne flagged down a taxi and once again we were on our way.

13

A Run of Bad Luck

I've never much liked Euston.

I got to know the area well during the sixteen years I worked on *Foyle's War*. I did a lot of the research at the British Library, just about the only modern building in the entire square mile with any sense of architectural style. I still don't understand how you can have a road that's only a twenty-minute walk from the centre of town, yet remains so inherently cheap and tacky. Or why there's been a traffic jam from one end to the other for the past twenty years. The shops are useless and you'd be mad to eat in any of the restaurants. Half the people you meet are tourists with backpacks. I should have known better when I heard that this was where Ahmet had his office. Theatreland it most certainly was not.

I brought Hawthorne to the front entrance, taking him down a flight of stairs concealed behind a row of dustbins to the basement of a tired grey house that had been sliced into flats. Light was streaming out of the windows below pavement level, but the glass was so dusty we couldn't see in. I rang the bell. It was ten to eight in the evening, but so dark that it could have been midnight. The April weather was showing no signs of improvement. It wasn't raining, but there was a thick fog that was doing the same job. Nobody came, so I rang the bell a second time. The door swung open to reveal Maureen Bates, dressed in a tweed skirt and mauve jersey with her glasses resting on her chest. She looked far from happy as she stood there, purposefully blocking the way in.

'I think Mr Yurdakul is expecting us,' Hawthorne said.

'I'm aware of that. Yes. But I have to tell you that this really isn't a good time.' Did she think we'd just turn round and leave?

'It's never a good time when someone has been killed,' Hawthorne assured her.

'I don't see how Mr Yurdakul can help you.'

'You'll find out when you let us in.'

With a pout of resignation, she turned and led us through the tiny hallway and into the office, where Ahmet was just finishing a conversation with a dark-haired man who looked uncomfortable in the armchair into which he had folded himself. As we arrived, he stood up and I saw that he was about six foot five, towering over the producer, twitchy and apologetic. I recognised him as the same person Ahmet had been talking to at the cast party. He had looked nervous then too. Cigarette smoke hung thick in the air, which was both unpleasant and, in modern times, rare. Ahmet was smoking. There was a packet of his L&M cigarettes in front of him, along with the onyx ashtray filled with at least half a packet's worth of butts.

The tall man was in a hurry to get away. He muttered a quick 'Good evening' to us and gathered up his laptop and papers, shoving them awkwardly into a leather briefcase. Maureen showed him out and I heard a brief snatch of their conversation at the door.

'I'll call you in a couple of days.'

'Thank you, Martin.'

'I'm so sorry. You know . . .'

'Don't worry. We'll deal with it.'

Not good news, then.

Meanwhile, I had introduced Hawthorne to Ahmet and he had taken the empty seat. Ahmet had stayed at his desk, half concealed behind a laptop and a great pile of letters and bills. As usual, he was wearing a suit, but had taken off his jacket to reveal an old-fashioned shirt and braces. His fingers were stained yellow with nicotine. It had even crept into his eyes.

'So, how are things?' Hawthorne asked cheerfully.

'Not so good.' The three words were like a death knell. I had never heard him sound so defeated. He looked at me like a dog abandoned by its owner. 'Martin, the man who was here just now – he is my accountant. A very reliable man. And what he tells me . . .'

'Are we going to have to close?' I asked. It was the inevitable conclusion. I just wanted him to get to the point.

He drew out another cigarette and lit it. 'I am fighting, Anthony. All my life I have been fighting.' He blew out grey-blue smoke. 'I will tell you. It was my ambition to produce for the theatre from the day that I joined the Really Useful Theatre Company. I was there for many years.'

'You worked with Andrew Lloyd Webber?' I asked. I was impressed. The Really Useful Group had been set up to look after Lloyd Webber's multibillion-pound musicals, but had since diversified into theatre ownership, film production and records. It was a fantastically successful conglomeration, but Ahmet had never mentioned he had been part of it.

'I worked for him in IT,' he explained. 'I helped to develop the box-office ticketing software they still use to this day!' For a moment, a smile flitted across his face and his eyes were far away. 'Database compatible files, easily imported into spreadsheets. Mail merge files and account reports. Online credit card verification. Publicity. Revenues. One of the first user-friendly onscreen seating charts! Do you know what I called it? Computer-Assisted Ticketing System. CATS! They told me that Sir Andrew smiled when he heard that. He was not a lord then. I don't know why they didn't use it. The name, I mean. The system is still very much alive.'

'Is that why you became a producer?' Hawthorne asked.

'Yes, sir. I looked at the enormous amounts of money these musicals were making. It was incredible! Do you know that a hundred and fifty million people have seen *Phantom of the Opera* and that it has made more than six billion dollars worldwide?' He pointed at me. 'And not all the reviews were favourable, let me tell you! There were critics who said that it was old-fashioned hokum. What did they know?'

'So we might be all right,' I said.

'No, no, no. They still liked the sets, the sumptuous costumes, the music, the performances. With *Mindgame* . . . not so much.' He gazed at me, tears welling in his eyes. 'I blame myself, Anthony. It is a wonderful play. It is original. Apart from the excessive violence – and we did discuss this – it is highly entertaining. I believed in it and it may be that in the end I did not do it justice. This is my fault. I have let you down.'

I should have argued with him but I was feeling too dispirited.

'You don't blame Harriet Throsby?' Hawthorne asked.

'Why?' Ahmet seemed genuinely surprised.

'I'd have said she had the loudest voice. Certainly, she was the rudest.' Hawthorne paused. 'And the first. That may be why she was the one who was stabbed to death.'

'You believe she was killed because of what she wrote?' Ahmet shook his head. 'I'm sorry, Mr Hawthorne. That is impossible. Sometimes critics upset us. Sometimes they make us angry. But we are never violent!'

'Jordan Williams was violent. He made threats against her.'

It was Maureen who answered. 'He did no such thing!'

'Tony was there. He heard him.'

'Jordan had been drinking and he was emotional. But it was obvious to everyone in the room that he didn't mean what he said. He was joking.'

'A strange sense of humour.' Hawthorne considered. 'How well do you know him?'

It was an innocent enough question, but Maureen turned away, leaving it to Ahmet to step in. 'This was the first time we had worked together. But we got to know each other during rehearsals. Of course he was angry. But I can assure you that he meant nothing by what he said. He was acting!'

'You were angry too,' Hawthorne pointed out. 'You said Harriet Throsby was a liar and that what she wrote was shit.'

Maureen visibly winced when she heard that. She didn't like bad language. Ahmet glanced at me sadly. 'Did you tell him that?' It was clear to me that he felt I had betrayed him. Jordan Williams had said the same. 'I was upset, of course. It was the first review. But I had no ill feelings towards her personally. She is a woman. She is doing her job. And sometimes, you know, there is nothing you can do. My company has had a run of bad luck. I can blame the critics. I can blame the audiences. But in the end, what good will that do? I made the choices. I blame myself.'

'You're going out of business,' Hawthorne said.

Ahmet didn't even try to deny it. He nodded. 'I was meeting with my accountant when you came in. Martin has told me there is no other option. It is not just *Mindgame*. We lost a great deal of money on *Macbeth*.'

'We should have taken out weather insurance,' Maureen muttered.

'We discussed this at the time,' Ahmet snapped back. 'It was either weather insurance or costumes.' He collected himself. 'That was just one in a sea of misfortunes. There are other plays, also, which I have developed and which have never reached the stage and these have also cost money. I have overheads . . . the rent on this office, the photocopier. Martin has persuaded me that we have come to the end of the road.'

'It's a crying shame,' Maureen exclaimed. She sounded more outraged than upset. Two circles of pink had appeared on her cheeks. 'Nobody has worked harder than Ahmet. I've known him twenty years and he deserves better than this.'

'Were you also at the Really Useful Company?' Hawthorne asked.

'No. We met at the New London Theatre. Ahmet organised a very special evening for me.' Hawthorne looked at her enquiringly and she realised she was going to have to continue. 'It was an anniversary.'

'My software told me that Maureen had seen *Cats* one hundred times,' Ahmet explained.

'I loved that show. I can't explain why.' Maureen looked into the far distance. 'It was the music, of course. "Memory"! "The Rum Tum Tugger". That always used to make me laugh, every time. There wasn't a song in that show I didn't know off by heart.' She stopped herself, aware that she might look foolish. 'It filled a hole in my life after my husband died,' she explained. 'I went once. Then I thought I'd see it again. And after a while I found that I was only happy when I was in the theatre. It was like a barrier against the world.

'I couldn't afford the best seats, but that night I got a surprise. I found myself in the front row. Ahmet had arranged that for me. I had a free glass of champagne in the interval and afterwards I went backstage and met some of the cast. It was a wonderful evening and after that we sort of became friends.'

'Maureen came to work for me when I set up on my own.'

'What were you doing before that?' Hawthorne asked.

'I was a secretary at Hewlett-Packard in Reading.'

Right then I felt a sense of guilt and sadness that might have been unjustified but which nonetheless affected me. Maureen and Ahmet truly were an odd couple. I'd known that from the start, but I'd been so eager to see *Mindgame* on the stage that I had ignored my misgivings and let them go ahead. But it wasn't the failure of the play that upset me. It was the sense that it was all my fault. I was the one who'd brought them down, and although I would go on to other things – there were other books in the pipeline – they'd come to the end of the road. Right then, I wanted to go back outside and never see either of them again. I hoped Hawthorne had found out everything he wanted and we could leave.

But he hadn't finished yet. He reached into his pocket and took out the crumpled packet of American cigarettes he had found at the theatre. 'Are these yours, Mr Yurdakul?' he asked.

Ahmet was puzzled. 'It's the brand I smoke. Yes.'

'I found this in the green room at the Vaudeville.' He opened the packet, showing Ahmet the three broken white tubes spilling out their tobacco. 'I wondered why you didn't finish the pack.'

'I don't remember. Where were they?'

'They were in the bin.'

'Maybe somebody found them and threw them away. I don't remember leaving them behind.'

'What have three broken cigarettes got to do with anything?' Maureen asked, scornful now.

'Probably nothing.' Hawthorne smiled and got to his feet. 'Thank you, Mr Yurdakul. You've been very helpful.'

'I'll show you out.'

We left the office and went back into the hallway. Maureen closed the door behind us as we came out. 'Mr Yurdakul is very upset,' she said in a low voice. She was almost admonishing Hawthorne, as if he had no right to come barging in with his questions. 'You can't possibly think he had anything to do with that woman's death.'

'He had the most to lose,' Hawthorne remarked, pragmatically.

'If he'd wanted to kill someone, he'd have killed Anthony.' I was shocked to hear her say that, but she had already turned on me with fury in her eyes and there was no stopping her. 'I warned him against your play. I said that it was too peculiar for a modern audience and that nobody would understand what you were trying to get at. Is it a comedy? Is it a thriller? What is it, exactly? But he had complete faith in you, and now you turn up with your detective friend and cast aspersions on a man who is absolutely blameless and wouldn't dream of hurting anyone. Mr Yurdakul has been wonderful to work with. I'd do anything for him! And just so you know, I've never seen him lose his temper . . . not once. He's a gentleman in every sense of the word.'

'So where was he on Wednesday morning?' Hawthorne asked, cutting her short.

She looked at him in disbelief. 'He was nowhere near Palgrove Gardens. He had a meeting at Frost and Longhurst at eleven o'clock.'

'Who are Frost and Longhurst?'

'His accountants. That was Martin Longhurst you met just now.'

'And where are they based?'

'In Holborn.'

Hawthorne sighed. 'Holborn is less than thirty minutes from Little Venice on the tube. That would have left him plenty of time to kill Harriet Throsby.'

Maureen stared at him with poison in her eyes. 'You clearly haven't listened to a word I've said . . .' she sniffed.

'You think she didn't deserve it?' He was deliberately provoking her.

'Just so you know, I agree with every single word she said – about the play, anyway. Maybe I wouldn't have couched it in quite those terms, but of course she didn't deserve to die. Nobody does.'

'Just out of interest, how did you know she lived in Palgrove Gardens.'

'I didn't.'

'You just said that Ahmet was nowhere near that address.'

Maureen took a deep breath. I thought she might be about to scream. 'The police told me where she lived,' she explained, simply. 'Before they came here, I knew almost nothing about Harriet Throsby. As far as I'm concerned, I never want to hear her name again.' She opened the door, allowing the cold air to rush in. 'I very much hope you won't come back,' she continued. 'We've got nothing more to tell you and as far as I can see, you're not helping at all.'

We walked past her and climbed back up to street level.

'Frost and Longhurst,' Hawthorne said.

'The accountants . . .' I muttered.

'The name doesn't mean anything to you?'

'No. Should it?'

'It's lucky you're not a detective.' Hawthorne glanced at his watch. 'Time for one more visit. If you're up for it.'

'Don't you ever eat, Hawthorne?'

'Ewan Lloyd is expecting us.'

Ewan Lloyd would complete the line-up, and perhaps he would shed some light on what had happened. For myself, I had no idea who had killed Harriet Throsby. It was always possible that her husband had finally got tired of being criticised day in, day out. It would have been easy enough to slip out of school, cycle home and kill his wife. Her daughter had made no secret that she loathed her mother and she didn't work too far from home either. Jordan Williams, Tirian Kirke, Sky Palmer, Ahmet Yurdakul, Maureen Bates and Ewan Lloyd were the six main suspects, all connected to her by the play. Any one of them could have got hold of my dagger and planted it in her chest.

It had to be one of them.

But which?

14

Premonitions

Ewan Lloyd's home was a mews house in every respect but one. It wasn't actually in a mews. It was compact and elegant, painted pale blue, with a flat roof and a front room that had been converted from a garage. It was wedged in between two very similar houses in a cobbled street with old-fashioned street lamps. But the street itself led somewhere. I could imagine it being used as a rat run by north London mothers taking their children to school. Finsbury Park tube station, one of the most depressing stations on the London Underground system, was just round the corner. It had been my nearest station when I was living in Crouch End and I might have rubbed shoulders with Ewan any number of times. It's amazing, really, the invisible process that can turn complete strangers into friends.

As Hawthorne rang the front bell, yellow light spilling out of the front windows and the sound of a Chopin nocturne being played on a speaker system, it struck me that this was exactly the sort of home I would have expected Ewan to live in. It reflected his single-mindedness, the way he presented himself, as if the light and the music had been arranged specially for our arrival. It was also the house of a divorced man. Ahmet had told me that he'd been married with four children and it was impossible to imagine them all living here. I wondered if he was still on his own.

The nocturne stopped mid-trill and a few moments later, Ewan opened the door and stood there, blinking through his round-framed spectacles. Hawthorne had told him we were on our way and he had dressed for the occasion in a velvet jacket with another long scarf dangling from his shoulders. At the same time, he wasn't happy to see us. He filled the entire door frame . . . but then again, it was a small door.

'Mr Hawthorne?'

'Yes.'

'I'm afraid I can only give you a few minutes. My wife will be home soon and I'm just cooking dinner.'

Well, that answered the question I'd just been asking myself.

'A few minutes is all I need.' Hawthorne replied. Of course, he would say that. Once he was inside, he would stay as long as he wanted.

The front door opened directly into the main living area, effectively a single space with an open-plan kitchen, modern furniture, a spiral staircase leading up to the next floor, and more than a thousand books. Like Harriet's office, these focused almost entirely on the theatre. I ran my eye across biographies of Trevor Nunn, Laurence Olivier, Peter O'Toole, Harold Pinter – and was surprised to see that he arranged his shelves alphabetically. There were framed posters from landmark productions that he might have seen when he was much younger: *Look Back in Anger*, *Who's Afraid of Virginia Woolf?*, *Rosencrantz and Guildenstern Are Dead*. No musicals or comedies. The awards he had won peeked out of various corners, but none of them were recognisable in the way of a Tony or a BAFTA. Over in the kitchen, a large copper pan sat on the flame, the lid gently rising and falling and something bubbling away at the edges. The smell of onions and spices permeated the room and I was reminded that Ewan was a vegetarian. I'd found this out when we'd had dinner together in Colchester.

'Can I get you a glass of wine?' he asked.

'No, thank you.' Somehow, Hawthorne had answered for both of us.

Ewan already had a glass of red wine. He gestured at a sofa shaped like an L, arranged around a crowded coffee table with a widescreen TV screen beyond. I took the short end, leaving Hawthorne with the full width. Ewan sat down in an armchair, setting his wine beside him. He took off his glasses and wiped the lenses with a handkerchief.

'This is such a horrible thing to have happened,' he began. 'I couldn't believe it when I heard.'

'And why was that?' Hawthorne asked, innocently. 'A woman like Harriet Throsby would have had a lot of enemies.'

'That's true. But even so . . .'

'And a death threat was made against her right in front of you.'

'You're talking about Jordan.' Ewan waved the idea aside. 'He was just letting off steam.'

'Really? He specifically announced his intention to put a knife in her . . . the same knife that was used, as things turned out.'

'I understood that it was a different knife.' Ewan had not taken to Hawthorne. I could see that already. And no matter how he felt about Harriet, he had an almost proprietorial interest in protecting his cast. 'Jordan is a good actor and a good man, the father of two children. If he has a fault, it's that he sometimes doesn't think through what he's saying. He can get angry. We all do. Theatre can be a very demanding business. But whatever he may have said that night, I can assure you he didn't mean it. If you think about it, Mr Hawthorne, if you were planning to kill someone, would you announce it to the whole world first?'

'Maybe someone else in the room got the idea from him.'

'I think it's very unlikely.' Ewan finished his wine. His little eyes blinked at us. 'I know the people in that room better than anyone, and I think I'm the best judge of what they might and might not be capable of doing. I remember working on an improvisation with Jordan – the scene when he attacks Nurse Plimpton – and I can assure you that he found it incredibly difficult to find the trigger . . . the well of anger inside him.'

'Was that before or after he nearly put her in hospital?'

'I think you're exaggerating. It was just a few bruises.' He paused. 'I'm not saying Jordan isn't emotional. Quite the opposite. It's not helped by the fact that he's having marriage difficulties at the moment . . .'

'I had no idea,' Hawthorne lied.

'Then I'm sorry I mentioned it. I just want you to understand that he would never hurt anyone.' He looked at me across the top of his wine glass. 'If you're going to start throwing accusations around, you might as well know that Jordan wasn't the only one. Anthony, for one, agreed with him.'

'I didn't!'

'I saw you nod your head.'

'Ewan – that's not fair. I thought what he said was awful!'

'I'm sure that's true. I'm just pointing out that we'd all been drinking, it was late, the end of an intense evening, and emotions were running high. I wish Sky had never told us she had the review. I don't know what she was thinking, anyway. She could have at least read it first.'

'How did it make you feel?' Hawthorne asked.

'The review? It made me angry . . . bloody angry.' So far Ewan had barely stammered, but he had to fight to get out the 'b' of bloody. He noticed the empty glass in his hand and went over to a trolley with its selection of bottles. 'Are you sure you won't have something?' he asked.

'We're fine, thank you,' Hawthorne said.

Ewan refilled his glass and came back to his chair.

'First of all, it was unfair. Lots of people enjoyed it when we performed it outside London and I think it was sharper and stronger when we came in. But even if there were some failings – in the script, in my direction, whatever – she had no reason to be so filthy.' He took another swig. 'Harriet Throsby chose her words carefully,' he continued. 'That was what was so appalling about her. It's one thing to criticise a play, but she did it in a very deliberate way, to cause the greatest upset. She was even at it at the party! I mean, you have to ask yourself, why would she even come to a first-night party? No critic does that. But she couldn't resist the opportunity because she enjoyed hurting people – she relished it. You heard what she said to me.'

'She hardly spoke to you,' I said.

'She said enough.' He put the glass down heavily, slopping red wine over his fingers. 'Perhaps you don't remember what she said about the Savoy Hotel. "Those big hotels don't exactly light my fire." Those were her exact words.'

'I don't understand.'

'You wouldn't.' I had never seen Ewan like this. He might have been unable to find a well of anger in Jordan Williams, but his own was spilling over, perhaps helped by all the wine he had consumed. 'My life was ruined by a fire.'

'Your production of *Saint Joan*!' Suddenly I remembered.

'Exactly. And you might as well know, she did the same thing in the review she wrote after the accident. There were plenty of newspaper stories, but none of the other critics actually sat down and reviewed the play. Why would they? It had already closed down. No audience was ever going to see it after the disaster on the opening night. But she couldn't resist it, gloating about what had happened. Not, of course, that she made it obvious. It was just one little line buried in the rest of it. "*Under Ewan Lloyd's over-fussy direction, the play never caught fire.*" You see? The same word!'

'Do you have a copy of the review?' Hawthorne asked.

'No. I wouldn't have that garbage in my house. You can find it online. Most of it was very sympathetic – or pretending to be. At the time nobody knew how badly Sonja Childs had been injured, so maybe that was why Harriet got away with it. In fact, she praised Sonja. "*I'm sure everyone in the audience will be wishing her the speediest recovery and we can't wait to see this talented actress back on the stage . . .* " But with every word she wrote, she blamed me. My ambition. My arrogance. My stupidity.

'I thought about suing her. The theatre fully supported me. But at the time, I was torn to pieces. I had a young, beautiful actress in intensive care with third-degree burns. I'd destroyed her career. How could I have any right to worry about my reputation when I knew that, at the end of the day, it had happened because of me? To this day I don't know what went wrong. Something short-circuited? A transformer overheated? Somehow a fake fire became a real fire and it was horrible, the worst day of my life – and Harriet Throsby made it worse still. I'll never forgive her for that.

'But I didn't kill her.' He had seen Hawthorne examining him and returned the stare. 'I was in this house all morning. I took phone calls. I can give you the names of people who spoke to me.'

'Did anyone see you?'

'No. My wife was at the surgery. She's a sports therapist. There was just me.'

'So if it wasn't you, who was it?'

'I've told you. I don't think it was anyone who was in the green room that night. Not Jordan. Not Sky or Tirian – they had no reason to kill her. She hadn't said anything bad about either of them.'

'You haven't talked very much about Tirian. What do you make of him?'

Ewan took off his glasses and turned them over in his hands, using them almost like worry beads. 'I can only answer that as a director,' he said. 'I don't really know him – and actually, that's the worst I can say of him. He's a loner. It was very hard to make him feel part of the company, but then he only joined the cast at the last minute.' He sighed. 'He's never had any professional training and that doesn't help. He doesn't know how to project. He gets bored too easily. It isn't easy giving him notes. From my experience, I don't think he's suited to theatre. He's one of those actors who need to be famous because then they can get away with murder.' He stopped himself. 'That wasn't appropriate, but you know what I mean. I have a feeling the camera will love Tirian. He's got real star quality. But that doesn't necessarily work on the stage.'

'Sky?'

'A trouper. We had an extremely difficult time at Middleham Castle, but she never once complained and I was thrilled she joined the cast of *Mindgame*.'

'What about Ahmet? And his colleague?'

'Ahmet's harmless.' Ewan smiled for the first time since we came in. 'As for Maureen, you know she saw *Cats* over a hundred times?'

'Is that relevant?'

'You tell me. I think it's rather delightful. And she dotes on Ahmet. She'd do anything for him.'

Hawthorne was about to ask something, but just then his mobile phone buzzed. He took it out of his pocket and glanced at the long message on the screen. It was something he had never done before – allow the outside world to interrupt his train of thought. He slipped it away. 'Thank you, Ewan. You've been very helpful.'

We both got to our feet.

Ewan did the same. 'You know, I was quite certain that something bad was going to happen on the first night of *Mindgame*,' he said, ruminatively.

'Oh, yes? And why was that?'

'I have premonitions. It's been the same all my life. I had a motorbike crash when I was at drama school and I knew it was going to happen even before I got on. The opening of *Saint Joan*, I was sick as a dog. It wasn't nerves. I had a horrible, twisted feeling in my stomach. And it was the same at the theatre, when I left the green room. I wasn't feeling great. I'd drunk too much. We all had. But I also had this chill in the back of my neck, like there was something following me.'

'Maybe it was the reviews,' Hawthorne suggested.

'I don't care about the reviews. It was worse than that. When the police told me that Harriet had been stabbed, I wasn't surprised at all—'

He stopped. Unexpectedly, the front door had opened.

'You're early!' Ewan was looking past us at a woman who had come in. For a moment, she was silhouetted against the street lamps and I couldn't see her properly.

'My last client cancelled,' the woman said. She sounded puzzled. Obviously, Ewan hadn't told her he was expecting visitors.

'This is Detective Inspector Hawthorne. He's asking questions about Harriet Throsby. And this is Anthony. He wrote *Mindgame*.'

The woman stepped into the room and I saw her clearly. My first impression was that she was very beautiful, with black hair sweeping down past her shoulders. Slim, wearing a thin, grey mac belted at the waist. Brown eyes. She could have been Italian or Eastern European. She had spoken with a slight accent.

Then she turned her head towards Hawthorne and I saw the terrible scars on the side of her face, a red trelliswork that climbed from her neck to her forehead, darkening around one eye. It wasn't a cold evening, but she was wearing gloves. I wondered what injuries they covered. I knew at once who she was and I was shocked.

'This is Sonja,' Ewan said.

Sonja Childs. *Saint Joan.*

'You're together . . .' I muttered.

'Yes.'

He had been responsible for her injuries and, subsequently, he had left his wife for her. I didn't know what to say.

Hawthorne stepped in for me. 'We won't take up any more of your time,' he said, cheerfully. 'You've been very helpful. Thank you.'

As far as I was concerned, we couldn't get out quickly enough.

There were all sorts of questions buzzing in my head as we sat in the taxi on the way back to the City – Farringdon for me, Blackfriars for Hawthorne. Had Ewan Lloyd begun an affair while he was still married? Had he moved in with Sonja because he was in love with her or because he felt responsible for what had happened? I very much doubted that I would ever learn the answers. That was the awful thing about the world in which I found myself. Who had murdered Harriet Throsby? That was what we needed to know. It was all that mattered. It suddenly occurred to me that I'd hate to be a detective, seeing life between such narrow lines.

Neither of us spoke. Hawthorne was deep in thought. I was exhausted after a series of interviews that I was quite certain had taken us nowhere. Of course, I was quite wrong. Between them, the various suspects must have provided us with plenty of clues. The trouble was, I hadn't seen any of them. I was hungry. I was wondering if there would be any food in the house or whether I would have to pop into the Nando's chicken restaurant that had just opened round the corner from my flat. That was the full extent of my thoughts.

It was only as we headed south down York Way, coming in behind King's Cross, that I remembered the text message that Hawthorne had received. I asked him about it.

'It wasn't good news,' he said, trying to dismiss the subject.

'What was it?'

'Do you really want to know?'

'That's why I'm asking.'

He took the phone out again. 'It looks like there's been a breakthrough. Cara Grunshaw may be on to something.'

'She knows who did it?'

'Well, there's new evidence.'

I was astonished. 'For heaven's sake, Hawthorne. What is it? Why didn't you tell me?'

He stared at the screen. 'There was a CCTV picture of you taken close to the Maida Hill Tunnel, just a few minutes away from Harriet Throsby's house. You were wearing a grey puffer jacket, but they can't be sure it was you because the hood was up. That said, they took a similar jacket from your flat.'

'What about it?' I was becoming uneasy.

'They found some blossom from a Japanese cherry tree . . . a couple of petals. They were lodged inside the hood.'

'Of my jacket . . .'

'Yes. You know, there are over three hundred different species of Japanese cherry . . . different varieties and hybrids. The police have been able to identify this one as *Prunus yedoensis*, the Yoshino cherry. Apparently, they're quite rare in the streets of London. They have pink flowers which fade to white around now.'

'And?' I was feeling the same twisted feeling in my stomach and chilled spine that Ewan had described.

'There's a line of them growing in Palgrove Gardens. There's one right outside Harriet's house.'

The taxi rattled through a set of traffic lights and continued past the station. Suddenly I wasn't hungry any more.

15

Clerkenwell at Night

Dinner was waiting when I got back to my flat. Jill had got in ahead of me and defrosted something that I'd cooked while I was writing my last book and which had been waiting in the freezer ever since. We opened a bottle of pink wine and sat down together and for the first time during that long day, I felt a sense of normality. This was my life. A marriage that had lasted thirty years. Two sons doing well in their careers. An elderly dog asleep in his basket. I looked at one end of the room, where the piano I had inherited from my mother stood, its polished surface gleaming in the light. I played it as a break from writing, moving from one keyboard to another. Behind me, a library of about five hundred books, half of them left to me by my father, stood on the shelves I'd had built for them. I'd added to them over the years: all the Bond novels, the 1946 Nonesuch edition of Dickens, a signed copy of *I, Claudius* that I'd found in Hay-on-Wye. Each book was a friend.

'What sort of day have you had?' Jill asked.

My sense of comfort and security disintegrated instantly.

'Not great,' I said. 'This morning I woke up in a police cell. Did I mention I'd been arrested on suspicion of murdering a critic who didn't like my play? I was locked up overnight at a custody centre in Islington and interrogated. I'm afraid it's not looking too good. They've got enough evidence to put me away for twenty years, including – news just in – petals from a Japanese cherry tree growing outside the house where the murder took place . . .'

Actually, I didn't say any of this, much as I wanted to. I'd just had the worst two days of my life and I was terrified that the next two were going to be worse still. What would happen if Hawthorne failed to find the killer before the DNA evidence came in? How was I going to tell my sons that I was about to be arrested for murder? Of course I wanted to tell her, but I couldn't bring myself to do it. Jill had enough on her plate running a company, currently raising the finance for an eight-part series based on my Alex Rider books. There was nothing she could do to help me. This was something I had to deal with on my own.

'I saw Hawthorne,' I said.

'Oh – really? I thought you weren't going to do another book with him.'

'Well . . . he's investigating something that might be worth thinking about.'

She was surprised. 'What about *Moonflower Murders*?'

That was a mystery novel – fiction rather than true crime – I had been working on for six months. I'd worked out most of the structure, but so far I hadn't written a word. Would they let me have a laptop in jail? I doubted it.

'I might write some of that tonight,' I said, vaguely.

That reminded her. 'Where were you last night?' she asked.

I'd known she'd ask me this and I'd already rehearsed my answer. 'I went to see Ewan Lloyd. He has a place in Finsbury Park. We had rather too many drinks together and he invited me to sleep over.'

I hate lying to Jill. We've been together so long and she's so much cleverer than me that it makes no sense to keep anything from her, and anyway, she always finds out. But this time I felt I had no choice. My one hope was that someone would say something or some clue would fall out of the sky and Hawthorne would work it all out. That was what I told myself. She would never need to know.

'Did you see that a theatre critic got killed?' Jill asked.

'No!' I was amazed. 'Which one?'

'I'm surprised Ewan didn't tell you about it. I heard it on the news.'

It was a wretched evening. We watched a TV show together: season 7 of *Game of Thrones*. I could never work out what was happening at the best of times, but given everything that had happened, I wasn't even able to enjoy the gratuitous sex and dismemberments. After an hour, I went up to my office and tried to work, but my thoughts were as blank as the computer screen in front of me. I was tired and wanted to go to bed, but knew I wouldn't sleep, so I abandoned my desk and took the dog – a chocolate Labrador – out for a walk. It might at least be a chance to clear my head.

It was a little after ten thirty and a particularly dark night in Clerkenwell. At least it was still dry, but the streets were deserted and the moon was hiding behind an impenetrable bank of clouds. One of the joys of living in this part of town was its sense of remoteness, the way it retreated into the nineteenth century as soon as the offices emptied and the pubs and restaurants closed. My flat was on Cowcross Street, literally where the cows once crossed on their way to the meat market. Nando's, Starbucks and Subway had all muscled their way in – our one bookshop had been forced out fifteen years ago – but the area still clung on to its sense of history, with St Paul's Cathedral watching over in the distance.

There were three little parks where I could take the dog. The one closest to my flat – St John's Gardens – had originally been a cemetery but the dead bodies had all been removed (to Woking, which must have surprised them) and what remained was an irregular space penned in by iron railings with a patch of scrubby grass, flower beds, paths and benches. The local council had taken to locking it at night to keep the drug dealers out, but occasionally they forgot – and fortunately that was the case tonight. I slipped inside and let the dog off the lead, then stood there watching him sniff around. The ground was wet underfoot, but I could feel a hint of spring warmth in the air, carrying with it the distinct scent of marijuana. There were empty offices on three sides of me, the back of a terrace of houses on the fourth. The dog ignored me. I felt very alone.

I don't know what spooked me first. It was the sound of footsteps, I think, coming up the narrow alley that led from Turnmill Street. There was nothing unusual about that. Other dog walkers used the park at night: I didn't know their names, although I knew their dogs'. However, these footsteps sounded too heavy, too slow and deliberate. Work on Crossrail was continuing day and night at Farringdon Station, which was out of sight around the corner, and they must have left a single floodlight on. A shadow stretched up the road towards me. It led to a single figure that suddenly stopped, silhouetted against the light, very much like Max von Sydow in the poster of the 1973 film *The Exorcist*. It was a man, standing there, silent and unmoving. And there could be no mistaking it. He was looking at me in a way that made me feel vulnerable, exposed.

'Lucky!' I called out. This wasn't an observation. It was the name of my dog.

The dog refused to come.

Despite everything that had happened, it had never once occurred to me that I might be in danger, that the smiling face of somebody I might have met even today could have been concealing the mind of a psychopathic killer and that they might have further designs on me. After all, one of them had walked round to a house in Little Venice and stabbed Harriet Throsby to death in her own hallway. That same person had tried to frame me. Suppose they now felt threatened? Suppose Hawthorne had said something during one of the interviews that had told them the game was up? They might not have any reason to kill me – but mad people don't need a reason. If they'd killed Harriet because of something she wrote, might they not do the same to me? In my case it would be *Mindgame*. She hated it. I created it. Maybe we both needed to be punished.

All these thoughts swirled in a sort of vortex through my mind. I tried to persuade myself that I was being ridiculous, that I was just a few minutes from my home and perfectly safe. But suddenly I had no desire to be out here on my own. I called the dog again and this time he must have recognised the anxiety in my voice because he padded over and allowed me to attach the lead. The man still wasn't moving. He looked enormous, slanting out of the pavement like some sort of golem.

'Good dog!' I muttered, cheerfully. I wanted the man to hear my voice; to let him know I wasn't frightened.

We began to walk out of the northern end of the park, up towards the Goldsmiths' Centre, one of the newer constructions in the area. At once, the man fell into step behind me. I heard his feet hitting the pavement and tried to quicken my own pace. Unfortunately, the dog wouldn't have it. He'd been distracted by an overflowing bin and although I tugged at the leash, he refused to move.

The top floor of my flat was in sight, poking over the other buildings. If I shouted loud enough, Jill might even hear. But shouting for help is one of the things people in horror films don't often do and it was the same for me now. I wasn't certain that there was anything to worry about. My imagination could be playing tricks on me. There was no one around to hear me anyway, and if I shouted, it might actually encourage whoever this man was to launch his attack. I glanced round and saw that he was holding something low down, at waist height. It glinted in his hand. A knife?

I made a decision, leaned down and released the dog. Wasn't he supposed to protect me? If he sensed the master was in danger, maybe he would turn round, bark and gnash his teeth.

The dog ran back to the bin.

Worse still, I'd got the timing wrong. By the time I stood up with the leash in my hand, I realised that the man had reached me. There he was, looming over me, his face a silhouette. I stared. Then he spoke my name and I recognised his voice.

'Jordan!' I muttered. 'What a lovely surprise!'

I wasn't sure what to say. Why was Jordan Williams here? Had he deliberately set out to frighten me? Why wasn't he onstage? No. The play would have finished forty-five minutes ago – ample time to get changed and take the tube across to Farringdon. He wasn't carrying a knife. Now that he was standing in front of me, I saw that it was a mobile phone in his hand.

'Hello, Anthony.'

'What are you doing here? I thought you lived in . . .' I realised I had no idea where he lived.

'I live in Hoxton. But sometimes I come home this way. When I need to clear my head.'

'How did the play go tonight?'

'It was good.'

'Decent audience?'

'We weren't full. But they enjoyed it.'

We stood there, face to face, slightly ridiculous in the open air with the dog scavenging for pieces of Kentucky Fried Chicken.

'I was hoping to see you,' he admitted. 'I was going to stop at your flat if the lights were on, but as I came out of the station, I saw you crossing the road with your dog so I followed you here.'

'Why?' I realised I was sounding defensive, but even though I now knew who I was dealing with, Jordan still seemed quite menacing. This was, after all, the man who had threatened Harriet Throsby, who had hurt Sky Palmer and was, I'd been told, on the verge of leaving his wife. If it had been Tirian or Ewan surprising me in an ex-cemetery in the middle of the night, I would have been much more relaxed. They were more my size. 'It's quite late, Jordan. Maybe we could talk tomorrow.'

'I happened to speak to Maureen Bates today,' he said, ignoring this.

'Oh really?' I replied, cheerfully. 'I was at her office this evening. She didn't mention she'd seen you.'

'We spoke on the phone. She told me that you might be writing a book.'

'A book?'

'About us. About Harriet Throsby.'

I wondered how Maureen had known this. I hadn't told her. With everything that was going on, I hadn't given it a moment's thought.

'Apparently, you've already written a book about that detective you were with. She said that was why the two of you were together.'

'Well, I haven't made a decision yet. If you really want to know, Hawthorne and I are out of contract.' It was stupid of me, but I couldn't resist adding: 'But I suppose it's always possible.'

That started him off again. 'You should have told me that before you came into my dressing room.'

'Why?'

'Because I don't want to be in your book. Do you understand me? If you'd told me that was what you were thinking, I wouldn't have spoken to you.'

'Why not?' I was genuinely puzzled. My only thought was that he had murdered Harriet and he didn't want it made public. After all, it wouldn't exactly help his career. 'Are you afraid of something?'

'I'm not afraid of anything!' He hadn't raised his voice but he was fighting for control. 'You have not asked for my permission to use any aspects of my life and I'm not giving it to you. I don't want my name in your book. I don't want to be any part of it. And that's the end of the matter.'

'Hold on a minute, Jordan.' I was angry too. He had no right to track me down in this way, to spring out of the shadows, half terrifying me in the middle of the night. Suddenly I was annoyed. 'Look, I may write about this. I may not. But either way, I don't think it's any business of yours. I don't see what right you've got to stop me.'

'So you haven't written anything yet.'

I couldn't lie to him. 'I may have taken notes.'

He jabbed a finger in my direction. 'You write about me and I will make sure that all hell comes in your direction. I have *my* life. I have *my* experiences. And you have no right at all to appropriate my story, turn me into a cultural stereotype, simply to embellish your own view of the world.'

'What are you talking about?'

'I'm talking about a privileged white writer describing things he knows nothing about, profiting – in every sense – from an experience he will never understand because he hasn't lived it. I have!'

'You're not being serious!' I couldn't believe what I was hearing. 'Are you saying that if I decide to write about the death of Harriet Throsby, I can't put you in the book, that I can't even mention you – because of your heritage?'

'How have you described me? In your notes? Have you said I'm a Native American?'

The ground had shifted beneath me and I suddenly felt sick. He was talking about cultural appropriation! I don't even like writing those two words. There's a reason why I never go anywhere near politics or social issues. I write to entertain people. If I have one determination in life, it's that I don't want to do anything that will upset anyone. I'm always aware of that great beast Twitter lurking on the sidelines, waiting to tear out my throat.

I desperately tried to work out an answer to what he had just asked me.

'I suppose I might have thought of you as a Native American. I mean, your background . . . being adopted . . . you told me everything yourself.'

'That didn't give you permission to use it. I only told Mr Hawthorne because I was under police investigation. I had no choice. You were there as an eavesdropper. You had no right to be in the room.'

'For heaven's sake, Jordan. You can't accuse me of cultural appropriation. I mean . . . I'm not saying it doesn't exist. Of course it does. It's terrible!' I realised I was burbling. 'I've been in the room with you loads of times,' I went on. 'I knew about your heritage before I even met you. What difference does it make? Are you saying I can't write about

Ahmet because he's Turkish? Or Pranav because he comes from India?'

'If you're talking about Pranav the stage manager, he's from Pakistan!' His eyes blazed. 'How have you described me? Have you mentioned the colour of my skin? My ponytail?'

'I may have mentioned them . . .'

'Those are more stereotypes.'

'You've got a ponytail!' I said. 'It's not my fault. And it's very nice. It suits you.'

'The other things I told you. Rosebud. Pomona. Are you going to write about all that too . . . ?'

'Why not? I didn't know about any of it. The way you were taken away from your family. The assimilation programme. The Carlisle Indian Industrial School. It's awful! Isn't it important that people know these stories and learn about them?'

'But they're *our* stories.'

'Yes, of course. I understand that. But the whole point about stories is that they're for sharing. That's the very nature of their existence. Stories are what bring us together. It's how we try to understand each other and understanding is exactly what my job is all about.' I didn't want to be having this conversation. I was tired. I wanted to be in bed. 'Are you saying you'd prefer it if I ignored what you told me? If I pretended you hadn't said it?'

'I'm saying it's none of your business. You have no understanding about how I feel.'

'And so I can't even try? What does that leave me with? We've already agreed that I can't write about Ahmet or Pranav. So presumably I can't write about Maureen or Sky either . . . because they're both women! Or Lucky because he's a dog! At the end of the day, if I listened to you, I'd only write about myself! A book full of middle-aged white writers describing middle-aged white writers being murdered by middle-aged white writers!'

We both drew a breath. And that was when the absurdity of it hit me.

'That's not why you're here,' I said. 'This has got nothing to do with cultural appropriation. You just don't want me to write about you because you're ashamed.'

'I have nothing to be ashamed of.'

'You threatened to kill Harriet! You stabbed a cake. There was that business with Sky. And you've had a row with your wife.'

Jordan visibly shrank. 'That's not true . . .'

'I'm sorry. I have absolutely no interest in your private life. But everyone's heard you shouting on the phone – and she didn't come to the first night.'

'I told you. She was working.' But even as he spoke, he sounded half-hearted and I knew that I was right. 'I don't want you writing about Jayne.'

I was disappointed with myself. I'd liked Jordan Williams from the very start and I was grateful to him. It had been a real breakthrough when he'd agreed to take the part of

Dr Farquhar and he'd thrown himself into it, supporting the play from the start. Only the week before we'd opened, he'd been on the radio, saying nice things about me. And here we were shouting at each other for no good reason at all.

'Look,' I said. 'Right now I'm not even thinking about the book. I don't even want to write it. All I care about is who killed Harriet Throsby.' I took a deep breath. 'And you might as well know that the police are convinced it was me. They kept me locked up for twenty-four hours and they interrogated me. I think, technically, that I'm out on bail. There! Now you know.'

'But I was the one who threatened her!'

'I know that. But it was my knife that ended up in her chest.'

He looked at me, puzzled. Then he remembered. 'You had it in the green room!' he said. 'I saw you with it.'

'You don't remember what I did with it?'

'I think you left it over at the side. Near the fridge. Yes! I'm sure I saw it there.'

'Was it still there at the end of the evening?'

'I can't remember.' He shook his head. 'Someone could have taken it.'

'That's why we were at the theatre today, asking you all those questions. Hawthorne's my friend. Well, he is sort of. He's just trying to save me from being sent to jail.' I felt empty, exhausted. 'I'm sorry if I've offended you,' I said. 'That really wasn't my intention.'

He smiled and at that moment I had the completely irrelevant thought that he would have been really good as Dr Who.

'I may be able to help you,' he said.

'How?'

'I may know who killed her.'

I stared at him.

'Tirian.' He went on hastily, before I could interrupt. 'I'm talking out of turn – and whatever happens, you didn't hear this from me – but you might as well know. Tirian was really worried about Harriet Throsby. I mean, worried sick! He thought she was going to ruin his career – his big break in that Hollywood movie.'

'How come?'

'You should know. You were right next to him!' Jordan moved closer to me as if he was afraid of being overheard. 'When Harriet came over to us at the party, Tirian was telling us about *Tenet*. Don't you remember?'

'He was saying it was no good.'

'That's right. He's full of shit really, because he doesn't know anything about anything, but he basically said the script was rubbish and the director – Christopher Nolan – didn't know what he was talking about.'

'And . . . ?'

'He didn't see Harriet creeping up behind him and by the time he turned round, it was too late. She'd heard every word of what he said! When we went back to the theatre later on, Tirian and me, I could see he was shaking like a leaf. I asked what was wrong and he told me. He was terrified she was going to write about him and repeat what he'd said.'

'In her review?'

'No. She didn't just write reviews. She had a diary column in the *Evening Standard*. She could have dropped it in there. Or she could have rung up Nolan's office and done the dirty herself, maybe in return for an exclusive interview. She was a monster. I wouldn't have put anything past her. And what do you think would have happened then? They'd have fired Tirian. He'd be one time-travelling secret agent who'd be heading right back to bit parts in TV. If they'd have him, that is. Nolan is Hollywood royalty. It could have been the end of him.'

'You think Tirian killed Harriet to stop her talking?'

'Look, I tried to persuade him not to worry. I said she had bigger fish to fry. And it's true: he seemed all right down there in the green room, at least until we read the review. But I don't know what was going on in his head. In fact, I never do. That's half the trouble, working with him. Maybe he went round the next day and . . .' Jordan mimed the rest of the sentence, the knife strike to the heart.

The dog whined.

'I have to go in,' I said.

'All right.' He held out a hand. 'I'm sorry, Anthony . . .'

'I'm sorry too.' I took his hand. 'If by some miracle I do end up writing about you, I'll change your name. And I can make you something else if you like. Korean or something.'

'No. I'll stay as I am.'

We shook. Jordan disappeared back across the park. I went home.

16
Frost and Longhurst

Hawthorne and I met the following morning at a busy crossroads near Holborn Station. He was sitting at a coffee shop – an outside table – lighting up what was almost certainly not his first cigarette of the day. I've often mentioned Hawthorne's smoking habit, and thinking about it, I'd say he was addicted not just to the cigarettes but to the very act of smoking itself, that he wasn't complete without it and the fact that it was unhealthy and antisocial only made him more determined to continue. For all his undoubted brilliance, Hawthorne was a very solitary man. He was separated from his wife and his teenaged son. I hadn't met any of his friends. Apart from Kevin downstairs and his rather eccentric book group, he had never mentioned having any. He lived on his own. It was as if he had recognised how few pleasures he had in his life, making him all the more determined to cling on to the few that remained. Murder and cigarettes. That about summed him up.

I got myself a hot chocolate and joined him. We were on a corner with commuters pouring out of the station and early-morning traffic crawling past in four directions; not the most salubrious place to meet, but at least the sun had finally come out. I wasted no time telling him about my encounter with Jordan Williams the night before. I'd hardly been able to get to sleep, thinking about what he'd said. I'd mistrusted Tirian Kirke from the start. Now Jordan had provided me with a clear motive for the murder.

Irritatingly, Hawthorne didn't agree.

'I'm sorry, mate,' he said, drawing on his cigarette. 'I know you're not that crazy about Tirian after he turned down your show. But it doesn't add up.'

'Why not?'

'Well, for a start, we can't be sure that Harriet did actually overhear what Tirian said at the party and nor can he. There were a lot of people in a small restaurant and from what you've told me, there must have been quite a bit of noise. Turkish music, people chatting, all the rest of it.'

'He didn't need to be sure. He could have gone round to her house and asked her.'

Hawthorne nodded. 'That's possible. But you've got to remember where the murder took place.'

'Palgrove Gardens.'

'I mean – which part of the building.' Hawthorne looked at me a little sadly. 'She was killed in the hallway.'

'What about it?'

'Look, Tirian might have been worried that Harriet had heard what he said about the film being no good. But there was always a chance she might not have taken it seriously. After all, it was a party. Everyone was drinking. And journalists don't usually report private conversations.'

'She wasn't a journalist.'

'Fair enough. But he'd still need to be one hundred per cent certain that she was going to write something nasty about him before he knocked her off – otherwise he wouldn't take the risk. So what would he do? Go round to her house, talk to her, try and explain himself, find out what she'd heard and what she was going to do. She'd said nice things about him in her review. Maybe he could persuade her to forget this little indiscretion. But if, on the other hand, she was determined to go ahead and ruin his career, then, all right, he would have a reason to put a knife in her.

'But the point is, Tony, would they have had the conversation standing there in the hallway? I don't think so. They were right next to the door to Harriet's study. They could have gone in there or into the kitchen and sat down over a nice cup of tea. "Hi, Harriet. I just wanted to tell you that I didn't mean that stuff I said last night. I was just being stupid . . . " That sort of thing.

'But it never happened. I'd say it's obvious that whoever arrived at the house that morning went there with one aim in mind, which was to murder her. No chat. No second thoughts. Harriet opened the door and that was the last thing she did.'

'And it wasn't Tirian.'

'It might have been. I got Kevin to do a search on him, by the way. All that stuff he told us about growing up in Wales, his parents dying in a car crash, moving to Harrogate, the National Trust . . .'

'And?'

'It all checks out. The episode of *Heartbeat* was called "Another Little Piece of My Heart". He didn't get a credit, though.'

'He was only an extra.'

'I think they're called background artists.'

My heart sank. 'Have you heard anything more from Cara Grunshaw?'

'She's not going to call me!'

'What about the forensic lab?'

'They haven't managed to sort themselves out just yet.' He half smiled. 'I thought you didn't approve of my friend Kevin.'

'I'm willing to make exceptions.'

Hawthorne ground out his cigarette and stood up. I was happy to leave my hot chocolate. It tasted of traffic fumes. 'Martin Longhurst is waiting for us,' he said.

Ahmet's accountant had been at the party; I'd seen him talking to Harriet Throsby. For some reason, he'd been nervous. And lying in bed at four o'clock in the morning, I remembered that hadn't been the first time I'd seen him either. He'd been sitting one row behind me at the first night of *Mindgame*. Even so, I still had no idea why Hawthorne was interested in him. We already knew that Ahmet was in financial difficulties. What else could he add?

Unlike their client, Frost and Longhurst were obviously doing well for themselves. They occupied a Queen Anne–style office spread over four storeys in a quiet backstreet. Theirs was the only name on the door and as we entered the reception area with its plush carpet and original oil paintings (horses and country villas), I couldn't help thinking of Ahmet's basement in the Euston Road. Why had they even taken him on as a client? This was an organisation more suited to high-end lawyers, businessmen, hedge-fund managers.

Martin Longhurst appeared almost at once, ushering us further into the building. At the first-night party, he had seemed awkward. When I saw him in Ahmet's office, I'd thought he looked ill, but that was probably only because he'd seen the advance ticket sales for the play. This was a different man. He was totally relaxed, in a Savile Row suit with his dark hair slicked back and gold cufflinks glinting in his sleeves. As we moved through his home territory, he stopped to show off a couple of the paintings ('That's an Edward Walter Webb. The horse won the 1840 Grand Liverpool Steeplechase . . .'). He led us into a conference room with an oak table that gleamed like a mirror, twelve chairs, and coffee and tea on a side buffet. We sat down and he poured coffee for Hawthorne and tea for me, talking all the while.

'I very much enjoyed your play, Anthony. I thought it was very entertaining. As a matter of fact, my daughter is a big fan of your work. She's too young for Alex Rider, but – I hope you don't mind – she'd love it if you'd sign another of your books.' I'd already noticed a well-thumbed copy of *Granny* on the table. If there's a book of mine in a room, it's always the first thing I'll see.

Longhurst took a seat. He moved very carefully, perhaps because he was so tall, sitting with a straight back and reaching for a bottle of sparkling water with elegant fingers. He was in his mid-thirties, with the easy confidence that comes from either inherited wealth or early success, a completely different man to the one I had met in Euston. Could it be that he changed his persona depending on the client he found himself with, that the richer and more established they were, the more suave and self-confident he became?

'So, how can I help you, gentlemen?' he asked eventually.

I had no answer. It embarrassed me that I still had no idea why we were here.

'Well, obviously we want to talk to you about Harriet Throsby,' Hawthorne said.

'I'm not sure I have anything to tell you.' Longhurst chose his words carefully. 'Certainly not in relation to her murder.

My client, Mr Yurdakul, told me about it yesterday and you can imagine my reaction.'

'How long has Mr Yurdakul been a client?'

'I first met him about eight years ago when he came in to develop a software system for this company. He did a very good job. When he decided to set up as a theatrical producer, he asked me if I would look after his accounts, and although I will admit he didn't quite fit the company profile – or the profile my partner and I were hoping to create – I agreed. I'm very sorry it hasn't worked out for him, but I'm sure he'll bounce back. He's nothing if not resourceful.'

'Did you know that Harriet Throsby would be at the theatre?'

'It had occurred to me that she might be there. I don't know why you're asking me that question, Mr Hawthorne. Do you think I'm in some way connected to her death?'

'Well, you were one of the last people to speak to her.' Before Longhurst could deny it, Hawthorne went on. 'I understand that the two of you met at Topkapi, the Turkish restaurant, after the play finished.'

Longhurst hesitated. 'I spoke a few words to her in a crowded room,' he admitted. 'We said nothing of any interest whatsoever.'

'Are you saying you'd never met her before?'

I saw the flicker of annoyance in the accountant's eyes as he realised that he wasn't going to be able to hide the truth. 'No. I haven't suggested anything of the sort. As a matter of fact, we did cross paths once, but that was a very long time ago. About twenty years, in fact, although I'd prefer not to discuss it.'

'I'm sure you'd prefer not to, Mr Longhurst. Unfortunately, when someone is murdered – and in a particularly brutal way – there are questions that have to be answered.'

'I didn't kill her.'

'But you had a good reason.'

'Did I?'

'She wrote a book about you.'

And there it was. As soon as I heard Hawthorne's words, I realised what I'd missed. There had been three books on the table in Harriet Throsby's office in Little Venice, all of them written by her. One of them was called *Bad Boys: Life and Death in an English Village*. Arthur Throsby had described it to us. *'It was about Trevor and Annabel Longhurst. You may remember them?'* Their son had been involved in the death of a teacher. Longhurst wasn't that common a name and Hawthorne must have made the connection immediately.

'Your parents are Trevor and Annabel Longhurst,' he stated now.

For perhaps half a second, Longhurst considered denying it, but he knew it would do no good. 'Yes,' he said.

'Your brother was called Stephen.'

'That's right.' He was still cradling the bottle of sparkling water. He twisted it open with a movement that was brief and almost violent.

Now Hawthorne was conciliatory. 'I'm sorry to have to bring this up, Mr Longhurst,' he said. 'I'm sure it's still very painful for you.'

'You have no idea at all of my feelings, Mr Hawthorne. I was eighteen when Stephen became the centre of attention for all the wrong reasons. He was very much my baby brother, eight years younger than me. Up until then, I'd had a normal childhood; I would say a very happy one. That single moment tore my world apart.'

'Your brother was responsible for the death of a teacher at his primary school.'

'No. I just told you. My brother was ten years old! Whatever the law may say, I do not believe he had reached the age of responsibility and he had no idea what he was doing. He was one of life's innocents. He fell under the influence of another boy a year older than him and that was where the trouble began. He was quite unlike the character that Ms Throsby described in her book – which was itself nothing more than a ragbag of scurrilous and ill-informed gossip put together by a hack whose only interest was in making money.'

'So, you didn't have that high an opinion of her, then.'

'You can taunt me if you wish. I'll admit that I should have disclosed my association with that woman as soon as you came into my office, but even now, all these years later, the wounds haven't healed.'

'It must have shocked you, then, meeting her.'

'It wasn't something I expected. I've already told you. I had a good idea that she might be at the theatre. But Ahmet wanted me to come to the first night – his financial future depended on it – and I felt I couldn't let him down. At the same time, I thought there was little chance of us encountering one another in an auditorium with six or seven hundred people. I saw where she was sitting and I made sure to avoid her.'

'Until you got to the restaurant . . .'

'Well, yes. That was a surprise. I had no idea that she would be coming to the first-night party. Indeed, I understand that it's a rare thing for a newspaper critic to attend. A very unpleasant surprise.'

'So what did you say to each other?'

'She saw me before I saw her,' Longhurst explained. 'Otherwise, I would have made my excuses and left. As a matter of fact, I'm quite surprised that she recognised me after all this time. But she didn't hesitate. She came straight up to me and introduced herself, reminding me who she was, as if I would take any pleasure in seeing her again. I didn't know what to say to her. I felt physically sick being anywhere near her. She asked after my parents. That was how she opened the conversation. I didn't know what to say. Part of me just wanted to walk out of the room. But I replied, briefly, that they were well.'

'And then?'

'She asked me if I'd enjoyed the play. That struck me as odd. She was the critic. Why would she be asking me my opinion?'

'What did you say?'

'I asked her the same – "Did you?" I didn't care, of course. I just wanted the conversation to be over. It was quite difficult to hear her, with the band playing nearby. Anyway, she gave me a queer little smile and ducked the answer. "That's my little secret!" I suppose she didn't want to give anything away until she'd written it down.'

He poured himself a glass of water and took a large gulp. I watched his Adam's apple travel up and down.

'I'm sorry to have to disappoint you, Mr Hawthorne. But that was it; the full extent of my conversation with her. I cannot begin to imagine what was going on inside her head or why she would think, even for a minute, that I would have any interest in ever seeing her again. I made an excuse and walked away. I left the party almost immediately.'

'Perhaps she was deliberately trying to upset you,' Hawthorne suggested.

'It's possible, I suppose.'

'So, tell me about the book. What was it that pissed you off?' In his own way, and despite his language, Hawthorne was at his most affable. 'The hard copy's out of print, by the way, but I picked up a copy on Kindle for nothing. I haven't had a chance to read it all yet, but from what I've seen so far, I don't think it's one I'll be recommending to my book club.'

'Do we have to do this now?'

'If we're going to find out who killed her, we need to move fast.'

I hardly needed reminding. The DNA, the fingerprints, the Japanese blossoms, the witness statements. Cara Grunshaw could be at my front door at any time.

Hawthorne had evidently created some sort of bond of trust with the accountant. Longhurst nodded slowly and put the water down. 'Very well.'

We waited.

'I can't tell you everything you want to know about the summer of 1998,' Longhurst began at last. 'You have to remember that this comes from the perspective of an eighteen-year-old boy and I wasn't even in Moxham when most of this happened. My parents had sent me to boarding school, to Marlborough College, and when this business with Stephen took place I was on my gap year, teaching football to children in Namibia. They wrote me a letter, explaining what had happened and urging me not to come home, even though that was my first instinct. They wanted to keep me out of the spotlight, to protect me, and they were largely successful . . . at least until that book came out.

'As I'm sure you're aware, my parents were fairly well known around the time of the millennium, which is to say they often appeared in the newspapers, in diaries or gossip columns. They had set up a business that started with children's clothes but then branched out into a much wider range of products – toys, books, furniture. You may remember the name. It was called Red Button. There were Red Button shops, Red Button restaurants and even Red Button holiday resorts and adventure centres by the time they finished. They were extremely wealthy and they were closely connected to centre-left politics, by which I mean, of course, New Labour. This was the same year that Peter Mandelson made that famous remark about being relaxed with people getting filthy rich, or words to that effect. He spoke for the prime minister . . . and it could have been my mother and father he had in mind.

'They had already given large sums of money to New Labour. They were major supporters of Tony Blair when he mounted his leadership bid in 1994, and they'd been with him in Downing Street when he won the election three years later. My father was involved in early talks relating to the Millennium Dome and might well have gone into the House of Lords if . . . things hadn't happened the way they did.

'My parents had moved to the village of Moxham Heath in the early nineties. I'm afraid I can't really describe what it was like, living in the middle of Wiltshire, because I wasn't there very much. I was either at school or I stayed in London. We'd kept our house off Sloane Square. To this day, I'm not sure why they'd decided that country life would suit them, particularly as they were opposed to so many of its traditions, but let me say at once that it was without any question the worst decision they ever made. It all went wrong from the moment they bought Moxham Hall, which was a quite unnecessarily large country house with a hundred acres just outside the village. Arriving by helicopter didn't help either. My father flew it himself.

'It was them and us – although not perhaps drawn across classical lines. This was a time when the Tories were losing power, and maybe there was a degree of resentment in what had always been a true-blue Tory shire. I don't know. My parents weren't just rich. There were plenty of rich people in Moxham. They were rich socialists. They supported the Labour opposition to hunting. They wanted to build a wind turbine, and you can imagine that that put a great many people's backs up. Spoiling the view! Killing a few birds before the locals had a chance to gun them down! My father had been part of the Campaign for Lead-Free Air, so having their own helicopter pad made them hypocrites too. I kept out of it, but I still remember there was one squabble after another. The swimming pool. The footpath they wanted to move ten metres. The church-hall restoration fund. The annual village fête. This was little England and the two of them were incomers and hypocrites . . . at least, that was the perception. Nothing they did was ever right.

'Maybe that was why they decided to send Stephen to the village school – Moxham Heath Primary. That was one of the things that Throsby suggested in her book. They were using him to ingratiate themselves with the villagers, to prove that they were "one of them". It was complete nonsense, it goes without saying. But she wrote it anyway.

'I need to describe my younger brother to you. Up to the age of nine – before he left London – he was a very quiet boy. He loved reading. He did well at school. He had plenty of friends. Harriet Throsby described him as spoilt and although it's not a word I would have used, he was certainly indulged. This was because to all intents and purposes he was an only child. My parents always used to say he was an afterthought – although he was much loved and cherished.

'Things changed almost as soon as he arrived at Moxham Heath. You can imagine how difficult it was for him. As I've explained, I was away. He'd lost all his London friends and he was having difficulty making new ones. My parents were launching Red Button in America and they were spending more and more time abroad. Stephen had a lovely nanny, an Australian girl who had moved to Wiltshire with the family, and she did the best she could. But looking back, I would be the first to admit that he was neglected. Things happened very quickly and nobody noticed until it was too late.

'Moxham Heath Primary School had a policy of taking in boys and girls from as wide a catchment area as possible. They didn't just want the offspring of local squires and bankers, and I'm sure this is something to be applauded. One of these boys, however, exerted a malign influence on Stephen almost from the start. His name was Wayne Howard and he lived on an estate just outside Chippenham, about eight miles away. He had no experience of village life and would probably have been much happier in a larger town.

Nonetheless, he was bussed in every day and he and Stephen became friends.'

He shook his head sadly.

'It's hard to believe that they were just nine and ten years old when they first met. They were children! But they formed what you might call a gang of two, with Wayne very much the ringleader, and soon they were out of control, always getting into trouble with the teachers at school, the neighbours, even the police. On one occasion they were reported for shoplifting from the village store, a place called the Ginger Box. After that, my parents went into the school and demanded the two boys be separated, but it was easier said than done in a small community. Really, that was when they should have seen the writing on the wall and taken Stephen back to London. But, as I've said, they were preoccupied and were inclined to think that "boys will be boys", that it was good for Stephen to have met someone of his own age and that eventually things would sort themselves out.

'It was a decision that led, inexorably, to the death of their teacher, Major Philip Alden.

'He was an ex-soldier, born in the village. He'd fought in the Falklands and when he left the army he trained to be a teacher and worked for a few years in Trowbridge before he applied for the job at Moxham Heath Primary School. He was the deputy head: getting on a bit, mid-sixties and eccentric, exactly the sort of character you'd expect to find in a little Wiltshire village. Very much into cricket. Ran a chess club. Kept a bust of Cicero in his study. It was a solid thing, made of marble. I believe he had inherited it from his father.

'Philip Alden was what you might call old school. He believed in discipline – not surprising, given his army background – and he came down hard on the children who didn't keep up with their work or who misbehaved in class. It wasn't long before he had both Stephen and Wayne in his sights. Things came to a head during the spring term. They were accused of doing something very stupid and unpleasant. They defaced a number of books in the library – tore out pages and scribbled obscenities in the margins. They both denied it, but he punished them by making them miss out on a trip to Bath Spa. I know it all sounds very trivial, describing it to you in this way, but in the end it was anything but.

'Wayne and Stephen decided to get their revenge by playing another trick on the major, this one the oldest in the book. It was Wayne's idea, of course. They sneaked into his study and balanced the bust of Cicero on top of the door, leaving it ajar. God knows how they got it up there because it weighed a ton, but there were a lot of books in the room, some of them on high shelves, and Alden used a small stepladder to climb up and down, so I presume they were able to use that. Later, they both claimed that it was just a joke and they didn't want to hurt anyone, but the long and the short of it was that Alden came into the room, the bust fell on him, fracturing his skull, and the next day he died.

'The two boys were sent to youth court and tried for manslaughter. By law, they'd both reached the age of criminal responsibility and they'd killed a war hero, for heaven's sake, so it was no surprise when they were found guilty and sentenced to five and ten years in different secure units. Stephen's lawyers were able to prove that he had been influenced by the older boy, so his sentence was shorter, but that made little difference as far as my family was concerned. Their names were released after the trial and the press, who had been fairly restrained up to that time, fell on us in a feeding frenzy. The effect on my parents was catastrophic. You can forget America! Red Button went bust almost immediately. You can't sell children's products when your own child is in jail. All their political friends turned their backs on them, of course. The pressure on them was enormous and a year later they separated. My father lives in the British Virgin Islands now. My mother went back to Vancouver. She was actually born in Canada. Stephen served four years at Warren Hill, a secure unit in Suffolk, and when he was released he was given special licence to live with her. They're still together in Vancouver now.'

There was a long silence. Hawthorne was looking more subdued than I had ever seen him, but then he had a thirteen-year-old son himself and the story must have resonated. 'Do you ever see them?' he asked.

Longhurst shook his head. 'Not as often as I would like. I took my family there a few Christmases ago, but it was quite difficult explaining to my daughters that this was their uncle who had killed someone. My mother has rebuilt her life and she made the decision that she had to do it without my father or me. That makes me sad, but I understand it, I suppose.'

'Do you know why Harriet Throsby decided to write the book?'

'Yes, I do, as a matter of fact. She was a crime reporter at the time, working for a newspaper in Bristol, but she knew someone who lived in the village.'

'Would that be Frank Heywood?'

'That's absolutely right. Yes. He was the drama critic on the same newspaper as her. She took over from him when he died a few years later. He was able to give her a great many insights into the people of Moxham, many of whom he knew socially. This is something for which I will never forgive him.' His eyes darkened. '*Bad Boy*s was nothing less than a complete travesty of the truth. It turned my parents into the villains of the piece. The court made it absolutely clear that Stephen had been completely under the thumb of the older boy. Their respective sentences demonstrated exactly that. But the way Harriet shaped her narrative, it could have been my parents who were responsible for Alden's death. They were too busy with their own jet-set lifestyle. Stephen was neglected but he was also spoilt. He was the child they didn't want, which was why they were so willing to turn a blind eye to his delinquent behaviour.

'She didn't stop there. It was all set out, chapter by chapter. They'd antagonised the villagers. They were arrogant and selfish. They had no respect for their neighbours. The footpath, the fête . . . she paraded all these trivial arguments as if they actually amounted to anything and she made it seem that the death of Major Alden was nothing less than a logical conclusion. It was a hatchet job, nothing more, nothing less – written cleverly enough to keep her on the right side of libel. My parents were still together when the book came out and maybe there was a chance they would have muddled through. Harriet Throsby destroyed them. I blame her at least in part for the breakdown of their relationship. You could say that I lost a mother and a brother thanks to her.'

He spread his hands, signalling that he had little more to add.

'I hated that woman. I won't deny it. Hatred isn't an emotion that I would normally entertain, but I believe that Harriet Throsby relished what she was doing. To use what was, at the end of the day, a tragic accident, a childish prank that went wrong, as an excuse to make money? To subvert or – at the very best – simplify the truth to sell books? I don't know how she lived with herself and I'd almost go as far as saying that whoever killed her did the world a favour.'

He smiled for the first time. But there was no warmth in it.

'I'm aware that I may have incriminated myself in your eyes,' he said. 'Do you want to know where I was at the time of her death? I believe the police are saying that it was around ten o'clock in the morning.'

'It would help,' Hawthorne said.

'I went to the Vaudeville at half past nine. I had to go through some papers which Ahmet had left there. He was given one of the dressing rooms as a temporary office. Then I came here, arriving just before half past ten.'

'You spent a long time at the theatre.'

'Not really. No more than forty minutes. I'm sure the stage-door manager will have seen me leave.'

'You signed in and out?'

Longhurst thought back. 'No. I don't think I did. The pen was out of ink. But you can ask . . . I made no attempt not to be seen.'

'Thank you, Mr Longhurst. You've been very open with us. I'm sorry we had to make you go through it all again.'

It was rare to hear Hawthorne apologise for anything and the moment we were back in the street, I had to ask: 'Did you believe him?'

We were walking along Queen Square, a private garden laid out on one side. The sun was still shining and the trees were in blossom, not that the sight of them did much for me. Hawthorne was already deep in thought. 'Believe what, exactly?' he said.

Why did he have to be so difficult?

'All along, we've assumed the dagger was taken after the party, at night,' I explained. 'But Martin Longhurst could have taken it early the following morning.'

'I haven't assumed anything,' Hawthorne said.

I ignored this. 'An hour and a half would have been enough time to go to Little Venice and back again. He could have killed Harriet Throsby and gone straight into work.'

'Covered in blood?'

'He could have worn a coat!'

'But why would he have wanted to frame you?' he asked.

'Well, you heard what he said. His client's going bankrupt. Maybe he blamed me for the play.'

Hawthorne stopped. 'It's just possible that Longhurst could have picked up the dagger when he went to the theatre the next morning,' he said. 'But there are three questions you've got to ask yourself. How did he know it was there, and if he happened to come across it, how would he know it was yours?'

'And the third question?'

'How did he get hold of a strand of your hair?'

It was true. 'Longhurst wasn't anywhere near me,' I admitted. 'He couldn't have got a sample of my hair . . . not unless he followed me into a hairdresser, and I haven't been to one for weeks!'

Hawthorne stopped. I could see the main road and Holborn Station ahead of us.

'Let's just suppose for a minute that the two things – the murder and your involvement – aren't connected,' he said. 'Let's imagine that you're completely irrelevant.'

'Thanks!'

'An old man died in the village of Moxham Heath. Two kids killed him. And Harriet turned it all into a book.'

'You think someone didn't like what she wrote?'

'Nobody ever liked what she wrote. That was her intention. But emotions always run high when someone dies. And you've got to ask yourself – what was that book doing, sitting on Harriet's desk?'

'*Bad Boys ...*'

'Maybe she was trying to tell us something.'

'We're not going to Moxham Heath, are we?'

'Tony, mate. Cara Grunshaw can't be too far behind. By the end of today, she's going to have everything she needs to nail you.'

One hour later, we were on the train.

17

Extract from Bad Boys *by Harriet Throsby*

They were, of course, very young boys. Nobody can say if they intended to kill Major Philip Alden, a twice-decorated veteran who served with the Royal Marines and who saw action in the Falklands, a family man and a teacher loved by all those he taught. When they balanced a marble bust of Cicero on the door of his study, I am sure they were giggling. Oh what a lark! The defence made much of the fact that an eleven-year-old would be unlikely to have the words 'fractured skull' in his vocabulary, although both the defendants would have seen episodes of *Casualty* and *Peak Practice* on TV.

When Philip Alden was laid to rest at the lovely Norman church of St Swithin's on a sunny spring afternoon – two weeks after his death on 19 April – the vicar spoke of forgiveness and understanding. Well, I'm trying to understand. That has been the purpose of this book . . . to make sense of a senseless waste of life. But like the crowd who packed into the little cemetery, with mourners coming from as far as Arbroath and Port Stanley, I struggle to forgive. Standing next to Rosemary Alden, Philip's widow, as she wiped away the tears only to have them replaced by more tears in a constant stream of sorrow, I reflected on the circumstances that had brought us here, to this ugly rectangular trench cut into the emerald sward.

Trevor and Annabel Longhurst had sent flowers. At least, their personal assistant had. Their wreath had to be bigger than anyone else's and it dominated the entrance to the church: £200 worth of white orchids and lilies tied with a black ribbon and the name of the donors on a label, writ large so there could be no mistake. The Longhursts themselves did not make an appearance. Out of decency or shame? one had to ask. Perhaps both, came the answer, echoing like a funeral bell.

Trevor and Annabel had never been popular and had become even less so when their son had taken one of Moxham's own. I have described how they had fought to move a centuries-old footpath simply because it afforded a view of their swanky new swimming pool. How the village fête that had always taken place on the sacred turf of Moxham meadow had found itself turfed out, redirected to the Waitrose car park. We have seen how, from the day they arrived, they had seemed to deliberately search out reasons to antagonise the long-suffering villagers.

Well, the flowers may have spelled out some sort of apology, just as other wreaths spelled out BROTHER, SOLDIER and ADIOS. But even as the old soldier was being sent on his final pack drill, serious manoeuvres were going on behind the scenes. The Longhursts had assembled, at enormous cost, a team of London's most aggressive and unsparing lawyers in what they had decided would be a fight to the death, determined that the death for which their son was partly responsible should be seen as unfortunate, accidental and definitely something for which he did not need to be punished.

I have spoken to a junior barrister at Blackwood Chambers who worked on the case. Speaking in the strictest confidence and with total anonymity, he told me that this was the agreed strategy. 'We had to separate the two boys. Wayne Howard was the older of the two. He didn't even live in Moxham Heath, but on the nearby Sheldon Estate, which was part of Chippenham. His father had been arrested for drug offences. He was physically larger, on the edge of puberty. It was evident from the start that he was a Machiavellian figure, even though he was only eleven, and that Stephen had been in thrall to him from the day they'd met. Our task was to make the judge see this, to prove the psychological manipulation which the older boy had exerted over the younger. Put simply, we set out to represent Stephen Longhurst as the victim he undoubtedly was.'

It helped that Stephen was physically small, with a voice that had not broken and baby blue eyes. Although it has never been proved, several reports have suggested that when his trial began (by video link), he was dressed in a set of Red Button clothes that had been specially created for him, but which were originally designed for seven-year-olds. He was clutching a copy of *The Lion, the Witch and the Wardrobe*, his favourite book. The aim was to make him look as sweet and innocent as possible.

As we have seen, this was only half the truth. There are the memories of Rosemary Alden, who helped at Moxham Heath Primary School and knew both boys, and the testimony of Stephen's nanny, Lisa Carr, who still carries the scars of her time with him. There's the evidence given by Police Constable Brownlow, who first encountered the two boys following the village allotment incident. And what does it all add up to? Simply this. That Stephen Longhurst was the archetypal spoilt brat, entitled, rude to the staff and cruel to animals. The best that can be said of him is that he was an innocent, waiting to be led astray. If Wayne Howard hadn't come stumbling into his life, it might have been someone else. And whose fault was all this?

Step forward, Trevor and Annabel Longhurst.

They had always made it abundantly clear that their second son was an afterthought, the unwanted child – and how do you think it affected Stephen, hearing this? Oh yes, they showered him with material wealth – the quad bikes, the computer games, his own horse before he was even nine – but they were never actually there, too focused on their investment portfolio, their business in America and their fashionable charity projects. Their home might be in Wiltshire, but their hearts were in London and New York. The ten-year-old had no relationship with his teenaged, self-centred brother who had spent the past five years at a top public school and was about to disappear on a 'charity' trip around Africa. Martin Longhurst really didn't need a gap year. The gap between him and his brother could hardly be more apparent.

Lonely and alone, surrounded by paid staff rather than people who loved him, Stephen Longhurst was the perfect target for a boy like Wayne Howard. Oliver Twist had found his Artful Dodger . . . in this instance, a young lout who had been born, quite literally, into a life of crime – slumbering in a pram that had been stolen from John Lewis. Wayne must have thought he had struck gold when he first set foot in Moxham Hall.

The two of them found common ground in vandalism and delinquency. They had set off on a road that could only lead to disaster. A violent and unnecessary death was just a few breaths away.

And yet, there is still a part of me that feels sorry for Wayne Howard. He may have been a bully and a bad influence, but I have to remind myself that he too was only eleven years old, brought up on a rough council estate. What chances had he ever had in life? A father with a conviction for dealing Class A drugs. A mother who spent her child benefit on cheap vodka and cigarettes. The social workers who visited the Howards' home on the Sheldon Estate – far too late, of course – described a scene of squalor. I can defend Wayne because one thing is certain. Nobody else did.

From the very start, it is clear that Trevor and Annabel Longhurst and their razor-sharp legal team had decided it would be perfectly all right to throw Wayne to the wolves if it would save their own boy. Ironic, isn't it! A group of socialists who had espoused the values of New Labour and who were loudly beating the drum for equality of opportunity and education were ready to pile onto a working-class kid who'd never had one-tenth of the privilege of their own son. That may not be my view, but it was one that was being cited as the funeral of Major Philip Alden ended and the first day of the court hearing drew near.

18

Moxham Hall

Like Hawthorne, I had managed to download Harriet's book on Kindle and I skimmed through it on the train to Chippenham. What was I to make of Harriet Throsby's writing style? It was a mishmash of treacly sentimentalism and sheer venom, worth every penny of the £0.00 that Kindle had attached to it. I had to agree with what Martin Longhurst had said. There was something deeply offensive about turning a tiny incident, a tragedy in an English village, into some sort of Mills & Boon morality tale, and reading it, I felt less bad about her review of *Mindgame*. It was one thing to trash a play at the theatre, but with *Bad Boys* she had done the same to people's lives and almost every sentence demonstrated to me what a thoroughly unpleasant woman she had been. Why should I care what she thought of me? It's an interesting paradox. The more humane the critics, the more hurtful their opinions.

For a crime reporter, she had an extraordinary knack of muddling up the facts, so that it was almost impossible to work out where her sympathies lay – although by and large she seemed to have a bad opinion of almost everyone involved. So Stephen was the younger boy who had been seduced, led astray by Wayne. He had been abandoned by his unloving parents. But he was still Little Lord Fauntleroy, the rich kid who deserved everything he got. Wayne Howard was his worst enemy, a bad influence, the instigator of all their crimes. And yet he was a victim himself . . . damaged by his upbringing and social status. Major Alden was a patriot and a war hero, but he was also a stick-in-the-mud, a martinet who should never have been allowed anywhere near a modern primary school. Rosemary Alden, his wife, fussed over the children but never took their side against her husband. And so on.

Hawthorne had brought his iPad with him, but he didn't read any of the book on the way down. Perhaps he had guessed that he would find nothing of value inside. It was nice, just for once, to be one step ahead of him, but even as I swiped the screen from page to wearisome page, I knew that *Bad Boys* wasn't going to help me very much either. Harriet distorted everything. It was a sort of ownership. She made the entire world her own – just as she had done with my play, her marriage to Arthur, the production of *Saint Joan*, all those first-night parties she had insisted on gate-crashing. I was finally getting the measure of the woman. It was just the identity of her killer that defeated me.

I only hoped that this trip wasn't going to be a complete waste of time. With the experts still battling away at the Police Forensic Science Laboratory, time was something of which I had very little left.

All along I had assumed that Harriet Throsby's murder was in some way connected to *Mindgame*. After all, the knife that had killed her had been stolen from the Vaudeville and there seemed to be no escaping the fact that someone had deliberately tried to frame me. That was still the biggest puzzle, as far as I was concerned. It was easy enough to understand why the killer hated Harriet Throsby. But what on earth could I have done to make them want to harm me? So far, Hawthorne had said very little about this aspect of his investigation. He might have blocked the DNA analysis of my hair, but he hadn't offered any theory as to how it might have got onto the body in the first place. The same was true of the dagger with my fingerprints, the CCTV images, the Japanese cherry blossom. Perhaps it was because he still suspected me more than anyone else of having committed the crime.

But what he had said outside the accountant's office was true. It was extremely unlikely that Harriet had been killed because she'd written a bad review. The events at Moxham Heath provided a much more likely explanation. A man had died. Two boys had gone to prison. A family had been destroyed. And Harriet had written about it all. Badly. Maybe someone had decided it was time she paid the price.

We took a taxi from Chippenham Station, moving from ring road to motorway to country lane. The driver had been glum at first, reluctant to come out so far, but he'd cheered up when Hawthorne told him that we'd be using him all day. I swear I've spent more on taxi fares than I've earned from the books I've written about Hawthorne, but for once I didn't complain. We'd just missed the eleven o'clock train from Paddington and we'd had to wait thirty minutes for the next one. This was the slow service, stopping at Reading, Slough, Swindon and another half-dozen stations I'd never heard of. As much as I'd tried to concentrate on the book, I hadn't been able to keep Cara Grunshaw out of my thoughts. I half expected to see her waiting on the next platform. I felt like a fugitive in a Hitchcock film.

We were travelling down a country lane, through a tunnel of beech trees sporting their new spring leaves and between verges scattered with wild flowers. The light had turned green and there were motes of dust dancing in the sunlight. Ahead of us, a drystone wall twisted into the distance as if beckoning us to follow. I'm always dazzled by the beauty of the English countryside at the start of spring, but Wiltshire has a particular trick of throwing you back in time. At that moment, there was nothing to suggest we were still in the twenty-first century, apart from the car we were sitting in.

'Hold it!' Hawthorne broke into my reverie, calling out to the driver. 'Turn right here.'

For a moment, I was puzzled. Then I saw that we had been about to pass an open gate with a faded stone lion standing guard and a wooden sign marked *Moxham Hall.* We must have arrived at the outskirts of the village. This was the house where Trevor and Annabel Longhurst had been living – at least occasionally – when their ten-year-old son had managed to kill his deputy head.

The driver had reacted too slowly and shot a few metres past the entrance. He muttered to himself as he reversed the car and then turned into a ribbon of neatly laid gravel that led us through the thick woodland purposely designed to hide the house from the road. After about a minute, we emerged into an estate that could have been described as a kingdom in itself. Moxham Hall was a sprawling nineteenth-century manor surrounded by perfectly striped lawns reaching as far as a low metal railing. Miles of grassland stretched out on the other side, different shades of green rising and falling over hills and continuing as far as the eye could see. As we swung round an improbable white marble fountain – Neptune holding a trident, fighting off an army of cupids and dolphins – my eyes took in rose gardens, ornamental gardens, vegetable gardens and rockeries. And there was the famous helicopter pad, a white H stamped into a circle of mauve asphalt. My first impression was that the house was beautiful, with its patterned brick and limestone façade, the rows of symmetrical windows, the grey tiles and chimneys. But as we drew closer, I noticed the modern additions: the out-of-scale conservatory, the fake portico around the front door, the glass and steel shell surrounding the swimming pool. There was something a little soulless about Moxham Hall. I could imagine it being rented out as a posh wedding venue. It wasn't somewhere I would want to live.

The taxi stopped. We got out.

'What are you hoping to find here, Hawthorne?' I asked.

'Nothing much, mate. But this is where Harriet's book opens. And since we were passing, I thought we might as well have a look.'

'I don't think anyone's around.'

And yet someone had to be working here. It was obvious from the lawns and the flower beds, the exaggerated neatness of everything. The house was being looked after – and with all this land, so many rooms, it was going to take more than one visit a week. Feeling very much like a trespasser, I followed Hawthorne to the front entrance and watched him press the doorbell. It made no sound, or at least none that we could hear from outside. We waited. Nobody came.

'What now?' I asked, thinking we ought to move on to the village.

I was answered by the sound of footsteps on the gravel and a man appeared from around the side of the house, a groundsman or a gardener by the look of him. He was wearing a jacket, waistcoat, yellow cravat and expensive wellington boots. All that was missing was the shotgun under his arm and the Labrador Retriever. As he drew closer, I saw that he was in his sixties, perhaps even older, beaten about by the seasons. The sun had left a red welt on the bridge of his nose. The cold had scarred his neck with ugly patches of psoriasis. The rain had drawn the colour out of his cheeks and the wind had thrown his hair into permanent disarray. Just looking at his face, I took in a whole year of Wiltshire weather.

'You looking for someone?' he asked in a voice that was not exactly friendly.

Hawthorne was not intimidated. 'Who are you?' he asked.

'I'm John Lamprey. I look after the house and the grounds for Mr Golinishchev.'

'He's the owner?'

'Yes. You're on private land.'

'Is Mr Golinishchev at home?'

'I'm afraid I'm not able to give you that information.'

'It doesn't look like it. But it doesn't matter anyway. We're interested in Trevor Longhurst and his family.'

Lamprey sniffed at that. 'What are you? Tourists? Or newspapermen? If so, you're a bit late. That all happened years ago and they're no longer in the area.'

'I'm a detective. I'm investigating the death of Harriet Throsby. You may have read about it in the newspapers.'

For the first time, Lamprey looked interested.

'Yes. I saw that someone had put a knife into her. You got ID?'

'Do I really need it?' Hawthorne had a way of judging people and there was something about his response that amused the other man.

'Maybe not,' he said.

'Did you talk to her?'

'Harriet Throsby? Yes, I met her. Although I wish I hadn't.'

'Then you may be able to help us . . . if you'll give us ten minutes of your time.'

Lamprey took a few moments to examine us both, then nodded his head slowly. 'All right. I don't see why not. You can come inside if you like.' He opened the front door, which hadn't actually been locked.

'So where are the Golinishchevs, then?' Hawthorne asked.

'They're only here three or four weeks a year,' Lamprey replied. 'They usually come in the shooting season . . . October, November. You think Miss Throsby might have been done in because of that book of hers?'

'It's one theory.'

'It wouldn't surprise me. Everything she wrote was a pack of lies.'

He took us in through the front door, into a hall with gilt mirrors, a modern steel and glass chandelier, Persian rugs . . . all of them as soulless as the showrooms from which they had come. Too much money had been spent on the house, making it too perfect. The paintings were not just abstract. They were indecipherable. None of the furniture quite matched. Lamprey led us into a kitchen that reminded me of Hawthorne's except that it was three times bigger. It was too clean and strangely uncomfortable. There was a fireplace, but no evidence that it had ever been used for a fire. If it hadn't been for the lawns visible on the other side of the windows, we could have been in Belgravia. We could have been anywhere.

'You live here?' Hawthorne asked. Perhaps he was thinking the same as me.

'I have a room in the annexe. There's a separate kitchen there too, but I thought I'd spare you the walk.'

'And you worked for the Longhursts.'

Lamprey nodded. 'I was one of the gardeners back then. After they left, I stayed on to look after the place. It was empty for three years. After that, it was owned by a local family, but it was too big for them and eventually they moved on. Then the Russians came. They completely renovated the house . . . put all this stuff inside. Spent a fortune! If they didn't like it, back it went again. Staircases, bathrooms, the lot! And now it is how it is.' He had made his judgement. There was nothing more to add.

'Were you here when the teacher, Major Alden, was killed?'

Another slow nod. 'I used to know the major. The whole village did. He was what you would call a bit of a character. Bald, moustache. Always wore a three-piece suit. A big supporter of the local hunt until the day he died. Not such a bad old stick really, although some of the kids might have thought otherwise.'

'You said that Harriet Throsby wrote a pack of lies. I'd be interested to know what you meant by that.'

'You've read her book?'

'Some of it.'

'She came over here from Bristol. She had a friend in the village – Frank Heywood – and he introduced her to me. That was my mistake. I assumed, because she came recommended, that I could trust her. I sat down and talked to her in this very kitchen . . . not that it looked like this then. The Hall was already being emptied by the time she arrived. The Longhursts had gone. Anyway, I couldn't have been more wrong. She took what I said, used the bits she wanted and distorted the rest. I reckon she'd already made up her mind what she wanted to write long before she got here.'

'What did you tell her?'

'I told her about the family. About the boys. I knew Stephen Longhurst, of course, but the other kid, Wayne Howard, was often round here and I got to know him too. The school. The village. Two hours we spoke, and it all went down in that little notebook of hers. Scribble, scribble, scribble. You're not taking notes?'

'I don't need notes, Mr Lamprey. What did she get wrong?'

'Everything!' He sniffed, then pinched his nose between finger and thumb. 'First, Trevor and Annabel weren't that bad. They were incomers and that was always going to lead to trouble in a place like Moxham. You know the trouble with this part of the world? It's full of retired bankers and lawyers with too much time on their hands. People who used to be important but now they've got nothing to do, so they just get busy blowing everything out of proportion. You know about all those disagreements she put in her book? The way she described them, they could have been the start of a third world war. But they didn't amount to much at the time.

'I mean, let's start with the village fête. If Mr Longhurst didn't want it on his front lawn just a few months after he'd moved in, that was his business. He'd have come round in time if they'd only sat down and talked about it. And the footpath! You could see right into the swimming pool, and Mrs Longhurst, she liked to go skinny-dipping first thing in the morning. Hardly surprising she wanted to divert the footpath – but she was only asking for it to be moved a few metres. She wasn't trying to redraw the map! If the two of them had a fault, it was just that they were in too much of a hurry, but then they were Londoners. Everyone does everything at the double in London. You have to slow down if you want to get used to the country way.

'As for the villagers, you read Throsby's book, you'd think they'd all banded together with flaming torches and pitchforks and come round here to burn down the house. It wasn't like that either. There were a few mutterings at The Bridge – the local pub – and at the golf club. The Longhursts weren't the most popular people in the county. They were rich and they were a bit brash, so of course there were some who were jealous. But I said this to the Throsby woman. You choose any village you want, you're going to get your moaners. People need something to complain about. But come the weekend, it's all forgotten. It comes and goes with the wind.'

'Tell us about Stephen Longhurst.'

'Well, that was the worst of it. Why didn't she listen to me? I told her the long and the short of it – about him and Wayne – but I was wasting my breath. When I finally saw that book of hers, I couldn't believe what she'd written, and there was my name on the acknowledgements page at the back, as if I was the one who'd made it all up. I wanted to tell her publishers to take it right out again. My wife told me to forget about it, but I never have. It was a disgrace.'

He drew a breath.

'She got it completely arse about face. You say you haven't read the whole book, so I'll tell you. The way she described it, Stephen was the innocent little kid who was corrupted by Wayne. He didn't know what he was doing. Of course, that didn't mean she had to like him. She said he was spoilt. She described that business with Lisa when she got pushed into a barbed-wire fence – although that was really just an accident, not like what she said at all.

'But the biggest lie she told was that Wayne was the one in charge. You've only got to look at this place to know that's not true. I mean, you tell me! A kid with all the privilege in the world goes over to an estate near Chippenham and ends up hero-worshipping some eleven-year-old whose dad's been in jail and who lives in three tiny rooms surrounded by unwashed dishes and garbage? Give me a break! It was the other way round! I was here and I saw it. Wayne was just an ordinary kid. He came to this house and he thought he'd died and gone to heaven. The swimming pool. The sauna. The private cinema. Fridges full of food the likes of which he'd never seen before. Horses and dogs . . .

'Wayne was the one in awe of Stephen. Stephen was a year younger, but he knew exactly what he was doing. I'm not saying he was bad either. But he was bored and he was angry that his parents had brought him here. He'd spent most of his life in the city and that was where his friends were. What was he meant to do out in the sticks? There are only so many times you can swim in a pool or bounce on a trampoline. If you want my opinion – and this is what I told the Throsby woman – he wanted revenge on his parents and on the world and it was the older boy who provided him with the opportunity. Stephen changed once he got here. I saw it for myself. Trespassing, shoplifting, little acts of vandalism. It was Stephen who decided what they were going to do. Wayne may have agreed to go along with it, but he was always two steps behind.'

'What about the cruelty to animals?' I asked. That was something I'd read in the book.

Lamprey dismissed the accusation. 'The two of them went on the quad bikes and they ran over a sheep. It was an accident! That was just one of a million things she got wrong. Lisa was from Melbourne, not Sydney. This house was built in the nineteenth century. Stephen rode an American Quarter Horse and its name was Bree with two e's – not like the cheese. And he didn't fall off it – that was Wayne! Maybe that will tell you something about the two of them. Wayne had never sat on a horse in his life, but Stephen made him do it – and the next thing you know, he's come off, flat on his face. I remember him sitting over by the fire, blood streaming out of his nose, crying his head off like any other eleven-year-old. He ended up in hospital after that one! He only did it because he didn't want to lose face, and I'm sure the same thing was true when they did that silly trick with Major Alden. The family managed to persuade the judge that Wayne was the one in control and he ended up with twice the sentence of the other lad. But that wasn't the case.'

'Did you tell this to the police at the time?' Hawthorne asked.

Lamprey shook his head. 'It wasn't my place. I was just the gardener. Anyway, nobody asked.'

He'd had enough. When he spoke again, there was a sheen of some distant memory in his eyes.

'Neither of them were bad boys,' he said. 'I'm not saying they were perfect. But they were kids! They needed each other. I used to watch them chasing each other around the garden or sitting together, plotting and scheming, out by the old lion. That was their secret place. And I saw it with my own eyes. They loved each other in the way that only kids can. I was talking to my wife about it once and you know what she said? They were saving each other from themselves. That's what she said, and she more or less got it right. They were both on their own, both of them abandoned. One of them was rich. One of them was poor. But when they were together, they were happy. I can still hear them laughing and shouting and just being kids.

'At least, I used to hear them. Not any more. That's what Harriet Throsby took away with that book of hers. She made them into the bad boys they never were and I'll never forgive her for that. It was a wicked thing to do.'

He showed us to the door. The taxi was still waiting for us and we set off back down the driveway. As we turned the corner, I looked back and saw John Lamprey still standing there, the great sprawl of the house lifeless and empty behind him.

19
Long Shadows

Once we'd arrived at the centre of Moxham Heath, Hawthorne asked the driver to stop and we got out and continued on foot. Neither of us spoke. Maybe Hawthorne was trying to absorb the atmosphere of the village, imagining what it must have been like for the Longhursts as they adapted, unsuccessfully, to their new home. Or perhaps his mind was dwelling on what John Lamprey had told us. Mine certainly was.

For somewhere that had been the cause of so much sadness, Moxham was strikingly beautiful, the sort of place that turns up in jigsaw puzzles or Harry Potter films. In the summer it might be crowded with visitors, but on this bright April day – not quite the weekend yet – it seemed completely authentic; less a tourist attraction, more somewhere to live. We had been dropped off at the bridge, which formed the centre point of the community, its two stone arches spanning a stream doing its best to pretend it was a river. The houses and shops on either side were constructed out of Bath stone, with that warm glow no other building material has ever replicated, and one by one my eye picked out the little details: the ivy, the mullioned windows, the chimneys, the stone urns with their spring flowers bursting through, the original lamp posts, the war monument and the stone trough for horses. I could imagine the Longhursts arriving here for the first time and seeing the gurgling water, the church spire in the distance. Perhaps it wasn't so surprising that they had decided to stay. It was hard to believe that Chippenham, with its ring roads and business parks, and the six-lane M4 motorway to London were just a few miles away.

There were only three shops. We passed a newsagent's and a butcher's-cum-grocery-store before we came to the Ginger Box, still open, selling sweets and souvenirs. This had been the target of Stephen and Wayne on their shoplifting spree and it reminded me that as much as I had fallen for the charms of Moxham Heath, it must have been insufferably dull to a rich boy who had grown up in London. There were a few people in the streets, none of them under sixty. A vicar walked past on the other side of the street and smiled at us. A vicar! Had I accidentally wandered into an episode of *Midsomer Murders*?

But as we climbed the hill towards the church, the twenty-first century began to impose itself. Suddenly there were yellow lines and – paradoxically – more parked cars. A modern house and a bungalow stuck out like teeth added by a blindly inept dentist. I was glad to see that the village had its own library, but it was a 1960s monstrosity. We came to the church – St Swithin's – and seeing the name, I wondered if we were going to visit the grave where Major Alden was buried. I should have known better. I don't think I've met anyone who was less of a sentimentalist than Hawthorne and he didn't even glance that way.

His destination was on the other side of the road: another old building, this one Victorian red brick, just one storey, with an ill-fitting glass extension on one side. A sign told us that this was Moxham Heath Primary School. The classroom windows would have a view of the graves; a vivid illustration of the transience of life, though one probably lost on the children. There were a few parents milling around on the pavement and, looking at my watch, I saw that it was five to three. Presumably the school day finished on the hour. We had timed it well. We lingered until we heard the class bells ring. The doors opened and the children streamed out, the girls in blue-and-white checked dresses, the boys in shorts and blue polo shirts. I watched them rush into their parents' arms, delivering the usual bundles of exercise books, curling watercolours and disparate objects made from cardboard. Suddenly the building was empty. We went in.

The school didn't have a lot of space for the forty or fifty children who went there, but there was still a generous reception area with a glass-partitioned office on one side, a visitors' book and security passes. Swing doors would have to be buzzed open to allow us access into the school itself. The arrangement reminded me of the stage-door entrance of the Vaudeville. Here, Keith's role was taken by a businesslike young woman in a blue suit. Hawthorne told her who we were and asked if we could speak to the head teacher. The receptionist looked doubtful but rang through anyway.

A primary school is about the only place where my name opens doors and less than a minute later, a large, energetic woman came bursting into the reception area to greet us. I could see at once that she was exactly the sort of head teacher I'd have liked to have when I was ten years old. There was just enough of the Miss Trunchbull about her to make her eccentric, but she was all warmth and smiles, middle-aged, her corded glasses tangling up with the beaded necklace around her neck. She introduced herself as Helen Winters.

'The children would have been so excited to see you here,' she announced, ignoring Hawthorne. 'Your books are very popular in the library.'

'I'm afraid I'm not here for a school visit,' I said.

'We're wondering if there's anyone here who was around when Philip Alden was killed,' Hawthorne said, getting straight to the point.

'Oh . . .' The head teacher faltered. This wasn't what she had been expecting at all. 'I'm afraid not. To be honest with you, we've tried to forget what happened all those years ago. It's not a nice memory to have in the school.'

'There are no teachers? Nobody who might remember Stephen Longhurst?'

'Absolutely not. We have quite a young staff here. I've only been at Moxham four years myself.'

'Do you work in the study that Alden used?'

'No. That's our quiet room now.'

'I wonder if we could see it?'

'I can't imagine why you would want to, Mr Hawthorne. Nothing is the same any more. All the furniture was taken away . . . even the bookshelves. It's been repainted.'

'It still has the door.'

I could see that Helen Winters was regretting she had ever met us. 'Well, all right,' she said. 'But I really can't see how it will help you.'

She led us through the double doors and along a corridor decorated with the children's paintings. As we went, I tried to cheer her up by admiring the artwork and talking about books. We passed the library, a bright space with miniature desks and beanbags. A plaque showed that it had been opened by Michael Morpurgo.

'Such a lovely man,' Helen said, a little caustically. The inference was clear. Unlike me, the former children's laureate hadn't come here investigating the half-forgotten death of the deputy head. 'Have you met him?'

'Many times. I'm a big fan.'

We reached her office – long and narrow, with papers piled high on her desk and certificates on the wall. The quiet room was next door. It had been modernised, carefully designed to soothe the more volatile children. Everything was soft: the sofas, the carpet, the beanbags, the stuffed toys and the lighting that faded from pink to mauve to green even as we stood there. One wall was covered with a mural showing an underwater scene and there were liquid lava lamps morphing away on low tables. Turning on the lights had also turned on music: the theme from the film of *War Horse*. Morpurgo's fingerprints seemed to be all over the school.

'This is where Major Alden worked,' Helen said. 'It was an office until I arrived, but we haven't had a deputy head for years and I decided to adapt the room to its present use.'

'Do you have a lot of difficult children here?' Hawthorne asked.

'We don't consider any children to be difficult.' Helen Winters replied in a way that suggested Hawthorne was once again straining her patience. 'All young people need to calm down from time to time. Modern society can seem very stressful when you're nine or ten years old. Children are under so much pressure these days. This room is a facility for everyone to use. I sometimes sit in here myself.'

Hawthorne had already turned his back on her. He was examining the door frame, which was unusually high. He opened the door and held it. I could see him working out how easy it would have been to balance the bust of Cicero above and for once I was sure we had both arrived at the same conclusion. There was no way one of the boys would have been able to set the trap on his own. They had to be working together. And the bust had a long way to fall. If the sharp edge of the plinth had been pointing in the right direction, it could easily have fractured Alden's skull.

'Have you seen enough?' Helen asked.

Hawthorne nodded. 'There must be people in the village who remember Major Alden,' he said.

'I don't understand why it's of such interest to you, Mr Hawthorne.'

'I should have explained to you, Mrs Winters. A woman was murdered in London two days ago, a theatre critic by the name of Harriet Throsby. She was stabbed in her own home. I believe her death may be connected to what happened at this school. I know it was a long time ago, but murders cast long shadows. I'm just trying to shed a little light.'

If he was being deliberately provocative, it had an effect. 'I never met Harriet Throsby,' she said. 'But I know who she was. She wrote a book about Moxham Heath and I don't think any of it was very kind.'

'She didn't visit the school?'

'Yes. I believe she did. But that was long before my time. I was living in Bath Spa when all this was happening. I only became aware of what had happened here when I became head teacher, and as I told you, I try not to let these awful memories intrude.'

'But there must be someone in the village who was here when it happened.'

Helen Winters considered. She quite probably didn't want to give Hawthorne a name, but at the same time it would be the fastest way to get rid of him. She made her decision. 'I suppose you could talk to Rosemary Alden.'

'Major Alden's wife?' I said.

'His widow. She still lives in the village. She was allowed to stay on in the house she occupied with Philip Alden when he worked here.'

'For twenty years? Isn't that a bit unusual?' Hawthorne immediately homed in on that one detail.

'She had nowhere to go and, to be fair to them, the Longhursts were very generous. They set up a trust in Philip Alden's name and bought Glebe Cottage so that she could continue living in it rent-free. It cost them a pretty penny, but I suppose it was the least they could do, given what had occurred.'

'And where is it?' Hawthorne asked.

'Glebe Cottage? It's just up the road from the Ginger Box. But I should caution you. She's quite elderly and her health hasn't been good. She had a stroke last year and she doesn't go out very much any more. If she agrees to speak to you, you'll have to be gentle.'

My eyes glazed over when I heard her telling Hawthorne that, but I said nothing.

She insisted on escorting us back to the main entrance. 'You never had any contact with Stephen Longhurst?' Hawthorne asked her as we made our way.

'No. Neither of the boys returned to Moxham Heath. There was a rumour that Wayne joined the army, and as for Stephen, he went to America after he came out of prison.' She stopped. 'I did meet his brother, though.'

'Martin Longhurst?'

'Yes.'

'He visited the school?'

'It was all a bit strange. This was a couple of years ago. He said he was thinking of sending his children here . . .'

That was strange indeed. Martin Longhurst was in his mid-thirties and it was perfectly possible that he had children of primary-school age, but he hadn't mentioned that he was planning to return to Moxham Heath. His business was in central London. And given its bad associations, the fact that the village had been responsible for the almost total destruction of his family, this was surely the last place he would want to be.

'I suppose you knew who he was?' Hawthorne asked.

'He told me his name and of course I made the connection immediately. He was a very tall man. Quite aggressive. I didn't feel at all comfortable with him.' We were passing the library a second time and that jolted her memory. 'As a matter of fact, he mentioned you.'

She meant me. 'Oh – really?'

'Yes. I have to say, it's a funny coincidence you being here, but maybe there's some sort of connection.' She thought back. 'He saw one of your books in the library and he mentioned that he'd loved reading it as a child.'

'That's nice.'

'Not really. I'm not sure I should be telling you this, but he went on to say that he'd sent you a fan letter when he was fourteen years old and you never replied. He was quite upset about it.'

This was something else he hadn't mentioned.

'I always reply to all my fan letters,' I told her.

'Well, you must have missed his – not, I'm sure, that you did it on purpose. But it's funny, isn't it, how some things matter to people.' We had set off again and a moment later we reached the front door. 'Glebe Cottage,' Helen reminded us.

'Thank you,' Hawthorne said, adding: 'It seems like a nice school.'

She smiled. 'We try to keep it that way.'

We set off back down the hill.

20
Past Crimes

'Mrs Alden won't see you!'

The woman who had answered the door at Glebe Cottage was short and ferocious. From her accent, I would say she was Eastern European. She had dark skin colouring, hair tied back, aggressive eyes. She wore a loose-fitting tunic with a watch pinned to her chest, which gave her the look of a nurse although she had introduced herself as a private carer. Hawthorne had told her who we were and what we wanted. She was uninterested.

'Mrs Alden is having her rest.'

'We won't keep her long. It's important. It's about her husband, Major Philip Alden.'

'She doesn't want to talk about him.'

Glebe Cottage was one of a row of three former almshouses nestling side by side just off the high street. Everything about it was half-sized, like a theatrical set. The roof sloped unevenly. The walls bulged. Shrink it further and you could sell it in a tourist shop, a perfect reproduction of what a Wiltshire cottage should be.

The carer was about to close the perfect oak door in our faces, but just then there was a movement behind her and Rosemary Alden herself made an appearance, supporting herself on a walking stick. 'Who is it, Tara?' she queried.

'They want to talk about Major Alden,' the carer replied.

'What about him?'

Hawthorne would clearly have liked to explain for himself, but Tara had imposed herself firmly between him and the hallway. 'They're asking questions.'

'What questions?'

'I've told them to leave.'

'No. Let them come in.'

The carer hesitated. She wanted to disobey, but there had been something in the old lady's voice that persuaded her otherwise. I'd heard it too – a steely determination that seemed odd, given that she had no idea who we were. Grudgingly, Tara stepped aside. We went in, through a hallway barely larger than the WELCOME doormat, and into the rather too cosy living room.

Rosemary Alden was already lowering herself into a high-backed chair, carefully resting the walking stick against the arm. She was surrounded by clutter, as if the contents of two or three different properties had been poured into this little space. There were ornaments everywhere: on the mantelpiece, the window sills, on occasional tables that had no purpose other than to display ornaments. Many of them were related to hunting and I remembered how John Lamprey, the caretaker at Moxham Hall, had described the major. *'A big supporter of the local hunt until the day he died.'* Well, here was the evidence. A silver stirrup cup above the fire. A porcelain fox wearing a bright red jacket. A riding crop pinned to the wall. Cushions with embroidered beagles. Several photographs of Philip Alden on horseback, often surrounded by fellow enthusiasts.

Rosemary's own life – or what was left of it – was interwoven into all this. She liked books; not modern paperbacks, but miniature volumes in leather bindings that might have been in her family for generations. She collected tiny silver boxes and crystal jars, porcelain animals and glass ballerinas. A bowl of hyacinths had been placed on a table next to where she was sitting. They were the very worst flowers to have in this confined space, their sickly smell permeating the overheated air.

And what of Rosemary herself? She must have been in her seventies, but she could have been ten years older. Age had shrunk her, tightening her arms and her shoulders, making the sinews in her neck stand out. She was not well. She could barely walk and the stroke that she had suffered a year ago had frozen half her face, the eye on that side bulging unpleasantly, like a marble. She was wearing a smart floral dress that came down to her ankles, clip-on earrings and a pearl necklace. Her hair had been groomed, her make-up carefully applied. I assumed all this had been done by Tara. She could have been about to go out – perhaps for tea or bridge – but it was unlikely that this was something she ever did. This was her entire world. She was living the illusion of a life.

'You can leave now, Tara.'

'Are you sure, Mrs Alden?'

'For heaven's sake, girl, I can look after myself!'

'I've put your supper in the oven.'

'I know. I know. Thank you, Tara.' It was not an expression of gratitude. It was a dismissal.

Tara was unhappy, but she knew better than to argue. She snatched a quilted jacket off a chair and went back out through the front door. Nobody spoke until we heard it close. Mrs Alden turned to us, examining us with that obtruding eye.

'I would like a whisky,' she announced. 'There's a bottle of Dalwhinnie over there in the corner. I'd like two inches with a splash of water, if you don't mind.'

She had a drinks trolley crowded with different bottles. I found the whisky and poured some into a heavy tumbler, then added water from a jug. I carried it over to her.

'Tara doesn't like me to drink. The doctor says it'll kill me, but he's a damn fool. I'm seventy-eight years old and look at me! I'm dying inch by inch. What difference do you think it will make?' Her hand trembled as she raised the glass to her lips. She swallowed with difficulty. 'You want to talk to me about Philip?'

'If you don't mind.'

'Why? I heard you tell Tara you were a detective. You don't look like a detective. You look more like an undertaker. Are you investigating me?'

It seemed an odd thing to ask, but Hawthorne didn't blink. 'No. We're looking into a death that took place in London. We believe there may be a connection with what happened here.'

'Whose death?'

'A woman called Harriet Throsby.'

'I remember her. She came here a while ago. She wrote a book about what happened at the school. I never read it.'

'It seems that a great deal of what she wrote was untrue.'

'Of course it was. She didn't know anything.' She smiled to herself, but only half of her mouth moved. 'Is that why you've come here? Because you want to know the truth?'

'I already know the truth, Mrs Alden, and so do you. I just wanted to hear it . . .' he glanced at one of the hunting photographs '. . . from the horse's mouth.'

She stared at him. At least, one of her eyes did. The other was fixed on something in the middle distance. 'That sounds very impertinent, Mr . . .' Her voice trailed off. 'What did you say your name was?'

'Hawthorne.'

'Hawthorne! How can you know anything about me? You've only just walked in!'

Hawthorne didn't reply.

Mrs Alden tilted the glass and finished the whisky. She handed it to me. 'I'll have another.'

'Are you sure?'

I didn't actually say the words, but I must have shown what I was thinking because she glared at me. 'What do you think I'm going to do?' she snapped. 'Get drunk and dance on the table? You can have one yourself, if you like. Perhaps it will make you a little less po-faced.'

When she spoke like that, I glimpsed the woman who had once patrolled the corridors at Moxham Heath Primary School as the deputy headmaster's wife. I knew exactly what she must have been like. '*Tuck in your shirt tail! Let's have a little less noise, please. No running in the corridor!*' We'd had a matron just like that at my prep school. We'd all been terrified of her.

I went back to the trolley and poured a second measure, but I made sure it was smaller than the first. Hawthorne wouldn't be too pleased if she passed out before she could tell us what he wanted to know. I gave her the glass and she took another swig. It was quite a performance, especially considering it was only four o'clock in the afternoon – but then I suspected that time had no meaning for her. There were no clocks in the room, perhaps deliberately.

'I'm not frightened of you, Mr Hawthorne.' She wasn't quite slurring her words, but the alcohol had certainly had an effect on her speech. It had released her inhibitions, emboldened her. 'Those two boys deserved everything they got. They crept into Philip's study and they put that bust on the top of the door and when he walked in, it fell onto his head and broke his skull. He went into a coma and the next day he died.' It took her a few moments to recover. 'I always told him to get rid of that stupid thing. He had no interest in Cicero. But he thought it impressed the children.'

'What sort of man was your husband, Mrs Alden?'

'Not an easy one.' She swirled the whisky in the glass, tempted to finish it. 'He took a long time to find himself when he came out of the army. He missed the camaraderie. He wanted to come back to Wiltshire because that was where he was born – he grew up in Corsham. His parents had the manor there, but their money had gone long before I met him. We were both poor as church mice. He had his army pension, but that never went very far. We didn't even have our own home.'

'You have this one. And you live here rent-free.'

She hesitated. 'Yes. The school has been very kind to me.'

'Why did your husband become a teacher?'

'He needed a job and we needed somewhere to live. I was the one who suggested it. Obviously, if Philip could get a job in a private boarding school, he would get accommodation, which would kill two birds with one stone. He did apply to several prep schools in the area, but they wouldn't have him, so he did a teacher-training course and after a couple of years in Trowbridge – dreadful place! – he ended up at

Moxham Heath Primary School. We rented a home to begin with, but when he was promoted to deputy head we were given Glebe Cottage. I've been here ever since.'

'Was he happy in Moxham Heath?'

'Oh, yes. He soon found his feet. In fact, he became quite a well-known figure in the village. He liked fishing.'

'And hunting.' Hawthorne made the words sound like an accusation.

'Well, you can see the evidence all around you. Yes. Hunting was his great love, even though he could barely afford it. It may surprise you to know that not everyone who goes out with the hounds is loaded. Philip rode with the Avon Vale Hunt. He hired a horse some of the time, but the master of hounds took a liking to him and often lent him his own chestnut. Philip made a lot of friends who looked after him, and the hunting community always was very generous . . . a bit like the army.' She pointed at a black-and-white photograph in a silver frame. It showed a boy, slightly out of focus, resting his hand against a horse. 'That's Philip aged twelve. He went hunting with his father in Corsham when he was a boy. He had so many memories. He never stopped talking about them!' She let out a sigh. 'He was never happier than when he was out on a frosty morning with all his friends, trotting down a country lane and then hurtling across the countryside, leaping over fences and streams, risking a broken neck every time. That's when he came alive. That was all he looked forward to.'

'He can't have been too fond of Stephen Longhurst, then.'

Rosemary Alden froze. 'I don't know what you mean.'

'His parents were close to the Labour government. They wanted to ban hunting.'

'That wasn't the child's fault.'

'Your husband may not have felt that way.'

'Philip didn't like the parents. Nobody did!' She had blurted out the words without thinking. She composed herself. 'It was very unpleasant,' she continued. 'There was lots of talk in the newspapers and on television. We even had saboteurs in the village, riding around on their motorbikes and trying to put the hounds off the scent. There were acts of vandalism . . . graffiti . . . one of the horses was hurt. And two of the loudest voices calling for a ban belonged to our new residents, Mr and Mrs Longhurst. They had come into this community, but they had absolutely no understanding of our way of life. They were the vipers in the nest. That was what Philip called them.'

'So you can't feel very comfortable living here, then,' Hawthorne said. 'Just now you told us that the school had been kind to you, letting you live here. But you must know that it was Trevor and Annabel Longhurst who paid.'

'I had no idea.'

'You're not a good liar, Mrs Alden.'

'How dare you call me that!'

'Then tell me the truth. The Longhursts bought this house and put it in trust just for you. Of course you knew.'

She drained the glass. 'I had nowhere else to go.'

Hawthorne waited for her to calm down. When he spoke again, he was more reasonable. 'Don't you want to get it off your chest, Mrs Alden?' he asked. 'Isn't that why you let us in? Seventeen years you've been sitting here, thinking about it. But that's the trouble with past crimes. They never let you go. And here you are, talking about dying and worrying that somebody's going to come and investigate you.'

She held out the glass. 'Another!'

'I think you've had enough.' Hawthorne reached out and took the glass from her hand. 'Let me tell you how I see it. First of all, I think Major Alden was wrong. That business with the library books . . . tearing out pages and all the rest of it. Stephen Longhurst would never have done that. It's the one thing we know about him. He loved books. If he and Wayne wanted to hurt your husband, it wasn't because he wouldn't let them go to Bath Spa, it was because he'd accused them of something they didn't do.'

'You're being ridiculous. How can you possibly know? And anyway, it was a tiny incident, a long, long time ago.'

'A tiny incident that led to your husband's death. Are you denying it?'

'I'm not saying anything!'

'Then let me tell you. Because there's something else I know. Wayne was the older of the two boys and, coming from a council estate, everyone assumed he was the one who instigated the bad behaviour. He was the ringleader. But in fact it was the other way round. Wayne was the innocent one. Stephen was the one in charge.'

'Why are you telling me this? Why does it matter any more?'

'Because Wayne got ten years in a secure unit and Stephen only got five.' Hawthorne paused, fixing her with his gaze. He leaned forward before he spoke again. 'Did you testify in court, Mrs Alden?'

Rosemary Alden caught her breath. The colour had drained out of her face, leaving her make-up sitting as if on parchment. At last she replied. 'I gave a statement. Yes.'

'A false statement. Because the Longhursts' lawyers got to you, didn't they? They told you to say that Wayne was the troublemaker, that Stephen didn't know what he was doing. And this is what you got out of it. This cottage. Somewhere to live. You supported their version of events and this place was your reward.'

'No!' Rosemary Alden was sitting bolt upright in her chair. It was as if she had been electrocuted. 'Get out of here!' she quavered, her voice catching in her throat.

'I'll leave when you've told me what I want to know.'

'Tara . . . !'

'Tara's not here. You sent her away.'

Hawthorne was ferocious. It didn't bother him that the subject of his interrogation was sick and in her seventies. I was seriously worried Rosemary might have a fatal heart attack or another stroke. Cara Grunshaw would love that. Another death – five minutes after I'd been in the room.

'Who defaced the library books?' Hawthorne asked.

'I don't know.'

'But it wasn't Stephen or Wayne!'

'I don't know who it was!' She struggled for breath. 'Nor did Philip . . .'

And there it was, finally, the admission.

'Philip knew it wasn't them,' she went on. 'He told me! He couldn't find the real culprits, so he decided to make them an example.'

'And the rest of it?'

'I don't know what you mean . . .'

'The lawyers.'

She nodded. All she wanted was to get Hawthorne out of the room. 'One of them came to see me before the trial. A smarmy young man with his hair greased back. He didn't tell me his name. He said that he represented the family and that maybe he could help me if I agreed to help them. I testified that Stephen was a good boy, that he didn't know what he was doing, that the other boy influenced him. I didn't lie. It wasn't *my* lie. All I had to do was support their version of the truth.'

'To commit perjury.'

'You can call it that if you like, but what was I to do? I was desperate. I would have had to move out. I had no job, no income, nowhere to go. Philip was in the cemetery and nobody cared about me.'

A single tear leaked from her good eye.

Hawthorne stood up. 'We'll leave you alone now, Mrs Alden. You did the right thing, telling us the truth.'

'Will I have to leave Glebe Cottage?'

'No. You can stay here. That wasn't why we came.'

He began to move towards the door, but she stopped him. 'Could you do something for me, Mr Hawthorne? If you ever find those two boys, could you tell them that I know what I did was wrong and I am so very sorry? Neither of them should have gone to prison. It was a prank. Can you tell them how sorry I am?'

Hawthorne stopped. 'I'd say it's a bit late for that now, love.'

He left the room. I gave her a half-apologetic shrug and followed.

21

The Jai Mahal

I thought we would be going straight back to London, but Hawthorne had called ahead and made one final appointment. Adrian Wells had been chief editor at the Bristol *Argus* when Harriet had written for it, first as a crime reporter, then as the drama critic. He still lived in Bristol and that was where we were now headed. We would take the train home from there.

I was feeling increasingly uneasy – and not because I was aware of time running out for me. On the contrary, things were happening at whirlwind speed. My play had premiered on Tuesday. Harriet was killed on Wednesday. Hawthorne had shown up on Thursday and today was only Friday. My problem was that although I knew we had achieved a great deal, I couldn't see how it would help.

We knew the truth about Stephen Longhurst. Contrary to what everybody thought and what the judge had clearly believed, he had not been the innocent that he seemed to be. We had learned of a conspiracy to pervert the cause of justice, with Rosemary Alden bribed by an anonymous London lawyer to perjure herself in court. Major Alden himself had been exposed as a vindictive bully. And then there was the strange behaviour of Martin Longhurst. What had he been doing visiting the school, and why tell a lie about sending his children there?

But what had any of this got to do with the death of Harriet Throsby? Hawthorne had suggested that the reason for Harriet's death might be found in Moxham Heath, but unless John Lamprey or the major's wife had travelled to London to take revenge (which seemed unlikely), it felt like a complete waste of time.

Adrian Wells was retired now and wanted the whole world to know it. He was sitting with his arms folded across his substantial belly, wearing an almost shapeless cardigan and slippers. His silver hair was long and tangled and he hadn't shaved. He was living alone in a flat carved out of a converted church in Clifton. Some of the stained-glass windows had been left behind and they suited him. He looked like a debauched saint.

'Of course I remember Harriet,' he was telling us. 'A frightful woman. Good writer, though. She never let the facts get in the way of a good story.' He laughed at his own cliché.

'What exactly do you mean by that?' Hawthorne asked.

'She didn't lie, but she embroidered the truth. She saw things a certain way and she made sure her articles reflected her own point of view – she didn't care if the entire world believed otherwise. So if she liked someone, she'd make them appear sympathetic, even if they'd hacked up their wife and stored the pieces in a freezer . . . which was actually one of the stories she covered.'

'Did she like the company of criminals?'

'That's a good question.' Wells laughed a second time. 'She certainly had a way of ingratiating herself with them – and, for that matter, with their wives, their husbands, their neighbours or their victims! That's how she was able to get so many of her insights. She went places other journalists never dared. I don't suppose the name Robert Thirkell means anything to you?'

'She wrote a book about him.'

'That's the one. He was a doctor who polished off half a dozen old ladies in various care homes. Well, he was under suspicion for two or three months before he was arrested and in that time she became good chums with him. I think there was a part of her that was attracted to people who kill.'

'She admired them?'

'I wouldn't go that far, but she was certainly fascinated by them.'

'She told me she found criminals dull,' I interjected. That was what Harriet had said during the brief exchange we'd had at the party. Once again, I reflected how strange it was that just a short while ago she had been standing there with a drink in her hand, alive.

'Harriet found everyone dull in the end. Her friends, her colleagues, her husband . . . me! That was because she had such a high opinion of herself.'

'Arthur Throsby also worked on the paper.'

'That's right. I was at their wedding. Since you mention it, I was surprised their marriage lasted as long as it did. A single man would never have been enough to satisfy Harriet and I'm sure Arthur knew she was playing the field.'

'She was having affairs?'

'Don't be so surprised, Mr Hawthorne. She was an attractive woman back then. I half fancied her myself! There was something about her – the energy, the ambition. I don't know. She used sex to get what she wanted. She wouldn't let anything stand in her way.'

'Was she having an affair with Frank Heywood?'

'I wouldn't be surprised. I can't really tell you, to be honest. They were certainly close. He often took her with him to the theatre and that was how she got the idea she wanted to be a critic. I told her she was barking mad. Why swap real-life drama for a bunch of tossers leaping about on the stage? Anyway, she was too old-fashioned to be a theatre critic, too set in her ways. The first play she covered after Frank died was a lesbian love story and she slated it – not because it was bad but because she didn't approve of the subject matter.

I think she'd have been much better off sticking where she was, but she wouldn't listen to me.'

'It was Frank Heywood who introduced her to Moxham Heath.'

'When the teacher got killed? Yes. That was Frank. He lived in the village.'

'Was there any kickback from the book she wrote?'

'God, yes! She had the Longhursts and their lawyers threatening her with libel. The Moxham Village Trust wrote letters. She even had the local MP involved. But it all went away, just as she knew it would. When you read her stuff, you may not like it. You may think it all a bit ghastly. But she knew what she was doing. She always judged it exactly right.'

'How long was she the drama critic on the *Argus*?'

'Less than eighteen months. She didn't wait long before pushing off, but I sort of suspected that she was only using her position on the newspaper as a launch pad for better things. I've already said – she knew what she wanted. I didn't want to give her the job, but she left me no choice. The week after Frank died – she wrote his obituary, by the way – she was in my office with her ultimatums. It was that or lose her altogether.'

'What can you tell me about Frank Heywood's death?'

Outside, it was getting dark. The stained-glass windows were slowly losing their definition, the Virgin Mary and her attendant angels fading into the shadows. Adrian Wells reached out and turned on an Anglepoise lamp.

'It's interesting you should ask me about that. I was talking about it only this week. I even suggested I might tip a wink to the police.'

'You mean . . . Cara Grunshaw?' I asked.

'Who? I don't know that name. It was just something that occurred to me . . .'

'What?' I hoped I didn't sound too alarmed.

'I'm sure you know, Frank Heywood died of food poisoning. Well, strictly speaking, the cause of death was heart failure. He smoked like a chimney and hadn't done any exercise since the year dot, so he wasn't in great shape. No surprises there. More to the point, he was eating at an Indian restaurant that was notoriously bad. The Jai Mahal near the St Nicholas Market. It was quite popular, particularly among Bristol students, but the health and safety mob had been in a couple of times and they weren't impressed at all. Our food critic called it the Die Mahal.

'Frank's fatal heart attack was brought on by a dodgy lamb rogan josh. Harriet was with him that night and she was taken ill too, although in her case it was just an overnight stay at St Michael's Hospital. She looked awful when I visited her a couple of days later, but the restaurant had been her choice and she felt terrible in every sense. She blamed herself for his death.'

'It was food poisoning,' Hawthorne said. 'And it was a long time ago. So why do you think the police might be interested now?'

'Because Harriet's been killed too!' He made the answer sound obvious. 'It made me think. You see, I heard a whisper that she may have been murdered because of something she wrote – a review. I know it sounds insane, but I'd had almost exactly the same conversation with Frank the week before he died. Some of the stuff he wrote – well, he could be a bit harsh. That was something Harriet learned from him, the pleasure that comes with the twist of a knife. So, the two of us were having a pint and he mentioned a play he'd seen – it was only a short piece – but he'd really taken against it. 'I wouldn't be surprised if the writer didn't come after me with a pickaxe.' He was only joking. But a week later . . . boom!

'Perhaps I'm letting my imagination run away with me. That's what comes of having too much time on your hands – but it does make you think. We made jokes about the Jai Mahal, but nobody had ever died there before. And there was no police investigation at the time because two people got sick – not just Frank – and anyway, it was his heart that did for him. You're a detective. What do you think? A disgruntled writer follows them into the restaurant and slips something into the curry. The revenge of the rotten review.'

'I don't suppose you remember the play?' Hawthorne asked.

'As a matter of fact, I do. It was only an hour long. It was set in a secure unit for juvenile offenders. It was a bunch of them putting on a performance of *The Importance of Being Earnest*. Frank said it was the most unlikely scenario he'd ever come across, and here's the rub – he suggested that the writer might be disturbed. The play was called *A Handbag*.'

'And do you know who wrote it?'

I cut in before he could answer.

'I did.'

22

Safe House

I didn't enjoy the journey back to London. Of course, Hawthorne hadn't believed Adrian Wells's ridiculous assertion that all along I had been a serial killer of critics who didn't like my work. Or so I told myself. He said nothing. He had taken out his iPad and was methodically thumbing his way through Harriet Throsby's book.

Incidentally, I was very proud of *A Handbag*, a short play I had originally written for the National Theatre's 'New Connections' programme and which had subsequently been performed for one week only as part of a youth theatre festival in Bath. As Wells had said, it was about a group of kids locked up in a secure facility. The one hope in their life is their performance of Wilde's masterpiece, which, they believe, will make them seem normal. Their tragedy is that they can't understand a word of it. It was a play about failure and the refusal to give in.

I had never read Frank Heywood's review.

We parted company at Paddington Station, Hawthorne promising that he would call me the next day, and I took the tube back to Farringdon. It was about nine o'clock when I climbed up to street level, and already dark. I was exhausted. This being a Friday, and the rain having finally subsided, the pavements were still crowded with office workers drinking outside the Castle and the Three Compasses. I was about to continue into Cowcross Street when my phone pinged. I took it out and looked at the screen. There was a message from Kevin Chakraborty.

> Anthony – bad news I'm afraid.
> Lambeth forensic lab is now up
> and running. Grunshaw has definite
> match on hair. Suggest you head
> for the hills. Kevin.

I was still staring at the screen when two police cars tore round the corner with their lights flashing. Because of the way the station was configured, with a pedestrian area in front of the entrance, they didn't see me. But I had a clear view as they screeched to a halt. Detective Inspector Cara Grunshaw and Detective Constable Mills burst out of the first car. Two uniformed officers appeared from the one behind. I watched in horror as they rang the doorbell. I hadn't told my wife about any of this. What was she going to say?

Before I knew what I was doing, I had turned round and hurried off the other way, putting as much space between myself and Cara Grunshaw as I could. I already had a weird sense of disembodiment. Just a moment before, I had been part of the crowd, making my way home. Now I was wanted by the police! I was on my own, but it was worse than that. I felt as if I was watching myself on a screen, recorded by some all-seeing camera positioned high above. I forced myself to slow down, recognising that I was already behaving like a fugitive. If someone saw the police cars and then saw me, the connection would be obvious.

I turned up the alleyway where Jordan Williams had appeared the night before and went back to the park where we had met. I needed somewhere to sit down and think and knew it was unlikely there would be many people there at this time of the evening. I couldn't go back to Tolpuddle Street; that was the uppermost thought in my mind. It wasn't just the dirt and the humiliation. If I was sucked back, it wouldn't be for twenty-four hours. There would be no Hawthorne arriving to rescue me a second time. Cara had her evidence. Would it stand up in court? Of course it would! Tolpuddle Street could quite easily be the first step on the way to life in jail.

The park was locked. I sat on the edge of the pavement in despair.

All of this was crazy. I hadn't murdered anyone. But then the dagger, the fingerprints, the hair, the Japanese blossom and the CCTV images said otherwise. I had a motive. I had threatened Harriet Throsby, according to one witness. I had agreed she deserved to die, according to another. And all of that was without taking into account my first victim, Bristol *Argus* critic Frank Heywood. There was no way round it. I think if I'd been on the jury, I'd have convicted me.

I don't know how long I stayed there. Perhaps Cara would have gone by now and I could slip in and hide under the bed. It was a shame that the flat had no back entrance, not even a window I could climb through. I didn't dare go back into Cowcross Street. There would probably be a police officer waiting for me all night. In the end, I did what I should have done in the first place. I took out my mobile phone and called my wife.

She answered on the second ring. 'Anthony? Where are you?'

'Is Cara Grunshaw still there?'

'Yes. She is.' She continued in the same breath. 'Why did you do it?'

'Do what?'

'Murder that critic!'

'What? I didn't go anywhere near her! You can't seriously think I had anything to do with it!'

'The police seem to think they have a very good case.'

'And you believe them, not me?'

'Well, I know how upset you get by bad reviews.'

'Not upset enough to kill someone!'

'And why didn't you tell me?'

'I didn't think you'd want to know.'

'You're right! This is very disappointing—'

I would have continued, but then the phone must have been snatched from Jill's hand and Cara Grunshaw came on.

'Where are you, Anthony?'

'I'm not telling you.'

'You won't get away. We've got the whole of London looking for you. It'll make it a lot easier for you if you just turn yourself in.'

'I don't want to talk to you. I want to talk to Jill.'

'She's very upset. She had no idea of the sort of man she's married to.'

'Why don't you just drop dead, Cara!'

'Are you threatening me now?' A pause. 'Are you somewhere near?'

I hung up. There was something in her last question that had scared me. Was it possible that she could be tracing the call? I'd watched that scene in lots of films where the police try to keep the suspect talking for as long as they can while they close in on the signal – in fact, I'd written it a couple of times myself. I'd often wondered how long it really took. Perhaps these days it was instantaneous. It was time to move. I got up and walked back the way I had come.

But not to the station. That was the first place they'd look for me. Instead, I made my way up towards Holborn. If I wanted to lose myself amongst thousands of people, I'd be more likely to find them in the centre of town, and anywhere had to be safer than Farringdon. I was annoyed now that I had dressed in jeans and a jersey. If only I'd put on a hoodie or a baseball cap; anything to cover my head. It's fortunate that writers are very rarely invited on television and it had been at least a year since my last appearance. I shoved my hands in my pockets and stared at the pavement, hoping that nobody would recognise me.

I'd walked for several minutes before I began to ask myself what I was doing. Where did I plan to spend the night? A hotel was out of the question. The front desk would report me before I'd even reached the room. I had various friends in the city, but I wasn't sure I wanted to involve them, possibly getting them into trouble with the police – and anyway, Cara Grunshaw had been holding my wife's mobile phone minutes ago. I wouldn't have put it past her to make a note of all her contacts and then go round door to door. Could I go and stay with my sister in Suffolk? No – that meant train stations and trains.

I'd just reached Chancery Lane when it hit me. I needed somewhere to hide out – a safe house – and there was only one that might open its door to me. Without a second thought, I headed down towards the river, backtracking to Blackfriars Bridge. That was where I felt most exposed, above the water and out in the open, with nobody else on the pavement and dozens of cars speeding past. I could see the lights of Doggett's pub ahead of me. That marked my destination. I quickened my pace, wanting to get this over with. The only question was – would Hawthorne let me in?

He was intensely private. I had only ever been into his flat four or five times throughout my time with him and his hospitality hadn't extended much further than a KitKat in the kitchen . . . although on one occasion he'd offered me a rum and Coke. I didn't even know if he had a spare room. Was it possible that Cara Grunshaw knew where he lived? It was unlikely. Hawthorne would never have given her his address and he didn't own the flat; it belonged to someone overseas. He wasn't paying any rent. There would be no record of his name . . . not on the deeds, perhaps not even on the utility bills. The more I thought about it, the more River Court seemed to be the safest house in London. I was still nervous. Hawthorne hadn't exactly been championing my innocence since this began, but surely he wouldn't turn me away in the night.

I reached the front door and pressed the bell. There was no answer and I was beginning to think that he might be out or asleep or simply refusing to answer, but then, distant and metallic, I heard his voice coming out of the speaker. 'Tony!' I hadn't needed to speak. He'd seen me on the video system. He didn't sound surprised.

I pressed my face against the speaker, injecting as much urgency into my voice as I could muster. 'I need to come in,' I said. 'Cara Grunshaw's at my flat. Kevin texted me. They've got the DNA. They want to arrest me. I need somewhere to stay!'

There was a pause.

'I'm sorry, Tony. But the answer's no.'

My heart sank. I should have known that he wouldn't let me in. At the same time, I realised I'd heard those exact words before and there was something about the way he expressed them, as if he was reminding me of something. And then I remembered. They were exactly the same words I'd used when I'd told him I wasn't going to write any more books. The bastard! He was choosing this moment to have his revenge.

For once, I almost lost it. 'Hawthorne, if you don't allow me into this building, I swear to God I will never speak to you again and you can forget about Alderney. I'll break our contract. I won't write the third book. It'll never happen.'

'I thought you'd already started.'

'I'll tear it up.'

'You sound like you're in a bad mood.'

'Of course I'm in a bad mood! I'm being hunted by the police. Let me in!'

There was another long silence. I wanted to scream. But then came the exhilarating buzz of the electric lock. I pushed and the door opened. I almost fell into the reception area. The lift arrived as I walked towards it and I wondered if Hawthorne had sent it down. I was grateful that there was nobody else around. Nobody had seen me enter. I dived into the lift and travelled alone to the twelfth floor.

Hawthorne was waiting in the corridor. He had changed into another grey V-neck jersey, but otherwise he was wearing the same clothes he'd had on all day. He was looking nervous. 'Move it, mate,' he whispered. 'Someone may see you.'

For half a second, I thought he was being serious. Then I realised that, in his own way, he was enjoying this. I remembered how dismissive he'd been when he first came to Tolpuddle Street. *'The only thing he's ever hit in his life is a computer keyboard.'* The idea of me being a fugitive from justice amused him. And right now, looking up and down the corridor and then stealthily closing the door behind me, he was playing a part.

We went into the living room. I noticed Hawthorne's iPad on the table, surrounded by the intricate pieces of whatever military vehicle he was currently constructing. He must have been reading Harriet Throsby's book when I rang the bell. That was something, anyway. He was still committed to the investigation.

'Hawthorne,' I said, trying to keep my voice steady, 'I need to stay here tonight. I can't go home. Cara Grunshaw was there. She was with my wife! I can't check into a hotel. I've got nowhere else to go.'

He looked at me sadly. 'I'm not sure, mate. If the police have issued a warrant for your arrest, I'd be breaking the law by sheltering you. It might make me an accessory.'

'You're worried about breaking the law?' I nearly screamed at him. 'You got thrown out of the police for pushing a paedophile down a flight of steps, and later on you persuaded him to commit suicide. You regularly hack into the police computer system! You are kidding me, aren't you? Apart from being a detective, you have no respect for the law at all. You've got to help me. I thought we were a team. I've been in hospital twice because of you. All the things we've done together – don't they mean anything to you?'

To my horror, I felt tears pricking at the back of my eyes. It had been another very long day. I couldn't believe that this was where I'd ended up.

'Relax, mate. You want a drink?'

'What have you got?' I prayed it wouldn't be another rum and Coke.

'I think I've got some grappa.'

'Grappa?'

'It's Italian brandy.'

'I know what it is.' I forced myself to calm down. 'Yes, please. I'd love some grappa.'

'Just wait here a minute.'

He left the room and I examined the model in front of me. It was either a tank or some sort of mobile rocket launcher. He hadn't assembled enough for me to be sure and I was in no mood to make sense of the eighty or ninety scattered pieces that remained. The rest of the room was as empty as it had always been. Hawthorne hadn't drawn the curtains. There were no curtains. I could just make out the glint of the River Thames. There must be a full moon, although I hadn't noticed it before.

He returned with a glass of clear liquid and a single lump of ice. He was holding a small bowl in his other hand. He set them both down. 'Here you are, mate. I thought you might like a Twiglet.'

'That's very kind of you.'

There were perhaps a dozen Twiglets in the bowl. They reminded me that I hadn't had dinner and why I was here. 'Hawthorne,' I said. 'Tell me who killed Harriet Throsby.'

He grimaced. 'I wish I could.'

'You must know! We've talked to everyone. We've been to Moxham Heath. You always know by now . . .'

'Well, this one's been tricky. I'll be honest with you. I've got three main suspects.'

'Don't tell me I'm one of them.'

He avoided my eye.

'I don't know why I bother.' I threw back some of the grappa. It was sweet and a little cloying. It burned the back of my throat. The alcohol had no effect on me at all. 'I might as well hand myself in,' I said.

'There's no need to be defeatist.' Hawthorne tried to sound cheery.

'What else can I do? If you're not going to let me stay . . .'

Finally, he seemed to take pity on me. 'Look, mate. I'm not used to having guests overnight. It's just not what I do. And there's only one spare bedroom.'

'I only need one bed!'

'It's not that . . .' He was wrestling with himself. Finally, he seemed to arrive at a decision. 'All right. I'll put you up for one night. But only because it's you. I wouldn't do it for anyone else.'

'Thank you.' I really meant it. I don't think I'd have been physically able to leave.

'You want some dinner?'

'I can't eat.'

'Just as well. There's nothing in the fridge.'

'Hawthorne, please tell me. Three suspects. Two if you don't count me. You must have a good idea . . .'

'Let's talk about this in the morning. I've got an early start.'

'But surely you've got all the facts!'

'Actually, mate, that's exactly the problem. The facts. That's what's been getting in my way. There are too many of them and they can't be right. That's what I need to sort out.'

I had no idea what he was talking about, but he didn't want to say any more and I wasn't going to push my luck by putting more pressure on him. I threw back the rest of the grappa, hoping it would help me sleep, and followed Hawthorne out through the kitchen and into a short corridor on the other side. There were three doors that I'd never seen before.

Hawthorne pointed to the one at the end. 'That's my room. There's a spare bathroom next door. I'll dig out a toothbrush for you. And you'll be in here.'

He opened the nearest door.

'I don't want you talking about how and where I live. All right? And I definitely don't want to read about it in your book.'

'I'm not writing a book.'

He didn't say anything. I went in.

It was his son's room. I saw that at once. The single bed with its Arsenal duvet. The stuffed giraffe. The Marvel superhero posters. The books. Unlike the rest of the flat, it was actually decorated, and suitable for a young boy. The room was small and cosy with a little desk in one corner. The walls were painted blue. There were stars and planets stuck on the ceiling.

I turned to say something to Hawthorne, but he had already gone, closing the door softly behind him. I felt bad that I had forced my way in here. I knew very little about his son, William, but Hawthorne had told me they had a close relationship. He slept over sometimes and it wasn't right, me being here in this room. I saw a photograph in a frame and picked it up. William was a good-looking boy who looked very much like his mother. I had met her once. He had fair hair and an engaging smile. The photograph had been taken at a zoo. William was with Hawthorne, the two of them holding hands, looking at giraffes. Perhaps that was when they had bought the stuffed toy. I wondered who had taken the picture.

It was too late to back out now. I undressed and got into bed. Before I turned out the light, I glanced at the bookshelves that ran the full length of the wall. Hawthorne had once told me that William didn't read my books, but there they all were, or at least fifteen of them: Alex Rider, the Diamond Brothers, my collection of myths and legends, *Granny*, Groosham Grange. They looked well thumbed.

To my surprise, I fell asleep almost at once. I suppose I was mentally and physically exhausted. And my last conscious thought as I lay in that narrow bed, with my feet sticking out from under the duvet, was that I was in Hawthorne's home and that he was also in bed, just a couple of doors away. A lot of strange things had happened in the last four days, but that was the most unlikely of them all.

23
Nothing Personal

I opened my eyes and saw stars. It took me a few moments to remember that they were glued to the ceiling of William's room and that it was his bed I was in. My feet were cold. The duvet only came down to my ankles. I also had a crick in my neck from sleeping in an awkward position, although it was a miracle I'd been able to sleep at all. A large glass of grappa on an empty stomach had obviously had its effect, although it had left an unpleasant taste in my mouth. I should have cleaned my teeth.

I turned over, hearing the springs creak underneath me. Hawthorne had bought his son an old-fashioned metal-framed bed that might have come out of a boarding school or an army camp. For a few moments, I lay there, taking in the complete silence that surrounded me. Every house has its own collection of sounds that become part of its daily rhythm for those who live there. In my Clerkenwell flat it would be the click of the pipework heating up, the whine of the dog waiting for his first walk, the whirr and thud of my wife on her running machine, the voice of Nick Robinson on the radio in the kitchen. Here there was nothing. I listened carefully but there was no movement at all and I wondered if Hawthorne had already left.

I got out of bed and perched on the edge, feeling self-conscious sitting in someone else's room in my T-shirt and shorts. I had no fresh clothes to change into, so I pulled on my jeans and jersey from the day before. Softly I opened the door and peered out into an empty corridor. The door to Hawthorne's bedroom was closed, but the guest bathroom was open and, going in, I found a single towel neatly folded on the toilet seat, with a toothbrush and a tube of toothpaste sitting side by side on top. The bathroom, incidentally, was immaculate, as if it had never been used. Presumably it was there for William when he visited and that told me something about Hawthorne I had known but never fully acknowledged. He was obsessively clean. Perhaps that was the reason he seldom ate out in public: a fear of germs.

I brushed my teeth and washed and then wiped down the sink, using the towel. I came out of the bathroom and softly called out Hawthorne's name. There was no reply. I reached for my phone and checked the time. It was almost nine o'clock. My first instinct was to call Jill and tell her where I was, but I was still nervous of the signal being tracked and decided against it. The last thing I wanted to do was bring

Cara Grunshaw to Hawthorne's door. I made my way down the corridor and into the kitchen. There was nobody there, but I saw that a plate and a bowl had been laid on the table. There were two croissants in a bag and a collection of those miniature cereal boxes you sometimes get in hotels. Hawthorne must have gone out and bought the croissants for me. The cereal, I suspected, was William's.

Hawthorne had left me a newspaper and a note.

Had to go out. Back about eleven. Help yourself to anything in the fridge – don't make calls and don't answer the door! In emergency, find Kevin.

Out of interest, I opened the fridge. There was an unopened carton of milk, a slab of butter and a small jar of marmalade. Nothing else. I'd had almost nothing to eat the day before and I was really hungry. I wolfed down both the croissants and then had a bowl of Crunchy Nut cornflakes, followed by a bowl of Coco Pops. I made myself a coffee and quickly searched through the newspaper. I was relieved to find there was no mention of me. I sat back and thought.

Things were a little better than they had been the night before. I was wanted by the police, but they had no idea where I was. For the time being, I was safe. Hawthorne's note hadn't said as much, but it seemed that he was on the case. Why else would he have gone out so early – and what would he bring with him when he came back? I hoped it would be the identity of the killer.

I folded up the paper. It was slowly dawning on me that I had been handed an amazing opportunity. Since the day I'd met him, I'd been trying to find out more about Hawthorne, but he'd stonewalled me at every turn. I'd managed to speak to a detective inspector who had worked with him, but he hadn't been very informative and he'd charged me £100 for his time. Hawthorne had been forced to talk about himself when we'd been at the Alderney Literary Festival, but he still hadn't given very much away and I wasn't even sure how much of what he had said was true. His almost paranoid secrecy had become more and more annoying as we'd worked our way through three cases and we'd often argued about it. How could I write about him if I didn't know anything about his past? Well, here I was, alone in his home. If I looked around, there must be any number of clues that might fill in the gaps in Hawthorne's life. What had happened in Reeth was number one on the list, but there were all sorts of things I wanted to find out. Where had he been born? Why had he become a policeman? What did he do when he wasn't investigating murders with me? What was the thing with the giraffes?

I sat at the table for a long time, reflecting on the dilemma I found myself in. Hawthorne hadn't invited me here. He had only allowed me in because I was in trouble and had nowhere else to go. I wasn't sure I could abuse his hospitality by ransacking his home. I mean, the first place I might start would be the bedroom. This is where all of us are most exposed. It's where we keep our clothes and underclothes, the books or magazines we read before we sleep, the things that are most personal to us. Even the way we make our bed tells us something about ourselves. Wrinkled sheets and crumpled duvet or puffed-up pillows, novelty cushions and rag dolls? But I already knew that I wouldn't even be able to open the door without despising myself. I might never be able to look at Hawthorne the same way again.

What about his study, then? I'd glanced inside the first time I was in the flat and it surely wouldn't hurt to take a quick look at the business end of things. I went over to the door on the far side of the living room. 'Hawthorne . . . ?' I still called out his name before I went in, knowing there would be no reply. It crossed my mind that there might be security cameras concealed in the flat and that even now Hawthorne or Kevin might be watching me. I tried to look casual. I just need a piece of paper to jot down a few notes about the case – that's what I told my invisible audience. There was no other reason for me to be opening the drawers of his desk. Nothing personal.

The study was exactly how I remembered it – a desk up against a wall, two computers with strange brand names I'd never heard of, different bits of machinery plugged into the various ports and sockets, a tangle of wires. There were no papers or notepads on the surface, just a paperback copy of *The Great Gatsby* with several corners folded down to keep the place. I guessed he was reading it with his book club. I examined the shelves, but his choice of books was too diverse to tell me anything: literary fiction, thrillers, classics . . . everything from Dan Brown to Dostoyevsky. Nothing here by me.

There were eight or nine framed photographs that were more interesting. Half of them were shots of William in different guises – at home, at school, some of them taken with his mother. Hawthorne also had a framed portrait of his wife that stood slightly apart from the rest. This wasn't a casual snap. It had been taken with a great deal of attention to the light, to the shape of her hair, to her pose. It was a picture you would take of somebody you loved. Three more photographs provided an intriguing record of Hawthorne's past life, although they didn't give me very much in the way of facts. Here he was aged about twelve, in short trousers, standing between two adults. One was a uniformed police officer – a sergeant, I think. The other was a woman wearing her Sunday best. His parents? They were both strangely old-fashioned, standing very formally – and they didn't look anything like him. As for Hawthorne, there was already something vaguely otherworldly about him. He was holding their hands, but there was no emotion in his face. It was as if he was simply doing what he was told.

The next image showed Hawthorne now dressed as a police constable, perhaps at some sort of graduation ceremony. He was trying to smile for the camera, but he only managed to look awkward. Physically, he hadn't changed much in twenty years: he had just become more menacing as time passed. And finally, here he was with a man of about his own age, both of them holding glasses. The picture had been taken at a pub – I could make out the umbrellas – with a river in the background. It wasn't the Thames. I got a feeling that this was outside London. I took out my phone and took a picture of the picture. Maybe I could identify the location another time.

I turned my attention to the desk. It had six drawers, but the first two were virtually empty – just odd bits of stationery, more computer accessories, an old phone, a digital recorder. I stopped myself as I reached down to open a third. I was behaving badly and it wasn't even as if I was being rewarded with any concrete information. This was wrong. I deleted the picture I had just taken and went back into the kitchen. The newspaper was waiting for me. I opened it and tried to read.

It was hard to focus on the news when I was worried that I might be news myself. I couldn't stop thinking about Cara Grunshaw and what she might be doing right now. Was it really possible that I might go to prison? What would Jill say? And what about Hilda Sharpe – would she drop me? I turned to the crossword, but, as with the murder of Harriet Throsby, the clues made no sense to me at all. After about an hour, I heard the lift ping open and I briefly thought it might be Hawthorne, back at last. But it was more than one person. I heard two men on the other side of the door. Their voices became more distinct as they walked past.

'River Court is something of a landmark on this part of the river, and being on the twelfth floor, you get the most amazing views.'

Whoever was speaking had the well-educated voice and the smooth enthusiasm of an estate agent showing potential purchasers a flat. I heard a few more words – 'Two bedrooms . . . very private . . .' – and then a door opened and closed further down the corridor and the voices were cut off.

I made myself another coffee and then went back to the crossword – but it was just so many black and white squares. I was beginning to feel nervous. Could something have happened to Hawthorne? It was already ten forty-five and he'd said he would be back at eleven.

There was a knock at the door.

I stood up. I was tempted to open it – but then remembered the instructions Hawthorne had left me on the note.

A second knock. A voice called out: 'Hello?'

A pause, and then I heard a key being inserted into the lock, the door opened and a man walked in.

He was about forty years old, in a suit, with curly hair and a shiny face. On first appearance he seemed overweight, middle-aged, ordinary, standing there with the sort of embarrassment that seems particularly English. I recognised him at once from the photograph in Hawthorne's study. He was the man with the drink. He blinked at me. 'Oh – hello!' he said.

I also recognised his voice. I had heard him walking past the flat. And yet there was something about him that didn't quite fit my image of a London estate agent. He was too old, for a start. From his crooked tie to his unruly hair, there was something careless about the way he presented himself. His brown suede shoes didn't match his grey suit. He was holding a large manila envelope, heavily sealed.

'Hello.' I smiled at him.

'Look, I'm terribly sorry. I didn't mean to bust in. I wasn't expecting to find anyone here.' He waved the envelope vaguely. 'I was going to leave this for Daniel.'

Daniel? I had never heard Hawthorne called that before. 'You can wait for him if you like,' I said. 'He should be back in a minute.'

'Well, I'm not sure . . .' He was clearly surprised to see me, waiting for me to explain myself.

I told him who I was. 'Hawthorne let me stay here last night,' I said. 'We're working together. I'm writing books about him.'

'Yes. I know who you are. I read *The Word Is Murder*. I enjoyed it very much, although I'm not sure you quite captured Daniel . . . at least, the Daniel I know.'

'You're his half-brother?'

Hawthorne had told me that his half-brother was an estate agent who had arranged for him to stay in the flat. It was a guess but an informed one and the man nodded. 'You could say that.'

'You haven't told me your name.'

'Haven't I? How very remiss of me. It's Roland.'

'Roland Hawthorne?'

'Yes. That's right.' He placed the envelope on the table. I could tell that it was quite heavy. It might contain thirty or forty sheets of paper. 'I'll just leave this here. If you could say I called in . . .'

'I'm sure he'd be sorry to miss you.' I gestured at the kettle. 'I was just making coffee. Won't you join me?'

'Well . . .'

I was on my way into the main kitchen area before he could stop me. I clicked the kettle on and spun round. 'Milk?'

'A drop, please. No sugar.'

He sat down reluctantly. I made the coffee as quickly as I could and brought it over to him. 'So you're an estate agent,' I said, adding: 'I heard you go past just now. You were with a client. Did you sell the flat?'

'I'm not selling.'

'Another caretaker, then?' He looked at me blankly. 'Hawthorne mentioned to me that he's looking after this flat for a foreign owner.'

'Is that what he said?'

'Isn't it true?'

'He's certainly helping us out.'

He was already regretting being here, I could tell. So I pressed on before he could make an excuse and leave. 'So what estate agent do you work for, then?'

'It's not exactly an estate agency. We provide more of a creative and business development service.' Why was he being so vague? 'We facilitate things for our clients,' he concluded unhelpfully.

Looking at the envelope and knowing as much as I did about Hawthorne, a thought occurred to me. 'Does Hawthorne work for you?' I asked.

It made sense. He had come to me to write the books because he needed the money. He had been kicked out by the police, so he had to have some way of earning a living, if only to support his less-than-lavish lifestyle. He was a private detective. The police were occasional clients. There had to be others.

'He doesn't work for me. No, no, no. I work full-time for the agency and he works for the agency occasionally and in this instance I'm just . . . sort of . . . the intermediary.' He was visibly tying himself in knots as he tried to explain how he came to be here.

'Is that a job?' I went on, glancing at the brown envelope.

'It is.'

'Someone's been killed?'

'Oh no. Nothing like that. Nothing you'd want to put in one of your books. It's actually quite pedestrian. An errant husband. Wife thinks he's seeing someone else . . . which he might be, although quite what they're doing in Grand Cayman—' He broke off, realising he had already said too much. 'I really ought to be going . . .' he muttered.

'When I asked you if you were his half-brother, you didn't seem sure.'

'Well, I know who he is. And I know who I am. But I'm trying to think. Half-brother is when one of your parents remarries, isn't it? That never happened.'

'You're not blood relatives.' They had no physical similarity.

'That's right.'

'But you have the same surname?' In his own way, Roland was as infuriating as Hawthorne. He didn't want to tell me anything. The only difference was, he was unable to stop himself. 'Are you adopted?' I asked. It was the only possible explanation.

'I'm not! Heavens, no!' He let out a snuffle of laughter.

'So he is?'

Roland was immediately serious again. 'It's quite private, you know. He doesn't really like to talk about it.'

'Your parents adopted him.'

The two people in the photograph. The police constable and his formally dressed wife. It didn't surprise me at all that Hawthorne had been adopted. It put everything I knew about him – right down to the Airfix models – in perspective. So why had he called Roland his half-brother? I suppose he didn't want to give too much away.

'That's right. I don't really think of him as an adoptive brother, though. I'd say we're closer than that. He's a marvellous man. We've known each other all our lives.'

'What happened to his own parents?' Roland was squirming, his coffee forgotten. I could see him eyeing the door, planning his escape. 'I think Hawthorne mentioned they lived in Reeth?' I was lying. Hawthorne had said nothing of the sort. I was fishing.

Roland took the bait. 'In Yorkshire. Yes.'

'And they died?'

'If they hadn't died, he wouldn't have needed adopting.'

'That's true, of course. It was very sad.'

'A terrible business.'

'How did they die?'

It was one question too many and I'd asked it too directly. I saw his eyelids come down like shutters. 'I really can't talk about it.' He got to his feet. 'Actually, I'd best be off. A great pleasure to meet you, Anthony. Daniel's told me a lot about you. Perhaps you can tell him I looked in.'

But there was no need. Just then the door opened and Hawthorne was there, looking suspiciously from Roland to me. Then he relaxed. 'Roland!' he said. He was more friendly as he greeted his adoptive brother.

'Oh – hello, Daniel. Everything all right?' He picked up the envelope. 'Morton asked me to drop this in for you. The Barraclough file.'

Hawthorne took it. 'You met Tony, then.'

'Yes. He just introduced himself. I was rather surprised to find him here.'

'He's hiding from the police.'

'Oh. That would explain it, then.'

'You stopping for a coffee?'

'Just had one, thanks all the same. Best be on my way!' He turned to me. 'I may pop in and see your play next week. *Mindgame*. It looks interesting.'

'It may not be on,' Hawthorne said.

'Oh. That's a shame. Well, goodbye!'

He left. Hawthorne and I were alone. 'Who's Morton?' I asked, casually. Hawthorne didn't reply. He wasn't showing any emotion, but I thought he might be angry. 'I didn't let Roland in,' I said. 'He had a key.'

'You been all right on your own?'

'Yes. Thank you for the croissants. And the Coco Pops.'

He didn't know how long Roland had been here. He didn't know that we'd been talking about him. I'd left no trace of my visit to his study. I saw him glance at the kitchen table with the coffee cups and the newspaper spread open on the surface. He decided to let it go. 'We should make a move,' he said.

'Where?'

'The Vaudeville Theatre.'

I'm not sure what it was about the way he said that, but suddenly I knew. 'Have you worked out who killed Harriet Throsby?' I asked.

He nodded. 'That's right, mate. They're waiting for us there.'

24

Back to the Vaudeville

Hawthorne didn't speak to me as we crossed Blackfriars Bridge, the river glittering beneath us in the sunshine.

He hadn't mentioned Roland and I was sensible enough not to ask him any more questions about his adoptive brother – or whatever Roland wanted to call himself. From the way he walked – his shoulders hunched, his eyes fixed on the road ahead – he seemed to be in a hurry to reach our destination and put this whole business behind us. He obviously regretted ever having let me into his flat and knew that I had managed to get through some of his defences.

And what exactly had I learned? That he had been born in Reeth. His parents had died, presumably at the same time and so, I would imagine, in traumatic circumstances. A car crash? As a result, he had been adopted by a serving police officer. He was the classic private detective, working part-time for an agency possibly run by a man called Morton. The nature of the agency was still a mystery. It clearly had some sort of connection with River Court. It appeared that Hawthorne was not caretaking the flat as he had told me. He was there for another reason.

I would make sense of it all later. Right now I had other thoughts on my mind. Hawthorne had worked out the identity of Harriet's killer! We were on our way to meet him (or her) at the Vaudeville Theatre. I tried to imagine who might be waiting for us in the foyer and pictured them, one at a time. Ahmet with one of his American cigarettes. Maureen in her fur wrap. Martin Longhurst, tall and twitchy. Then I remembered something Hawthorne had said to Roland just before we left. My play might have come off by the following week. Did that mean one of the cast members was about to be arrested? Or Ewan Lloyd, the director?

We reached the other side of the bridge and turned into the Strand. 'Where were you this morning?' I asked.

Hawthorne took a few more steps before answering. 'I went over to Petty France,' he said.

That was in Westminster. It was where a number of government offices were located. I remembered that the Passport Office had been in the same street, although even assuming they were still there, they would surely be closed on a Saturday. 'Is that where you found the answer?' I asked.

'It was where I found what I expected to find.'

'Well, I'm glad that's sorted, then.' I hated it when he was so cryptic.

The theatre was ahead of us. As far as I could see, the play was still running. In fact, there would be a matinée performance at three o'clock that afternoon. Hawthorne opened the front door for me. I went into the foyer . . .

. . . and stood there with my heart pounding, my stomach shrinking and a sense of complete despair as DI Cara Grunshaw and DC Mills lurched towards me. Grunshaw was grinning victoriously. Her assistant was contenting himself with an unpleasant smirk. They had both been expecting me.

'So you kept your word,' Grunshaw said. She was talking to Hawthorne.

'Hawthorne—!' I couldn't believe he had done this to me.

'I'm sorry, mate. Detective Grunshaw called me this morning. Somehow, she'd worked out where you were – which is surprising as working things out has never been her strong suit – and she made it clear to me. I can't be seen to be obstructing the course of justice.'

'But I thought we were friends!'

'I'll come and visit you in jail.'

'I'm not going to jail. I didn't kill anyone.' I was close to tears. It wasn't just the notion of being charged with a crime I hadn't committed. It was Hawthorne lying to me, leading me into a trap.

'I saw your play last night,' Cara said. 'I took Mills. What did you think of it, Derek?'

'Not a lot,' Mills said.

'I quite enjoyed it myself. I think Harriet Throsby was very unfair. In fact, I might have been tempted to murder her myself if I'd been the writer. Anyway, shall we get the formalities over and done with?'

'You do not have to say anything—' Mills began. It was the second time he had given me an official police caution.

'Hold on a minute,' Hawthorne cut in. 'I think you're forgetting our deal, Cara.'

'What deal?' I grasped at the straw. Maybe they were going to let me run away.

'Thirty minutes. I explain how it all happened. Then you make the arrest.'

'We know how it happened,' Cara growled.

'That was still the deal we made.'

She sighed. Her ample chest rose and fell. 'All right then, Hawthorne. But I haven't got all day.'

'Not here,' Hawthorne said. 'Inside.'

'In the theatre? I didn't have you pegged as a drama queen, but I don't mind sitting down. I've been on my feet since breakfast and they're killing me. Let's get on with it.'

We went down the stairs, back into the auditorium and down the red carpet to the condemned cell . . . that was how it felt. But when we entered the stalls, I stopped in surprise. I looked past the long stretch of empty seats to the stage. The curtain was up and there were nine people waiting for us on the set of *Mindgame*, some of them sitting on the furniture used in the play, others perched on plastic seats that had been brought from backstage. Absurdly, the human skeleton that was part of the action stood in the corner.

The cast was on one side: Jordan Williams next to Sky Palmer, then Tirian Kirke. Ewan Lloyd was nearby but on his own. Ahmet Yurdakul and Maureen Bates came next, sitting side by side, uncomfortably close, on a sofa. Martin Longhurst, their accountant, was behind them. Arthur Throsby and his daughter, Olivia, had also been summoned to the theatre and were over by the window that during the play turned into a wall. They must have been waiting for us for some time and weren't looking too pleased as the four of us made our way down the aisle. That was when I noticed that Keith, the deputy stage-door manager, had been summoned too. He was sitting, half-hidden, in the wings.

We reached the front of the stage.

'You stay here,' Hawthorne said. He was addressing Grunshaw and Mills. He turned to me. 'You come with me, Tony.'

A flight of steps had been placed against the apron. While the two detectives settled themselves into the first row of the stalls, we climbed up. I noticed an empty chair had been placed centre stage, presumably for me. I sat in it. I was aware of everyone examining me and kept my gaze fixed on the empty auditorium, the invisible audience somehow more unnerving than a real one, all those imagined eyes watching me. Meanwhile, Hawthorne had taken off his coat. He was completely at ease, even enjoying himself. But then in his own way he always had been a performer. He was in his element.

'Thank you all for coming,' he began. 'I know it was a bit short notice, but Detective Inspector Grunshaw here only works until lunchtime on Saturdays.'

'What is this all about?' Jordan asked. Typically, he was more annoyed than anyone else.

'Well, obviously, it's about the murder of Harriet Throsby. We haven't come here to rehearse. All of you were involved, one way or another, and I thought you might like to know how it happened.'

'Do you know who killed my wife?' Arthur Throsby asked.

He was considerably less mournful than he had been just two days ago when we had first met. He was wearing brand-new clothes, for a start: a colourful blazer and tie. He'd had a haircut. It seemed to me that he'd not only got used to his wife's death, he had adapted to it and perhaps even found that it suited him. Next to him, Olivia was quiet, clearly nervous.

'I wouldn't have called you all here if I didn't,' Hawthorne replied.

He hadn't even started and Grunshaw and Mills were already looking bored.

'If you'll forgive me, Mr Hawthorne, why do we all have to be here?' It was Tirian who was speaking. 'It's the weekend. We have two performances today. There are other places I'd rather be.'

'I'm sorry to have spoiled your morning,' Hawthorne said, not sounding sorry at all. 'There are still a few questions that have to be answered by all of you. The funny thing about this murder is that it's much more complicated than it needs to be. Someone knocked on the door at Palgrove Gardens and killed Mrs Throsby. I think it's fair to say that every single one of you on this stage had a good reason to wish her dead.'

'How dare you say that!' Arthur Throsby remarked, although he didn't sound particularly outraged. 'Do you really think that Olivia or myself—'

'Forget it, Dad!' Olivia interrupted her father. 'Of course we're both suspects. We both hated her.'

'But I wasn't at home when it happened. I was at school.'

'I've talked to your school,' Hawthorne remarked. 'You had no lesson from nine thirty to ten fifteen. You told us nobody would have seen you if you'd left, but in fact it would have been easy. You had your bicycle. Ten minutes each way and two minutes to get rid of her . . .'

Arthur Throsby fell silent. 'I didn't touch her!' he muttered.

Hawthorne was unmoved. 'Any one of you could have done it,' he continued. 'And as it happens, none of you can fully account for your movements at the time she died. Easy enough to slip out of Starbucks without being noticed.' That was Olivia. 'You could have gone on a cigarette break.'

'I don't smoke,' Olivia said.

Hawthorne ignored this. 'Martin Longhurst has ninety minutes unaccounted for between leaving this theatre and arriving at his office. We don't know where Jordan Williams was at that time.'

'You didn't ask me,' Jordan protested.

'You want me to ask you now?'

'I was at home, in bed.'

'I wish people wouldn't tell so many lies. It does make my job very difficult.' Hawthorne shook his head sadly. 'But we'll get to all that in a minute. The point is, the crime itself was very straightforward and, more than that, the killer was obvious from the start. He'd threatened Harriet on the night of the party and he'd made it clear that he thought she should be dead. He knew where she lived. He was seen on CCTV near her flat. He used a murder weapon that could only have belonged to him and he stupidly left his fingerprints on the hilt. He dropped a hair at the scene of the crime and he managed to get some cherry blossom, identical to the sort that grows in Palgrove Gardens, on his coat. Worse still, it turns out that Harriet may not have been the only theatre critic he's killed.'

'Who are you talking about?' Sky Palmer asked.

'I think you all know who I mean.'

'He's talking about Anthony,' Cara Grunshaw called out, her voice expanding into the great emptiness around her. 'So if you've said your piece, Hawthorne, maybe we can arrest him and everyone can go home.'

There was a brief silence. I could feel everyone looking at me.

'I always knew it was him,' Maureen said. She turned to Ahmet. 'The first time he walked into the office, I warned you against him. All the violence in that play! You can't write things like that without being disturbed.'

'That's not true,' Ewan remarked, unexpectedly taking my side. 'Shakespeare wrote some extremely violent tragedies. Look at the blinding of Gloucester in *King Lear* or the multiple killings in *Titus Andronicus*, some of them utterly disgusting, and yet—'

'I think we can manage without a lecture in English drama, thanks all the same,' Hawthorne cut in. 'The point is, if it was Tony, why are there still so many unanswered questions?'

'What unanswered questions?' Cara demanded.

'I can think of half a dozen straight off.' Hawthorne counted them out on his fingers.

'Why were there three broken cigarettes in the dustbin in the green room? Why did Ewan Lloyd have a premonition that something bad was going to happen as he left the theatre that night? Why was a light bulb deliberately broken on the ground floor? How did Sky Palmer manage to read Harriet's review when it hadn't been posted on the internet? Why did Jordan Williams lie about the time he left the theatre and why did Maureen Bates agree to help him?'

'I did nothing of the sort!' Maureen sniffed.

'But let's imagine for a minute that, as improbable as it sounds, DI Grunshaw got it wrong and Tony didn't commit the murder. Now we've got another, bigger question to consider. Why did someone deliberately set out to frame him? A lot of the evidence is circumstantial. The CCTV camera only shows someone wearing a jacket that's similar to Tony's. There are actually quite a few Yoshino cherry trees in different parts of London including, as it happens, one in St John's Gardens, which is where he walks his dog. Did he know Harriet's address? Perhaps not. But the knife with his fingerprints and a strand of his hair found on the body. There's no arguing with that. Either he was incredibly clumsy or they were deliberately planted. So what had he done to upset anyone so much that they wanted to see him in jail?'

'He wrote the play,' Tirian said.

'That seems a bit harsh,' Hawthorne replied. 'Like killing Harriet because she wrote a bad review. Maybe I'm biased, but I don't believe Tony did it and I certainly don't think he did it because he was pissed off by a review.

'And here's the last thing. How many murders are we investigating here? Harriet Throsby was the start. But she also wrote a book about a teacher who was killed in Wiltshire and it turns out that one of the killers was Martin Longhurst's kid brother, Stephen.'

'You have absolutely no right to bring Stephen into this.' Longhurst leaned forward in his chair, speaking for the first time. 'It's bad enough dragging me into your petty accusations, Mr Hawthorne. But Stephen was the victim in all this and you should leave him out of it. He's completely irrelevant.'

'I would have said Philip Alden was the victim,' Hawthorne replied. 'He was the one who ended up dead with his skull caved in. And as for relevance, let's not forget that Harriet Throsby wrote a very nasty book about your parents and what happened in Moxham Heath. You told us that you blame her for the break-up of their marriage and the impact that had on your life. You also blamed Frank Heywood, the drama critic of the Bristol *Argus*. He knew Harriet and brought her into your lives. He fed her the information she needed. And that brings us to our third death, because he was killed too, apparently by food poisoning in an Indian restaurant. That was a very long time ago and we'll never be sure, but maybe it wasn't quite the accident it seemed.'

'I've never heard of Frank Heywood,' Grunshaw complained.

'That's because you haven't done your job,' Hawthorne returned. 'You might have asked yourself why Harriet had her book out on the morning of her death. *Bad Boys: Life and Death in an English Village*. Maybe she was trying to tell somebody something.

'You see what I'm getting at? All these complications! Quite frankly, it does my head in.'

Hawthorne fell silent.

When, after a lengthy pause, he still hadn't continued, it was Derek Mills who called out from the stalls. 'So if it wasn't Tony, do you know who did kill Harriet?'

'Oh yes.' Hawthorne smiled. 'That bit is easy.'

25
Final Act

'You know what I never understood?' Hawthorne asked. 'As I've said, every single person on this stage had a good reason to kill Harriet Throsby. But why frame Tony? I mean, that's just stupid. Not only is he completely harmless, but it's obvious he wouldn't commit a murder. At least, it's obvious to everyone apart from DI Grunshaw and DC Mills. If anyone was going to be framed, it should have been Jordan Williams. He was the one most upset by the review and he announced it in front of everyone. "*I'll kill her, I swear to you ... Someone should put a knife in her!*"

'And here's another thing. Why use Tony's knife? If Harriet Throsby had been stabbed with a kitchen knife, there could have been a million and one suspects. Anyone in London could have killed her. But by using one of the *Macbeth* daggers, the killer narrowed the number of suspects down to the people who are here today.' Hawthorne swept his hand across the whole group of us. 'Only one of you sitting in this theatre could have got your hands on the *Macbeth* dagger.'

'I couldn't have got it,' Olivia said.

'That's true,' Hawthorne agreed. 'But someone could have got it for you.'

'And who might that have been?'

'Your friend, Sky Palmer.'

'We hardly know each other.'

'Really?' Hawthorne went over to her. 'When we were at your home, you told your dad he didn't need to pretend any more.'

'So what?'

'So why are you still pretending now? What are you afraid of? Your mum isn't here to call you out any more.'

'What are you talking about?' Arthur Throsby demanded.

It was Sky Palmer who answered. 'He's talking about me.' She stood up and went over to Olivia, resting her hands on her shoulders. 'You might as well tell him. He knows.'

Olivia glanced briefly at her father, then placed one of her own hands on Sky's. 'We're together,' she said, simply.

Sky glared at Hawthorne. 'Who told you?'

'Nobody needed to tell me. It might have just been a coincidence that Olivia was wearing a T-shirt printed with a well-known gay icon at the first-night party. But obviously the two of you were close. She'd been round to your place loads of times.'

'I never said that,' Sky protested.

'No. But when we met at the theatre you mentioned all the CCTV cameras along the canal, which meant you knew the flat was near one. And you must have been there because you'd seen them.' Sky said nothing, so he went on. 'Why else would Olivia have bust into her mum's computer and sent you the review? I did wonder why you were hiding your relationship – I mean, these days, two girls like you should be out having a nice time – but it all made sense when I talked to Harriet's old editor in Bristol. He said that Harriet slated the first play she ever reviewed because she hated gay relationships. I could imagine that would have made life awkward for you.'

These last words had been addressed to Olivia, who nodded. 'I couldn't tell her. It would have been more trouble than it was worth.'

'I hate to say this, but it does give you both a real reason to want to do away with her.'

Sky looked Hawthorne straight in the eye. 'I can't disagree with that.' She dragged another chair from the side and sat down next to Olivia.

Hawthorne walked back to the centre of the stage.

'It's a funny thing about you theatre people,' he went on, 'but nothing is ever straightforward, is it! These two aren't the only ones lying about their relationships. What about Jordan and Maureen? Now there's an odd couple if ever I saw one.'

'What are you insinuating?' Maureen was outraged.

'Don't worry, darling. I know you two haven't been to bed together. But are you going to tell me you're not just a little bit in love with him?' Maureen made no reply, so he went on. 'When we were in your office, you leapt in to defend him – what he'd said about Harriet in the green room at the theatre. He was joking. He didn't mean it. You wouldn't even consider that he might have killed her, even though secretly you believed that he'd made good on his threat and done exactly that.'

'How can you possibly know that?'

'Because he'd asked you to cover up for him the night before the murder and you'd agreed. He never actually left the theatre. You know that. You lied to the police . . . and to me.'

'Leave her alone!' This was Jordan Williams, getting angrily to his feet.

'Are you going to deny it, Jordan?' Hawthorne smiled. 'We know you'd been arguing with your wife. We know she didn't come to the first night. And there were a whole load of clothes in your dressing room . . . You'd even brought along your wedding photograph – the two of you outside Islington Registry Office. You'd had a fight, hadn't you? You had nowhere else to go, so you were camping out at the theatre.'

'This has nothing to do with the death of Harriet Throsby!'

'No? You threaten to kill her – and the night before it happens, you ask Maureen to lie on your behalf—'

'I didn't!'

'—and she agrees because she must have met you when you were playing Mr Mistoffelees in *Cats*. Maybe it was you who met her backstage that night when she saw it for the hundredth time.'

Jordan took a breath. 'It was,' he admitted.

'He was brilliant!' Even now, Maureen couldn't resist a whisper of excitement.

'Which is why you could be sure she'd agree to sign you out of the theatre that night.' Before anyone could interrupt, Hawthorne went on. 'Keith didn't really know who was entering and leaving. He didn't see Tony leave either.'

'I can't see everything!' Keith complained, still half concealed in the wings.

Hawthorne ignored him. 'It was easy enough for Maureen to register that you had left five minutes before her, at ten to one. She made just one mistake. Everyone else had used the twelve-hour clock. You yourself had written that you'd arrived at ten thirty p.m. But she used the twenty-four-hour clock. She arrived at twenty-three twenty-five and left an hour and a half later at zero fifty-five. And she wrote down zero fifty for you.'

'I was there all night,' Jordan admitted in a hoarse voice. 'Jayne and I had had a stupid row – maybe that was why I was so emotional about the review. After the party, I went back to my dressing room and fell asleep almost at once. It had been a long day and I was exhausted. The next morning,

I slipped out, using the fire exit downstairs. I went straight home and – Jayne will tell you – I was there by half past ten . . .'

'Still enough time to make a detour via Little Venice.'

'I wasn't thinking about Harriet Throsby! I wanted to see my wife . . . to apologise for the things I'd said.'

'All of you were thinking about Harriet Throsby! We already know about Martin Longhurst and her book. Her review was the first nail in the coffin for Ahmet and his production company, and Maureen wouldn't have been too happy about that either. Tirian would have had his career screwed if she'd repeated the comments she'd heard him making about Christopher Nolan . . .'

I thought Hawthorne had dismissed this when I had suggested it to him. But maybe he was just trying to needle Tirian. It worked. 'That's ridiculous!' Tirian snapped. 'She couldn't have heard a word I was saying, and why would I care if she did? It was a private conversation. She wouldn't have been allowed to write about it.'

'And then there's Ewan,' Hawthorne went on. 'He had a particular loathing for Harriet because of what she'd written about his production of *Saint Joan*.'

'That was a long time ago,' Ewan said.

'Yes. But as you told us, she chose her words very carefully and she deliberately baited you when you met at the party. It was as if she was mocking you. "*Those big hotels don't exactly light my fire.*" Given that you're now in a relationship with the actress who suffered those injuries, it would hardly be surprising if you were goaded into taking revenge.'

'Sonja and I have learned to live with what happened. Harriet meant nothing to me.'

'So you say.' Hawthorne sounded doubtful.

'You've been talking for a long time, Hawthorne. Is this actually going anywhere?' The interruption came from the stalls, of course, from Cara Grunshaw.

Hawthorne beamed down at her. 'Don't worry if you're finding it hard to follow, Cara. I'll go through it all again later.' He turned back. 'We all know where we are now,' he concluded. 'But before I can tell you who killed Harriet, we need to look at the other two deaths: Frank Heywood and Major Philip Alden. Both of those men were connected to Harriet, so you have to ask – did they in some way inform her murder all these years later?

'Let's start with Heywood, the drama critic who supposedly died of a heart attack after eating a dodgy lamb curry at a restaurant called the Jai Mahal. He was a close friend of Harriet's and it may even be that they were having an affair. That's what Adrian Wells, her editor, believed. He also told us, by the way, that she always got what she wanted, which I think we already knew, but it does make me ask – if she wanted to take over as drama critic, did she also want him dead?

'I can't be certain. This all happened years ago and there are no witnesses. The police never suspected foul play, but then why would they even have looked? Both Harriet and Frank were poisoned. The restaurant was well known for its dodgy cuisine. Anyway, Frank died of a heart attack.

'But one thing we do know. Harriet chose the restaurant. Wells told us that when we met him. She knew it had a bad reputation, so why did she want to go there? And here's something else to consider. When she was writing her first book, *No Regrets*, she managed to get close to the main suspect, a man called Dr Robert Thirkell who was eventually arrested for poisoning a series of old ladies using rat poison – active ingredient, arsenic. Is it too far-fetched to suppose that she might have got a couple of doses from him just in case she might need it one day?'

'Are you saying that my wife might have killed Frank Heywood?' Arthur Throsby demanded.

'That's exactly what I'm saying,' Hawthorne replied. 'A big dose for him. A smaller one for her. The curry will disguise the taste. And the restaurant will get the blame. Do you really think it so unlikely?'

Arthur Throsby thought for a moment, then he gave a sniff of laughter. 'I wouldn't put it past her!' he exclaimed. 'She was capable of anything, my Harriet. If she slept with him, it was only because she wanted something from him.' He thought back. 'You know, it's very strange, but now that I think about it, I remember walking into her bedroom the next day, after she'd been released from hospital. She was sitting up in bed, writing Frank's obituary for the *Argus*.'

'What was so strange about that?' Olivia asked.

'He hadn't died yet.'

There was a shocked silence.

'So much for Frank Heywood,' Hawthorne continued. 'But what about Philip Alden? There's no mystery about who was responsible for his death, even if the whole truth has never really come out. It was Stephen Longhurst who thought up the trick that killed him because it was Stephen Longhurst who really hated him.' Hawthorne approached Martin Longhurst. 'Did you know the truth about your brother, Mr Longhurst? That he was the one in charge, not the other boy?'

'I only knew what my parents told me.'

'Your parents, or their lawyers, bribed one of the witnesses. They perverted the course of justice. A poor little kid got the bigger sentence – ten years in jail – when it should have been Stephen who took the rap.'

'I had no idea.'

'Why did you go back to the school? Why did you pretend you were going to send your own children there?'

'I can't answer that, Mr Hawthorne.' Longhurst bowed his head. 'All my life, I've been haunted by what happened at Moxham Heath Primary School. It tore my family apart. Even if Harriet hadn't written her book, it would have destroyed us. I just wanted to see where it happened, to try to understand. I couldn't explain myself to the head teacher, so I made up a story about my own children. I suppose you could say I was trying to lay a ghost to rest.'

'I'd like you to know, incidentally, that I did write to you,' I said. I couldn't resist chipping in, even if no one on the stage had a clue what I was talking about.

Nor did Martin Longhurst. He looked at me blankly. 'I'm sorry?'

'The head teacher said you used to read my books. You wrote to me and you didn't get a reply.'

'No.' He scowled. 'She's got that wrong. It wasn't you. It was Michael Morpurgo.'

'Oh.' I felt my cheeks burning and twisted in my seat.

Fortunately, Hawthorne had already moved to the front of the stage, working his way towards the final act. 'Are you still awake, Cara?' he called out.

'This had better be good, Hawthorne.'

He turned his back on her.

'The reason Harriet Throsby was killed had nothing to do with the play and nothing to do with Tony,' he said. 'The big mistake I made at the start was to believe that somebody had tried to frame him. His hair. His dagger. That made no sense at all. Worse than that, it twisted the whole crime out of shape. I should have listened to my instincts, which told me he was irrelevant. But it was only after I'd talked to all of you that I got the complete picture and realised what had happened.

'Jordan Williams had said he wanted to murder Harriet Throsby. He'd shouted it out in front of everyone. So it made complete sense for the killer to frame him. But that's what went wrong. Tony was a mistake.

'Think what happened on the night of the party. Tony arrives, soaking wet, and Jordan hands him a towel.'

'I dried my hair!' I said.

'Yes, mate, and at your age you're losing some of it too. Later on, someone went into Jordan's dressing room and picked a hair off his towel, thinking it was Jordan's. But in fact they took yours. Simple as that.'

'And they left it on the body!'

'Yes. As for the knife, that was another mistake. Keith came down and took Jordan's dagger and carried it over to the sink. Meanwhile, Tony had left his own dagger somewhere in plain sight and, once again, the killer took it, thinking it was Jordan's. Of course, the killer was careful not to add his own fingerprints to the hilt and since nobody else had handled it from the moment Tony unwrapped it from the tissue paper – wiping it clean at the same time – only his own fingerprints appeared.

'So the question we have to ask ourselves is not who would want to frame Tony, but who might have had it in for Jordan? And I think everyone here knows the answer to that.'

Suddenly, he was standing in front of Tirian.

'I like you, Tirian,' he said. 'I sort of feel sorry for you. But I've got to tell you. I know everything.'

'No. You can't.'

'I wish it could be otherwise, mate. But you can't hide any more. I know.'

Tirian gazed at him for what felt a very long time. Then, to my astonishment, tears appeared in his eyes and when he spoke again he sounded almost like a child. 'But I was so clever!' he wailed. 'I got it all right!'

'That's not quite true. You mucked up with the hair and the weapon, just for a start.'

'Apart from that!' The tears were flowing freely down his cheeks.

At once, Cara Grunshaw was on her feet. 'Tirian Kirke killed Harriet Throsby?' she exclaimed.

'Well done, Cara! You got there in the end!' Hawthorne smiled at her. 'You just needed a bit of help.'

'But why? Because she didn't like the play?'

'Haven't you been listening? How many times do I have to tell you? It had nothing to do with *Mindgame*.'

'Then . . . why?'

Tirian was slumped in his chair, silent, crying. He hadn't even tried to deny what Hawthorne was saying. The other actors, Martin Longhurst, Ahmet and especially Maureen were staring at him in horror.

'Let's start with the night of the party,' Hawthorne suggested, calmly. 'Tirian had decided to kill Harriet before he even left the theatre. We'll come to the reason in a minute. When Jordan Williams made his death threat, it provided Tirian with an opportunity he couldn't ignore. Jordan would be the scapegoat. Easy enough to nip upstairs and nick one of his hairs off a brush or a towel – but he also needed the dagger with Jordan's fingerprints. That would be the clincher.

'He was the first to leave the green room – at about twenty minutes past midnight. He signed out at twelve twenty-five. But he knew he'd have to come back when the theatre was locked for the night and there was only one way in: the fire exit, which only opened from the inside. So what he did was, he nicked a packet of Ahmet's cigarettes, which he was going to use as a wedge. He'd push the bar to open the door into the alleyway and then slide the packet underneath to make sure it never completely shut.

'But he had a problem. He knew that Keith was sitting in front of the TV screens in the stage-door office and the lights in the basement corridor were too bright. When he opened the door, light would spill outside and there was a good chance that Keith would see it – even on a black-and-white TV, a shaft of light is one thing you can't miss – and maybe he'd come to investigate. So he nipped upstairs, probably stole the hair from Jordan's dressing room at that time, and then smashed a light bulb.' Hawthorne glanced at me. 'He didn't do it to darken the corridor. He was just creating a diversion. Immediately afterwards, he ran back down and opened the fire door while Keith was dealing with the broken glass. Now everything was set up. He waited a moment or two, went back upstairs and left through the stage door – making sure he chatted with Keith so that everything would look normal.

'He didn't take the train to Blackheath. At least, not then. He came back to the theatre in the middle of the night, by which time he assumed everyone had left – although he didn't realise that Jordan was sound asleep in his dressing room. That didn't matter. He snuck back in through the fire exit, chucked the crumpled packet into the bin and stole the first dagger he saw, which happened to be the wrong one. Incidentally, one person noticed that the fire exit was open when they left the green room. That was Ewan Lloyd. He told me that he had a chill at the back of his neck – he thought it was some sort of premonition. He didn't realise . . . It was a cold night and all he'd felt was the draft from the slightly open door.

'The next morning, Tirian went round to Harriet's home. He'd got the address from an article in a magazine. She wasn't surprised to see him. She'd been expecting him.'

'How do you know?' Arthur asked.

'Because of the three books on her table. She was killed in the hall, so she must have taken them off the shelf before he arrived. They were her credentials, if you like. All three of them were a reminder of her days as a crime reporter, but the one that was actually relevant was *Bad Boys*. That was what she would have shown him if she'd lived a few minutes more.'

Hawthorne took a breath. Tirian was still crying. I had watched Hawthorne expose several killers in my time with him, but I had never witnessed such a complete collapse.

Part of me felt sorry for him, but at the same time there was something quite horrible about it. Harriet Throsby had described him as childish in her review. She'd obviously seen something that I hadn't.

'So that was how it was done. But I'm sure all of you – especially Cara – want to know why.'

'Don't push your luck, Hawthorne,' Cara growled.

'To understand that, we have to go back to the party itself. Tony described it all very precisely for me. It was almost like I was there.

'Harriet Throsby, of course, *was* there. She made a habit of crashing first-night parties because she liked screwing with people's heads. I think we all know by now that she had a malicious streak as wide as the Gulf of Mexico. There are two more things we have to remember about her. Ewan has already explained how she used words like weapons. She expressed herself in a way that was deliberately hurtful. That thing about lighting her "fire", for example. And there was something else. Tony told me that she was avoiding his eye when she was talking to him. She was "*looking over my shoulder as if hoping someone more interesting had come into the room.*" That's what he said. And he was half-right.

'She wasn't talking to him. She was talking to Tirian. And once you understand that, everything falls into place.

'What did she say? "*I never forget a face.*" She was pretending to be talking about an actor in some thriller she'd seen on the stage. But I bet you she was looking right into

Tirian's eyes then. And a moment later, Olivia mentioned Tony's Alex Rider books, and how did she describe them? "*They were stories about a young assassin.*" That's not quite true. They're about a young spy. So why that description?'

'She recognised me!' Tirian sobbed out the words.

'That's right. And just to make sure you knew that she knew, she even had to rub it in when she wrote her review. Not once but three times. "*Most disappointing for me is Tirian Kirke, whom I recognised from the first time I saw him . . .*" There you are. She's telling him she knows who he is. "*His performance is quite childish.*" Odd choice of word, don't you think? Childish. But then, she'd known him when he was a child. And that last line: " . . . *surprisingly, he is completely unconvincing when things turn violent.*" Why surprisingly? Unless Harriet knew that he had committed an act of violence in which a man had died . . .'

'So who is he?' Derek Mills had also got to his feet and was leaning against the front of the stage.

'Do you want me to tell them, Tirian?' Hawthorne asked.

Tirian nodded, unable to speak.

'His real name is Wayne Howard.'

Martin Longhurst stood up, his own seat falling backwards and crashing to the floor. 'He and Stephen—'

'That's right.' Hawthorne was merciless. 'He's the boy your parents stitched up for the death of Philip Alden. Wayne and Stephen were best friends in Moxham Heath and it was your brother who inspired him to choose the name he uses now. When Stephen was on trial, he had a Narnia book with him. *The Lion, the Witch and the Wardrobe*. According to the gardener, the two boys used to meet by a statue outside Moxham Hall. That's another lion – and in the book, lots of animals are turned into stone. Stephen called his horse Bree. He appears in the fifth Narnia book – *The Horse and His Boy*. And while we're on the subject of horses, take a look at Tirian. He's got a crooked nose, which he must have broken at some time in his life. I think he got that when he fell off a horse at Moxham Hall after Stephen persuaded him to take a ride.'

'Tirian Kirke . . . ?' I was trying to remember where I'd come across that name.

'King Tirian is a character in *The Last Battle*. I know all the Narnia books because I've read them with my son. And Digory Kirke turns up in three of them! When I first heard the name, I thought there was something dodgy about it. That's why I asked him where it came from, but it was only when we went to Moxham Heath that I got the full significance.'

'Wait a minute!' I hated breaking in again, but there was one thing I had to know. 'You're saying that Tirian Kirke is really Wayne Howard. But you told me that you'd checked him out and everything he'd told us about himself was true.'

'No, mate. I said I'd done a search on him and that everything he'd told us checked out. That's not the same. His whole life story was fake. And for what it's worth, that puzzled me too. When Tirian was telling us about himself, why did he have to throw in so many facts? The car accident that killed his parents involved a delivery truck. His aunt lived in Harrogate in a converted vicarage on the Otley Road, five minutes from the town centre. His drama teacher was called Miss Havergill . . . and so on. It was like he was blinding us with science. I told you when you were at my place – there were too many facts and they couldn't be right.'

'He made it all up!'

'No! Wayne Howard had been in the newspapers. He was the subject of a book. When he was finally released, he had to be protected and that was the job of MAPP: Multi-Agency Public Protection. They would have been the ones who set him up with a completely new identity, starting with his choice of a new name. There was no way he could go back to Moxham Heath – but he did have a relative in Harrogate, which is why he went there. He didn't live with her, though. He was in an approved hostel. Just so you know, I have a mate in the Prison and Probation Service in Petty France and I talked to him this morning. He managed to dig out the truth.

'Wayne was on special licence after his release. He'd have been made aware that he was always at risk of recall. He wouldn't be allowed to contact anyone connected with Philip Alden or the Longhursts. The south-west would be permanently out of bounds. And he'd have regular meetings with his probation officer, who'd be conducting risk assessments every step of the way. That still continued even when he became an actor.' Once again, Hawthorne caught my eye. 'That's why he had to turn down the part in your TV show, Tony. He wouldn't have been allowed to play a young offender; there was too much of a chance he'd be recognised. It also explains why he's never been to France. You might have been a bit surprised when he told you that. But then he'd never had a passport and wouldn't have been allowed to go abroad until he got cast in that big film. A lot of this was for his own protection. He had to get special permission to perform in *Tenet*, but at the same time the probation service wouldn't have wanted to hold him back. Rehabilitation is what it's all about.

'Unfortunately, *Tenet* was what caused all this trouble. You can imagine how terrified he must have been after his encounter with Harriet Throsby.'

'She was going to tell!' Tirian could barely get out the words.

'That's what she was threatening. Actually, I think she was just playing games with you. She was nasty. But you could see your big opportunity disappearing and your entire career falling apart. Killing her was the only way out.'

Hawthorne had nearly finished. Mills and Grunshaw had taken the steps up to the stage and were waiting to take hold of Tirian.

'I had a feeling there was something wrong about Tirian the moment I saw his dressing room,' Hawthorne said. 'He had so few cards, no photographs, no sense of family or friends. And the way everything was so neat! The cushions exactly ten centimetres apart and the towels folded into perfect squares. That was a pretty good sign of someone who's been institutionalised. It's hardly surprising the rest of the cast never got close to him. Jordan called him a cold fish. Ewan said he was a loner . . . and that's what he was. He was completely alone.'

Hawthorne went over to Tirian. He had stopped crying at last and was slumped in his chair, exhausted. He laid a hand on the younger man's shoulder. 'You shouldn't have done it,' he said. 'There was no need.'

'I was just so scared!'

'I know. But you don't need to be scared any more. It's over now.'

Hawthorne stepped away.

The two police officers moved in.

26

The Dotted Line

I didn't see Hawthorne for a while. After everything that had happened, I needed a break – and I also owed Jill an apology for all the upset I'd caused her. We booked a small hotel in the South of France, in a fortified village called Saint-Paul-de-Vence, and spent ten days in the sunshine, walking, swimming, visiting art galleries and drinking pink wine on the edge of a dusty square where the locals gathered to play boules.

Tirian had been arrested – with the inevitable result that *Mindgame* had closed at once. By then, I just wanted to put the whole thing behind me. I felt very sad. The failure of my play was part of it, but, strangely, it was thinking about Tirian that upset me more. I don't usually have sympathy with murderers, but he'd never had a chance, chewed up by Trevor Longhurst's lawyers and spat into a system that wasn't really designed to help him. I've visited many juvenile prisons – or 'secure centres', as they are now called – and I've always had my doubts about putting young people behind bars, particularly when both the costs and the reoffending rates are so high. It goes without saying that there are children who are a danger to both the public and themselves, and I've encountered them too. They were the inspiration for my play *A Handbag*. But the majority of them are mentally unwell rather than criminal and they need help, not punishment. Whatever the newspapers may say, and despite the title of Harriet's book, every one of the young offenders I've met has been more sad than bad. It seems crazy to me that the prison system educates them until they're eighteen, but then feeds them into adult jail where any good will be undone. Like Tirian, most of them will come out utterly unprepared for normal life.

I also couldn't help wondering what it must have been like for him negotiating his new career. He had been more than an actor. Everything about him – his accent, the motorbike, the private-school veneer – had been an act. Poor Wayne Howard. He had spent his adult life trapped in a different sort of prison and only by killing Harriet Throsby had he eventually released himself.

Anyway, I finally got back to London relaxed and refreshed, and although I took care not to walk past the Vaudeville – now 'dark', as they say in theatreland – my own life felt as if it had returned to normal. I was still working on my new novel, *Moonflower Murders*, and I immersed myself in the opening chapters, trying to remember all the clues I had already worked into the structure. It wasn't easy. How had Jordan Williams met Maureen Bates? What had Lamprey said about Stephen Longhurst and how did the statue fit into the story? No – that was real life. The fictional village of Tawleigh-on-the-Water, the setting of my new novel, refused to let me back in as my head was still too full of the events of two weeks before.

It was while I was sitting at my desk, struggling, that my phone pinged and I found myself reading a text from Hilda Starke, asking me to look in and see her that afternoon. This was a surprise. I didn't see my agent that often and as far as I knew, there was nothing we couldn't have discussed over the phone. But she was based just round the corner from the Charing Cross Road and it would be pleasant enough to browse in the two or three second-hand bookshops that remained. I walked over, hoping the fresh air would clear my head.

Hilda's office was in Greek Street, above an Italian café that had been there for ever. I went through the side door and up a narrow flight of steps that could just as easily have found itself in a haunted house. This was a successful agency with several big-name writers, but it always felt cramped and old-fashioned. My books were not on display in the reception area. A young receptionist behind an antique desk greeted me with a smile.

'I'm here to see Hilda Starke,' I told him.

'And you are?'

She'd only been my agent for four years. I told him my name and he rang through. 'Yes. She's expecting you. You know where to find her?'

'Yes. I think I can find the way.'

As I approached the door at the back of the building, there was a sound that I wasn't sure I'd ever heard before. Hilda was laughing. I think, occasionally, I'd seen her smile when she was reading the bestseller lists, but she usually focused on whatever business was at hand and left any sense of merriment outside the door. I knocked and went in.

Hilda was not alone. Hawthorne was sitting in an armchair, his legs crossed, holding a cup of coffee. Both of them were wearing suits and I suddenly felt very scruffy in T-shirt, jeans and trainers. It took me a moment to remember that Hawthorne was now represented by Hilda. It seemed like an age had passed since he'd told me that he had come to an agreement with her. What were the two of them doing here together? And why did they need me?

'You look well,' Hilda said. She herself was showing off a luminescent suntan from her recent holiday in Barbados. 'Have you started your book about Alderney yet?'

'You know I'm working on *Moonflower Murders*,' I told her. I sat down in the other empty chair. 'Did you see my play?' I asked.

'As a matter of fact, I had tickets to the Saturday matinée. I was going to take the whole office, but when we got to the theatre they said it had closed that very day.' She sniffed. 'At least we got our money back.'

'What is this about?' I asked, a little tetchily.

'How are you doing, mate?' Hawthorne looked across at me. He was unusually cheerful too. 'I was just telling Hilda about the murder of Harriet Throsby.'

'Yes. You know, for once I actually got it right!' I hadn't meant to blurt it out like that, but it was true. When I'd left his dressing room, I'd named Tirian Kirke as the killer.

'You didn't exactly,' Hawthorne returned. 'You only thought it was him because he'd refused to do your drama on TV.'

'Well, I didn't trust him. I was right about that.' While I'd been in France, I'd had time to think about what had happened and now I couldn't stop myself asking, 'Why did they all gang up on me, Hawthorne? I mean, Jordan said I agreed with him when he was making his threat to kill Harriet. Ewan said the same. Olivia told you I threatened her mother. And Sky Palmer said I'd seen Harriet's address in the magazine. None of that was true!'

'Basic psychology, mate. All four of them felt under pressure. Olivia probably blamed herself for nicking her mum's review and sending it to her girlfriend. Sky felt guilty about reading it out. Ewan was defending Jordan, and Jordan . . . well, he'd started the whole thing. It was the same for all of them. Deflection! They accused you to stop me accusing them.'

'There's something else.' This had also been on my mind. 'On the first night of the play, Martin Longhurst was sitting right behind me and I was sure I felt something prick at the back of my neck. All along, I thought he was the one who might have pulled out one of my hairs.'

'Why didn't you mention it?'

'I don't know. I couldn't be sure . . .'

'Well, he had nothing to do with it. It was probably first-night nerves.'

'Or you could have nits,' Hilda suggested.

'I don't have nits,' I growled.

Hawthorne smiled. 'Anyway, Tony, it's all over. And I've got to tell you, if it wasn't for me, you know where you'd be right now.'

'That's true.' I couldn't deny it. 'You worked it all out, Hawthorne. You stood by me. I owe you a big vote of thanks.'

He coughed quietly. 'Actually, you owe me a bit more than that.'

'What do you mean?'

'Well, you hired me. This time, I wasn't helping the police. You were the client. I put four days into this and Kevin helped too.' He held up a hand before I could protest. 'Don't worry. I'll do it for mate's rates. I can give you a ten per cent discount—'

'Hawthorne! I don't believe you're saying this. It's outrageous.'

'I don't see why. If it wasn't for me, you wouldn't have a career any more. I was just talking about that with Hilda.'

'I don't think it would have been a good look, being arrested for murdering a critic,' Hilda agreed.

I stared at Hawthorne. 'So that's all there is between us? You just think of me as a client?'

'You were the one who said you didn't want to write any more books.'

He let this sink in. Suddenly, I knew where this was heading.

'I've spoken to Penguin Random House,' Hilda chipped in. 'They were very saddened by your decision. *The Word Is Murder* has done much better than any of your other books, and you know how keen they are on series. Hawthorne asked me to call them on his behalf – I didn't want to trouble you while you were away – and I have to say, they've made an extremely generous offer.'

'An offer?'

'Four more books once you finish *A Line to Kill*.' She opened a drawer in her desk and took out a contract. 'Of course, it's entirely your decision. I wouldn't want you to do anything you weren't comfortable with.'

She handed me the document. I read:

Memorandum of Agreement dated 20 April 2018

between Anthony Horowitz ('Author'), c/o Hilda Starke Limited ('Agent') of the one part; and

Penguin Random House ('Publisher') of the other part, concerning 4 (four) original works of fiction of 90,000 words each at present entitled:

Hawthorne Investigates ('Book 4')
Untitled Hawthorne Book 5 ('Book 5')
Untitled Hawthorne Book 6 ('Book 6')
Untitled Hawthorne Book 7 ('Book 7')

(hereinafter referred to as the 'Work', together or individually as the context provides)

Whereby it is mutually agreed as follows:

That was as far as I got. There were half a dozen more pages of legalese. Is there an author in the world who goes through all this stuff and understands it? But that wasn't the point. I'd already read enough.

'I am never calling any of my books *Hawthorne Investigates*!' I said.

'It was only a suggestion.' Hawthorne shrugged. 'It'll be easy to write,' he went on. 'Not too many suspects. Everyone likes the theatre. And why do you think I gathered everyone on the stage like that? I did that for you, mate. It's a terrific end – just like Agatha Christie!'

Acknowledgements

This was an uncomfortable book for me to write and I want to start by thanking my therapist, Dr Lisa Beach, for helping me work through my experiences. I also sought advice from Graham Bartlett, a former detective and author, who explained much of what happened at Tolpuddle Road and gave me useful information about MAPP and the Prison and Probation Service.

I am grateful to Graham Thompson, the theatre manager at the Vaudeville, who showed me round the theatre quite some time after *Mindgame* had closed, so that I could refresh my memory. I think it's only fair to mention that the backstage area has been redecorated and modernised since the events described in this book. I also owe an apology, I think, to the director Christopher Nolan. I could not disagree more with Tirian's view of *Tenet* and note that he had clearly not seen the finished script as, ultimately, no scenes were shot in Paris.

Before I began writing this book, I had a memorable lunch with Michael Billington, who gave me many insights into the world of the drama critic and assured me that Harriet Throsby was really one of a kind. I am also grateful to Paterson Joseph, a wonderful actor (who has worked with my wife), who helped me come to grips with and not to be afraid of the issues discussed in Chapter 15.

Sophie Comninos is not the real name of the woman who killed her husband (mentioned in Chapter 8), but a generous supporter of the National Youth Theatre who bid at a charity auction to appear in this book.

My relationship with Hilda Starke has come under a lot of strain recently and it's only thanks to the work put in by her assistant, Jonathan Lloyd, that I have remained with the agency. I am glad to say that Steve Frost (of Frost and Longhurst) has agreed to help me with my tax affairs. My own assistant, Tess Cutler, organises my life and keeps me sane. I couldn't have written this without her support.

My wife, Jill Green, has been as brilliant as she always is, somehow finding time to read the manuscript between running a production company, moving house and managing the family. She has forgiven me for not telling her about my arrest and interrogation. And my sister, Caroline Dow, really was the first person to believe in *Mindgame*, so everything that happened was her fault.

Finally, my thanks to my brilliant publishers – not just a company but a bunch of supremely talented people who all deserve to be named and who therefore appear on the next page. For what it's worth, there were at least thirty errors in the finished book. My dear editor, Selina Walker, spotted them all!

Writers often feel isolated and alone but the truth is that producing a book is a huge team effort.

It's my pleasure to acknowledge the fantastic support I've been given in the long journey from idea to manuscript to finished publication.

PUBLISHER
Selina Walker

EDITORIAL
Joanna Taylor
Caroline Johnson
Charlotte Osment

DESIGN
Glenn O'Neill

PRODUCTION
Helen Wynn-Smith
Tara Hodgson

UK SALES
Mat Watterson
Claire Simmonds
Olivia Allen
Evie Kettlewell

INTERNATIONAL SALES
Richard Rowlands
Erica Conway
Laura Ricchetti

PUBLICITY
Charlotte Bush
Klara Zak

MARKETING
Rebecca Ikin
Sam Rees-Williams

AUDIO
James Keyte
Meredith Benson

About the Author

ANTHONY HOROWITZ is one of the UK's most prolific and successful writers, unique in being active in both adult and YA fiction, TV, theater, and journalism. Several of his previous novels were instant *New York Times* bestsellers. His bestselling Alex Rider series for young adults has sold more than nineteen million copies worldwide and has become a hugely successful show on Amazon TV. His breakthrough murder mystery, *Magpie Murders*, will be on PBS. He lives in London with his wife and dog.

MORE FROM
ANTHONY HOROWITZ

HAWTHORNE AND HOROWITZ MYSTERIES

"Horowitz shows no signs of ceding the spotlight. He's having too much fun and, as a result, so are his readers."

—*LOS ANGELES BOOK REVIEW*

JAMES BOND NOVELS

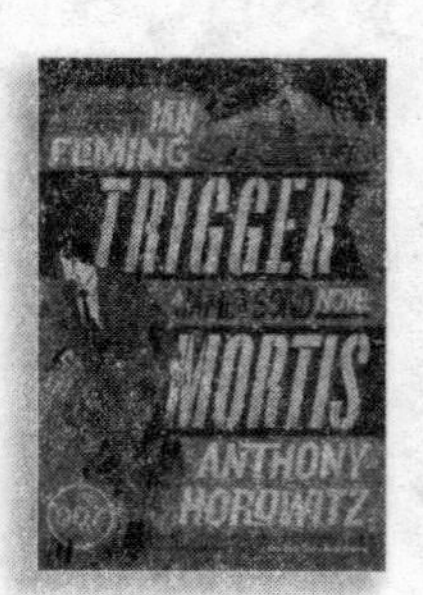